Sarah Hopkins is the author of two previous novels, *The Crimes of Billy Fish*, which was highly commended in the inaugural ABC Fiction Awards and shortlisted for the Commonwealth Writers' Prize, and *Speak to Me*. Sarah is a criminal lawyer and lives in Sydney.

Sarah Hopkins

This Picture of You

Author's note: This is a work of fiction. Some characters and places are inspired by real people and events, but the incidents described in the book are the product of imagination.

First published in 2014

This project has been assisted by the Australian Government through the Australia Council,its arts funding and advisory board.

Allen & Unwin
83 Alexander Street
Crows Nest NSW 2065
Australia
Phone: (61 2) 8425 0100
Email: info@allenandunwin.com
Web: www.allenandunwin.com

Cataloguing-in-Publication details are available from the National Library of Australia
www.trove.nla.gov.au

ISBN 978 1 74331 940 6

Quoted material from WE'RE GOING ON A BEAR HUNT
by Michael Rosen and illustrated by Helen Oxenbury
Text © 1989 Michael Rosen
Reproduced by permission of Walker Books Australia

Set in 11.5/16.5 pt Sabon LT Pro by Bookhouse, Sydney
Printed and bound in Australia by Griffin Press

10 9 8 7 6 5 4

The paper in this book is FSC® certified. FSC® promotes environmentally responsible, socially beneficial and economically viable management of the world's forests.

For my mother

For my mother

Part One

From his seat at the sunroom window, Martin watched Maggie walk from the house through the open gate that never shut: barefoot and straight-backed, a swimmer's shoulders. He watched as she crossed the street and stepped up to the footpath and as she walked over the grass, where her silhouette met the sea, still grey beneath a rising orange sun. And, finally, when she stepped over the rocks down to the ocean pool—her white towel tucked around the waist of her swimsuit, goggles and cap in hand—he edged forwards in his seat to keep her in view for as long as he could.

The rhythm of it . . . his Maggie. She stepped in time with her heartbeat, always had.

And here in this place that was their home she formed part of the landscape, like the black cockatoos that mobbed the sky, back again, yellow-tailed and screeching for the highest branch of the banksias. Maggie had wished for birds with a more beautiful song. Finnegan said they sounded like chimpanzees. But if the cockatoos were to be likened to another creature, Martin thought as he watched the smaller birds deserting the low-lying bush, it must be to a bat. The wide, steady span of their wing: the black bats of day.

The other weekend when he had slept over, Finnegan had counted the birds in the trees: 'Twelve plus nine cocka-monkeys.' He liked the yellow spots on their cheeks but thought that they were bullies. 'They push out the rosellas,' he said, creases denting his little forehead. But Martin shook his head. 'Maybe,' he said. 'Or maybe the rosellas just choose to leave.'

It was Sunday. Slowly the list formed; the family was coming at midday. Maggie would prepare the paprikash before going to the store for flowers. While she was gone he would sweep the path and light the barbecue so she could char the peppers. And for now he would make them tea and toast.

When she returned from her swim, he was standing at the fridge with a jar of chutney in his hand. She surprised him there at the door, and when he looked back to the jar it was just a dark brown jelly in cold glass without a label, like it was playing a trick on him. He shook his head and put it back.

'The strangest thing . . .' he said.

'What, darling?' The purple indentations of goggle marks were still around her eyes.

He smiled then. 'Nothing. How was the water?'

'Like ice.'

'And they're coming at midday?'

'Yes, midday.'

He picked up the paper. On seeing the date, and remembering the occasion, his eyes brightened. 'It is our anniversary,' he said. 'Happy anniversary, my girl.' They had never married, but it was thirty-seven years since the day she knocked on the door to his loft. There had been years when it went by unacknowledged, and then years of gifts and surprise dinners, and many, like today, somewhere in between.

'The look on your face when you stepped into the garden,' he said. The place he spoke of was a garden between the tenements in New York, which he had taken her to on the day they met. 'I can remember it, you know.'

'Of course you can.'

'Yes, but it is strange lately; it's as though the day were creeping back to me.'

'Why strange? What do you mean?' she asked.

'It's on my mind, that's all—strange in that the memory's so clear. The other night I dreamt of it. I think it's one of those recurring ones; I think that's what's happening.'

Maggie looked perplexed, but didn't press it, nor did Martin want her to. What he didn't try to explain to her was that in recalling the memory he was getting lost in it somehow, that when he returned to the here and now, the light had changed, dimmed—as though he had left the room for just a moment and someone had come in and messed it all up. At the very least, the ground was shifting. If it reminded him of anything in his past, it was the feeling one had at the end of an acid trip, the unsettling sense of not knowing exactly where one had been. (Unsettling, yes, though in some respects his favourite part.)

'I knew it then,' he said. 'I knew it.'

'You knew what?'

'From the look on your face: I knew you were for me.'

She began to shake her head but smiled instead. Martin pushed himself away from the table to stand, then walked around and kissed her forehead.

'Marry me, why don't you?'

She laughed but held on to his arm, and when he kissed her a second time she leant into it with lovely cool, salty lips.

'I have an idea—an anniversary gift from you to me. Before I get old and ugly . . .' He was asking her to paint his portrait, as he had been asking ever since her last exhibition. She went to protest but he stopped her. 'I know, I know: when you are done with the next commission, when the students are finished for the year . . .'

'I love you,' she said. 'And the garden was beautiful. The thrush had its nest in the walnut tree. We ate string beans and blackberries. And the daffodils were in bloom.'

'So they were, yes. Dave barrowed the dung.'

'And we spread it in the bed behind the Chinese Empress tree.'

'You hiked up that little skirt and knelt down in the horse shit.' He smiled. 'It gave us the excuse to take off your clothes . . .'

'Rubbish,' she said. 'It did no such thing.' She was right. The clothes came off later. 'Now go have a shower and get dressed.'

'What time will they be here?'

She hesitated. 'Midday.'

'Then let's get a move on.'

Later in the morning, Maggie returned with flowers just as the wind picked up and the sky darkened with muddy cloud. Out front, Martin was sweeping the path.

'Shame,' she called to him. 'What happened to our perfect winter morning?'

Martin peered out to the blurred horizon and the white-capped sea, and then turned to look behind him. 'The rain won't reach,' he said, and went back to his work.

Over the years, she had learnt not to argue about the weather with a fisherman. But looking out to the same sea, the water's surface disappearing before her eyes in the haze of a distant downpour, she shook her head.

'I'll move the barbecue undercover, just to be safe.'

He stopped his sweeping. 'No, you won't,' he said. 'Do the flowers, Maggie, then come back out.'

When she did, they sat together on the front fence and watched the dimpled surface of the ocean reappear under a clearing sky. Glancing at his face in profile, tanned and weathered like the cliffs, still handsome, she leant into him before swinging her legs over to face the house.

'I still think the colour is too dark.' It was French navy with white skirting, a Californian bungalow.

'I told you we never should have messed with it in the first place.'

Remembering the peeling paint on the walls and the window frames, she laughed. 'I don't think judges are meant to live in rundown houses.'

That was when he'd agreed to it, the day after his swearing in. She had wanted to do more—move the living areas to the front to capture the view, and knock down internal walls and join the open-plan movement along with the rest of the neighbours responsible for the architectural masterpieces and monstrosities now lining the South Coogee street—but Martin had put his foot down. It was still a house with separate rooms, and with rooms (even the kitchen) that had doors. Maggie could do what she wanted with her precious treasures—the coffee table inset with travertine, the carved-wood chandeliers, her vast collection of ornaments and figurines—but when it came to the rooms, Martin liked to know that behind him there was a wall and, if he so chose, he could close the door.

As for the exterior paint, blistered and bubbling, he had been sad to see even that scraped away—though beyond 'I like it the way it is', he hadn't been able to explain why. And so it was, French navy, perfect render. A mistake from the start.

'God, look at those windows,' Maggie said. But on that they had a deal. While others had darkened the glass of their front windows for the sake of privacy, Martin and Maggie were content to rely on the film of salt that coated theirs. It did the job; nature did the job, and did it for free. And the black glass, they both agreed, was an eyesore.

The salt was thick enough for Finnegan to wet his finger with spit and play noughts and crosses with himself. And in the corner of the left pane were the pictures he had drawn: a smiley face and a tree beside a giraffe, and dwarfing them all, the plumed head of a cockatoo.

As soon as Ethan pulled up at the house, Finn leapt from the car shouting, 'Grandie,' and ran to Martin, whispering feverishly in his ear.

'No fishing today,' Ethan said as he reached them, pointing more at Martin than the boy.

Martin shrugged. 'It isn't the right wind for it, Finny.'

'Hey, where's my hug?' Maggie held her arms out and Finn fell into them, tipping his cheek up to take the kiss before running inside to see if there were chips on the table.

Laini handed Maggie a bottle of wine and wrapped her free arm around her shoulders.

'Is that one of your special ones?' Maggie held up the label and feigned delight when Laini confirmed that it was: biodynamic, preservative-free. That was all Laini could drink because the regular stuff messed up her sinuses. No one else liked it, but it didn't matter because they didn't have to drink it; lately Laini was polishing off the better part of it herself. And though Ethan had thought the sinus problem might have more to do with the quantity rather than the quality of the wine she drank, he never said it. A good session with a bottle (biodynamic or otherwise) did a number of things to his wife, none of which he found objectionable: not the cute honk in her laugh or the skin on her chest flushed pink. Over the last couple of months—ever since she'd started beating up on herself—it was the only thing that seemed to let her live in the moment again, and what that meant for Ethan was that later at home, after Finn was asleep, she would pull him into bed and let loose like she did in the good old days.

He watched them walk inside, mother and wife, arm in arm, Maggie grumbling about Martin's rock fishing to Laini's tut-tuts.

'You're not silly enough to keep at it, are you, Martin?' Laini said as she found a place in the fridge for her salad.

It was a couple of months since Martin had been washed off the rocks fishing at dawn, and Maggie had been fighting with him about it ever since. The arguments were strong on both sides. He'd been fishing from the same rock for ten years and until that freak wave nothing had ever happened. But if you believed what they said about the sea levels, there were going to be more freak waves. Nature was taking its revenge et cetera, et cetera. Either way, Maggie was probably right: his father was lucky to be alive.

Martin appeared to consider Laini's question a minute before deciding to enter the fray. 'I suspect the answer, Laini, is yes—yes, I am quite silly enough.' He looked at Maggie, and as the two held eye contact throughout the long second of silence that followed, Ethan watched, waited, relieved that Martin was the first to blink, clapping his hands and declaring that it was time 'to crack open that bottle'.

'And how are you doing, Dad?'

'Never better, son.'

'Finn! Enough chips!'

Then Maggie: 'Tell me about the violin, darling.'

'Violin?' Martin asked. 'I thought he played the piano.'

'He does,' Maggie said. 'Violin too.'

'Violin too? So how many are we up to now? Soccer, gymnastics, kung-fu . . .'

'Tae kwon do,' the boy corrected him, puffing with pride. 'I got my blue belt. You wanna see?'

'You have it here?'

'No, Grandie, not the belt, the sequence. You wanna see my sequence?'

'Of course we do,' Maggie answered.

Like her son, Laini sprang to life. 'He needs more room.'

Obediently they shuffled out to the living room and sat on the couches, all except Finn, who took centre stage in the middle of the room and without any further prompt leapt into warrior stance, raised his arms in the air and fanned them around in a circle and back down to his sides. Ethan sat forward in his chair. On his son's face was the same look he wore when they wrestled: like he wanted to rip the world apart in a pretend kind of way, like a character in a video game. Ethan loved that look. When Laini talked to him about the importance of adults retaining the child within, that was how he imagined it, his own inner child. Kick-arse fearless. Game on.

There he was, his boy, standing in front of a room and doing his thing. He punched both arms forwards and shouted 'Keeyah!' so loud Maggie jumped in her seat. Next came the kicks—one out to the side with either leg and then on to the trickier move: his right leg out to the front as high as his head, leading into the spin to get him to the second kick, the left leg—higher again. He usually only did the spin once, but he was on a roll with a captive crowd so he went again, with another 'Keeyah!'

Only this time his foot kicked the bookshelf and the 'yah' didn't stop.

'Yaaahhhh . . .'

The boy curled into a ball on the floor, rolling back and forth. Ethan got there first, swept him up in his arms. *Christ.* A different look on his face, a different kind of anger—the blaming kind. He had kicked a bookshelf and he was staring at it now like it was a rabid dog that needed to be put down. Wasn't that what Ethan had taught him when he was little, when he stubbed his toe against a wall? *Bad wall. Bad table.* And Finn would smack it with his chubby little hand and feel all the better for it.

'We should've moved the shelf, buddy . . .'

Then Laini pulled him onto her lap and made him wriggle all five toes, and when the crying trickled into a sniffle, Maggie offered her own solution. 'How about Nana gets you some ice cream?'

Ethan came into the kitchen as Martin was mid-sentence.

'. . . soccer, violin, piano, tae kwon fucking do . . .'

Busy scooping ice cream, they hadn't heard him come in. 'Oh, Martin, come on, be nice . . .'

'Yeah, Dad,' Ethan said. 'Be nice.'

Martin didn't flinch. 'I am nice; I am perfectly nice. I'm just wondering what kind of super-boy you are trying to create here.'

Ethan shrugged. He could see his father's point. 'The other kids do it too. It's different these days.'

'But do you ever stop to ask why? I mean the way she runs him place to place after school now . . . Whatever happened to mucking around? Isn't that what seven-year-old boys are best at?'

'Look, it's Laini's thing. Don't give her a hard time.'

'It's not our business, Martin,' Maggie said. 'You just miss having him back here in the afternoons.'

'He misses it too! He loved fishing.'

'So fish from the beach.'

'I would if he wasn't at some bloody guitar lesson.'

'He doesn't do guitar.'

'No, not yet. I mean, for Christ's sake, one instrument's got to be enough . . .'

Laini's voice came from behind them. 'We let him try everything, Martin. We don't make him do it. If he expresses an interest we open the door, that's all.'

'Oh, Laini, I didn't mean . . .'

She smiled in sufferance. 'You didn't mean for me to hear.'

Maggie put her hand on Laini's shoulder in a gesture of reparation.

'I just thought I'd grab some ice for his foot,' Laini said. 'And look, to be honest, I don't mind. I'm glad you care, Martin. I'm glad you have an opinion.'

'It was different in my day, like Maggie said, that's all. I was lucky if my mother asked how my day was; I was lucky if—'

'Ah, here we go,' Maggie cut in, 'the poor neglected child in the Mosman mansion . . . Let me get out the violin.'

'Well, I never played a violin, I can tell you that for certain.'

'There you have it,' Laini said. 'And you could have been a concert violinist, for all you know.'

Martin mulled that over before speaking again. 'So is that what this is about? To find out if he is good at anything?'

Laini closed her eyes, and when she opened them the humour had drained from her face. 'For Christ's sake, Martin, he *enjoys* it. I just want him to know what is out there. I just . . .' There was a quiver in her voice. 'I just . . .' Ethan knew that quiver; the tears began to well.

Maggie shot daggers at Martin as she herded him out along with the melting ice cream.

Ethan put his arms around his wife. 'Come on, babe . . .'

'I don't know what's wrong with me. Am I one of those crazy mothers? I don't want to be that woman.'

'You're not that woman. You're not crazy.'

'I always said when he went to school, I'd start something then, but God, it's been two years . . .'

'What about your blog?'

She shook her head. 'You're working so much. I don't have any headspace.'

What they had also planned on by the time Finn was at school was another baby, but this wasn't the time to remind her again. He filled her wine glass. 'You've got a lot on your plate. We'll work it out, hon. You can go back to uni.'

After high school she had started a vet science degree then transferred into communications for a year before dropping out altogether to travel through South America. When Ethan met her she was thinking of starting a business importing Aztec healing clay. She was twenty-two. He was twenty-eight and had just been made a senior associate.

On her face now was a vacant look, like she was a world away. 'Sometimes I get these thoughts, Ethan. And I think . . . Is it us? Is there something wrong with us?'

He held her face in his hands. 'It isn't us. It isn't you. You are a great mother. I love you. Fuck Marty.'

Their eyes were locked. 'I want another baby, I do, and I know you do, but first I've got to work out what I'm doing with my life. I need you to be okay with that.'

'Sure, I am. I'm right behind you.'

Then she smiled. 'I love your dad,' she said. 'But yeah, fuck him.' And after a gulp of wine: 'Let's eat.'

Laini put her salad down in the centre of the table, a large round dish of chickpeas and roasted tomatoes on a bed of rocket and mung beans. She scooped a spoonful onto everyone's plate before filling her own, leaving no room for meat, wheat or dairy. Maggie admired her for her discipline, but had no interest in the theories behind it—blanket bans on food groups were to Maggie a form of sacrilege. For the rest of them it was a Hungarian Sunday lunch, one of Maggie's mother's best—chicken paprikash and spicy garlic sausages with bell peppers and fried potatoes.

Maggie asked Finn about school and he told her that a boy in his spelling group got sent out of class for telling the teacher she had fat ankles and not saying sorry.

'Is the hall finished yet?' Ethan asked.

Finn shook his head.

'The builders haven't been there all week,' Laini said, rolling her eyes as Ethan began his rant against the faceless bureaucrats, but offering up no argument against it.

Maggie smiled at the boy. 'Well, it'll be wonderful when it's done, darling.'

'We're going to have a special celebration assembly,' Finn said.

'Speaking of celebrations,' Martin chimed in, 'we're up for one right now. It is our anniversary. Maggie's made cake!'

Finn clapped and Ethan tapped his glass with his fork.

'Finnegan, I bet you can't guess how many years ago Nana and Grandie met.'

'Eighty?'

Maggie laughed. 'So how old would that make me now?'

'Tell us the story about the toast and honey,' Finn said.

Martin leant in over his plate towards Finn, and over Maggie's plea that he didn't, he did: 'In the olden days, at least a century ago, in a faraway land, there was a young man who was minding his own business while cleaning his kitchen sink when there was a bang on the door, a loud bang. He opened it, expecting the sound to have come from a giant fist, but instead he saw a pretty girl who told him she was hungry and demanded to be fed . . .'

'I did no such thing.'

'And in she came and ate the last of the poor young man's bread.'

'I had four bits of toast.'

'*The last of his bread and his honey*, which he was happy to share because though pretty, very pretty, the girl was a bit pale and had spent all her money.'

There were jokes then—'Hungry from Hungary'—and boasts from Finn that he himself could eat eight pieces of toast and a whole jar of honey. 'You should see how much maple syrup I can put on my pancakes.' But when the boy finished his lunch and left the table for his computer games, so went any fond reminiscing around the story of Martin and Maggie. As had become the family custom, it had been presented in its best light. The day they met: Martin was living in New York, Maggie was travelling. It began with a visit to the Japanese pigeon lady and ended with a sleepover in a garden that grew out of a rubbish heap. Ethan and Laini knew better than to probe into what happened next, into the logistics of long distance and the birth of Ethan. It wasn't until now that Finn was old enough to ask that they told this story about toast and honey. Like so much of adult life, the truth was no story for children's ears. It had been packed up and put away, the simpler version wheeled out this same day every year.

Only this year, it was not just today; it was yesterday and it was last week. In a feat of blinkered nostalgia, Martin was cheerfully retelling the story as though in his mind he had managed to extract it from what came after. Even this morning: 'I knew it then,' he had said. 'I knew you were for me.'

The garden between the tenement buildings that used to be the rubbish heap—yes, they had marvelled at that place, but he hadn't known then. Given what came after, it didn't make sense. And yet this morning she had watched him sip his tea, and she had listened to him savour a memory, a memory or a re-creation; either way, she could see no point in correcting him. She understood the lure of the lie, the reason to craft a story out of a larger, less manageable truth. And hearing it again over lunch, she asked herself the question: What did it matter now? After all this time, what did any of it matter?

'Maybe it's time he went to a private school,' Ethan was saying.

'Why, because the school hall isn't finished?'

'No, Laini, not because of the hall, because he would have an art teacher and a science lab and a swimming pool.'

Maggie put a hand up to stop him.

'I'm fine, Maggie, really,' Laini said. And to Ethan: 'Just give me until high school . . . Then you can feed him to the dragons.'

'Three years they've had that money. You've got to admit, they are fucking hopeless. That headmistress is a complete idiot.'

With that it began again, the grumbling: the waste of public money sector by sector, the bloodless knifing of a sitting prime minister and the despicable vote-grab from all sides as the election loomed—and with the grumbling, the same dinner-table tendencies Maggie had observed—at the Johnstons' on Friday and last Sunday at their friend Annie's. People were quicker to empty their glasses, she'd noticed, when listening in disagreement, as a method of self-soothing, or in preparation to do battle. And when the disagreement was most vehement, the more exaggerated the nodding became—clearly not in response to what was being said, but to the argument formulating inside the combatant's own head. Perhaps that, she mused, was the reason for the drink: they were toasting themselves in anticipation of a point well made.

'Leading the world?!' Ethan shouted across the table at his wife. 'You think China's going to give a damn what we do with our emissions? We are pissing in the wind, end of story.'

Laini began her retort with the first of a series of dot points, each prefaced with a number. All in all there were six, through which Martin nodded and emptied his glass. And Maggie listened, shuddered, not at the criticisms that were being made—politicians were manipulating the uncertainty, no question—but at the way the convictions, once voiced, were held like property, hoarded and protected. What was it they said? *The older I get, the less I know.* Though once a participant, more and more she felt the only role she could manage these days was that of observer, her perspective anthropological more than anything else. Why bang on and on with all the reasons you were right and someone else was wrong? Why count the ways? Surely there was a time to give it up, to shut up and plant some trees . . . and to stop your family from ruining another lovely lunch.

'How about some good news?' she said. 'Dad and I are going to Morocco.'

'You just got back from . . . where were you again?'

Copenhagen. They had been in Copenhagen for a judicial conference in April. 'We're not going until March. But we've settled on it.'

'It's fantastic the way you two travel,' Laini said.

They had always loved it, and every year since Martin was appointed a judge they'd taken an overseas trip.

'How's the centre going, Mum?' Ethan asked.

'We've got a new coordinator, an ex-lawyer from Melbourne.' The centre was the youth centre in Newtown; as a barrister Martin had given them some pro bono advice and now Maggie volunteered there in the office once every so often.

'Ha, you didn't tell them how they nicked your wallet!' Martin hooted, sufficiently well oiled to slam his glass down on the table. And when Ethan asked who the culprit was, he pointed his finger in the air: 'One of those kids.'

'*Those* kids?' Maggie interjected. 'We don't know who it was. It could have been anyone—a cleaner, for all we know. I was stupid and left it out. My fault really . . .'

'Here we go.' Ethan rubbed his eyes as he spoke. 'It's *your* fault . . . You give them your time for nothing and they steal your money—that's their thank you. That's just priceless, that is.'

'Listen to you both! What's happened to you? And you, Martin, of all people . . . If that's the sort of mindset you have as you sit on the bench, heaven help us all.'

'Oh, come on, Mum—we're just having a bit of fun.'

She stopped herself, took a breath. This was their argument, hers and Martin's. Ever since Ethan was at university, they had shaken their heads at their son's conservatism, but even Martin now, something had crept into his thinking, sitting on high in a red gown with a gavel in his hand, day after day, year after year. It was inevitable, she supposed. His job was to pass judgment on the masses. His job was to be right and to be righteous.

'Not conservative,' he would argue, 'just clinical.' He had taken emotion out of his deliberations.

'And with it your ideals.'

'Well, those that spring out of emotion, sure. Guilty.'

And so they would argue about the events of the day, and more and more he would find a way to shut it down. What became clear to her was that over the years his disdain for politics had come to match his disdain for religion. And perhaps in this, perhaps now, they weren't so different after all: along different routes they had arrived at the same place.

Today she had been drawn back into the ring, and now she would step out. 'Ethan,' she said, 'tell us, how is work?'

'Fine. Busy. Fine.'

'Busier than usual?'

'A little. Moira left. It's taking her replacement a while to get the hang of things. You don't realise how much someone does until they're gone.'

'Moira was a godsend,' Laini chips in. 'This one's a dill.'

'Well, I don't know . . .'

'She sent out the wrong affidavit.'

'It was a bit of a disaster.'

'And Ethan just kept his cool.'

Martin, without looking up from his stacked fork: 'Well, I'd imagine that's the best way to deal with it.'

'She only just started,' Ethan says. 'I mean, if it happens again . . .'

Laini: 'You'll slap her wrist.'

'Well, no. She'd have a claim if I did that.' He looked at his mother and father. 'And on the scale of personality defects in the office, hers aren't so bad.'

At this Martin's ears pricked up. 'Tell us about the other defects.'

'Come on, Dad—I'm not going there.'

Ignoring him, Martin went on. 'I'm sure you're right about that, Ethan. I wonder if it's not the nature of the beast.' And in an audible whisper to himself: 'It is family law, after all . . .'

Maggie put her hand over his. 'Stop it, Martin. There's nothing the matter with family law.'

At this Martin shook his head like a child refusing to eat. 'Don't tell me about the law. What are you doing there, son? That's a place you go to die.'

Ethan smiled wearily, the terrain too well trodden. 'That isn't why I go there. Dad, let's not do this today. Let Mum have a good day.'

'Quite right,' Martin said. 'And a special day it is: it's our anniversary.'

'We did that already.'

'We did the cake?'

'No, Dad. We haven't done the cake.' Ethan looked from Martin to Maggie. She shrugged. 'I think that's enough wine for you . . . How's that appeal matter coming along? The people smuggler?'

'They are trying to introduce fresh evidence. He is an interesting fellow, not what you'd expect.' Until the judgment was handed down that was as far as conversations about cases generally went around a lunch table.

'Well, you can bet he made a pretty penny out of it,' Ethan said. 'It's bloody criminal the sort of sums these people are charging.'

'Well, I suppose that's what I'm there to determine. I'm not sure it's always the case.'

Ethan shook his head. 'Come off it, Dad—kids in leaking boats . . . This isn't the time to go soft.'

Martin looked perplexed by his son's words, perplexed and then concerned. 'Well, there were no children on this boat in particular. There is evidence, in fact, that this fellow gave cheap passage to a mentally disabled man. If that man was not here, he'd be sitting in a camp in Indonesia.'

Ethan threw his hands in the air. 'There has to be some sort of process. You know that as well as I do. And what, it's all okay because he gave some guy a cheap boat ride? I'm not buying it.'

Maggie could feel Martin stiffen as he listened to his son lament the inequity of queue-jumping. Finally he cleared his throat, leant his weight into his hands at the edge of the table as though preparing to stand. But he did not stand; he sat back in his chair and waited for Ethan to finish. When he had, Martin folded his arms and posed a question: 'Do you know, Ethan, what they do with a mentally ill man in Indonesia?'

'Sorry?'

Martin repeated the question.

'No, Dad,' Ethan said, wary now. 'What do they do?'

'Once he has become enough of a public nuisance, they take him to some out-of-the-way place and tie him to a tree, or to a post, and they leave him there to eat the food that is thrown on the ground and to piss and shit and sit and howl in his piss and shit, and . . .' His eyes glazed over as he spoke, staring at the centre of the table. Ethan went to speak, but Maggie shook her head, held up her hand. Martin fell silent, lost in the mire of his thoughts.

When he looked up, he squinted across the table at his son. 'What on earth am I talking about?' And before anyone could answer, he turned to Maggie. 'I am tired,' he said. 'Do you think I could have a little nap?'

'Of course, darling.'

Laini jumped up. 'I'll clear.'

'We'll take a walk down to the beach,' Ethan said.

Maggie went with Martin to their room, and lay down with him on the bed. She rested her head on his chest and felt its warmth on her cheek as it rose and fell.

'You know, when I close my eyes,' he said softly, 'I see you in younger skin. You are standing at the wall in the loft, studying my face, a piece of charcoal in your hand. And I can see the picture that you draw. Strange to think of it now buried beneath layers of paint. Perhaps we could go and find it, peel it back.'

The arm cradling her shoulder went limp. Maggie sat up and kissed his cheek, this man she had spent a day with thirty-seven years ago, this man who fed her toast and posed for his portrait and took her on a walk to a garden between the tenements on the Lower East Side of Manhattan.

He was stressed about these last judgments, and he hadn't been sleeping and he might have had one wine too many—that was what she said by way of explanation when she caught up with the others on their walk.

'I'm sorry,' Ethan said. 'I went too far.'

Maggie put her hand on his shoulder. 'Don't you worry. He can be a grumpy bugger.' And she repeated it, the answer to his outburst—'a grumpy bugger'—as much to convince herself as to convince Ethan.

Martin opened his eyes.

He had left the lunch table, and before that he had said things he shouldn't have. He hadn't meant for Laini to hear in the kitchen. As for the table, he couldn't be sure now what had sparked the outburst—if that's what one would call it. Whatever it was, I am fine, he thought. All is well.

Thank God for Laini. He remembered the night of their first meeting. 'I'm not really a private sort of person,' she said after downing her third glass and letting loose with the extraordinary details of her adolescent love life. 'It is a bit of a scream now when I think of it.'

'Oh yes,' Maggie said. 'A hoot.' Only part-snide; the truth was Laini could tell a bloody good story. And later, on the drive home, Maggie had already come around: 'God, this could work! Who'd have thought Ethan would fall for someone that . . . flamboyant?'

It was the right word. Her hair that first dinner was the colour of a ripe apricot. By the second it was a plummy purple. (Martin had to look twice to check it was the same girl.) But whatever the colour of her tortured tresses, what was clear to both him and Maggie by the time they were eating dessert was that Ethan—who was not predisposed to happiness—was, indeed, happy.

'Yin and yang,' Ethan had endeavoured to explain months later after telling his father over a beer at the pub that they were going to be married.

'Ah yes,' Martin replied. 'Darkness and light.'

Ethan smiled. 'Exactly. Like you and Mum.'

'Oh, come on, matey . . .'

'Yeah, yeah, you're right: you're more murky than dark.'

'And this is how you speak to your poor old dad?' For a moment he held the eyes of his son. Of course, he had no real complaint with him. Given the way it had started—the quiet little boy holding out his hand—Martin could only be grateful to be accepted, later loved and now, God forbid, understood. 'You've seen enough now, Ethan. Do it better.'

As he got out of bed, Martin resolved to apologise if required, in a roundabout sort of way—something about the verbal incontinence of old men. *Older* men—he was not so old. He didn't feel it, not now. Sixty-five was the new fifty, didn't they say? He paused in the mirror to confirm that there was something still to admire, and smoothing his silver-grey hair, he felt energised: fit as a fiddle and ready to eat cake.

Out in the hall it was dead quiet. The faces of his family lined the walls: a stilted portrait of his parents with their plump sons, Maggie's mother as a girl standing on a bridge in Budapest, Ethan at every stage of his well-documented life alongside Maggie's painting of him, aged six, the small face surrounded by fantastical animal avatars and spirit guardians. And Finn, of course, the photo of the two of them on the rock platform, the fish in the boy's hands, his eyes bursting with pride and wonder. Maggie was always having a new picture framed, moving paintings closer together to make room. If you looked closely you could see the spots of putty in the plaster.

To the right of the hall was the dining room, straight ahead the living room, and to the left, the kitchen. Martin walked into each of them, and found each empty. In the living room he sat on the couch and thought about the boy's tears, and afterwards the kitchen conversation. What lay behind his questions was not just a concern that Finny was doing too much. These last weeks he had noticed something, a sadness in the boy's eyes, just a flash of it before he blinked it away. Maybe it was because he was being made to jump through all of these bloody hoops . . . Maybe, but Martin sensed there was something more. He got up from the couch and went back to the kitchen where the cake sat on the table—Finny's favourite, cream-cheese icing. He scooped a bit from the side of the plate with his finger.

Had someone said something about a walk?

Martin's plan was to follow his family down to the beach, to make things right. What stopped him was the sight of Ethan's keys on the ledge at the front door. He picked them up. In the middle of the clinking mass, there was a larger key in a black casing, the car key.

'You are forgetting things,' she had said. 'That makes you dangerous, Martin.' She was crying then, driving him home from the service station, telling him they needed to go to the doctor. In the car he couldn't find the words, but later he explained: 'I just got lost. There was nothing dangerous about it.'

She listed the infringements over the last months: going through a red light, disobeying the no right turn, failing to indicate, enough so almost all his points were gone. 'You are a judge, Martin. The papers would have a field day if anything went wrong.'

There it was now, the key in the palm of his hand. As it pressed into his skin, he felt a pulse beating in his wrist—beating as though to remind him there was a reason to get into the car.

Later the argument had been repeated, this time with Maggie shouting. She didn't shout very much. She'd walked out of the house into the dark and come back feeling better and he'd promised he wouldn't drive again. He'd promised, but still she'd hid the keys like he was a child who couldn't be trusted; it had made him angry because he had promised. A promise was enough. And anyway, she had been wrong. He could remember; he could remember things she had forgotten. He could remember the word list his grandson learnt last week. He could remember the day they met; he could remember her kneeling in the horse manure and what she had said to Mrs Bess. And once he was there it was clearer than yesterday, clearer than today.

The problem of late, he told himself, must be the wine. He didn't have the stomach for it anymore, or the head. It was slowing him down, clouding the days. Perhaps he'd have to give it up. He cringed at the thought.

When he walked outside he did not turn right and head towards the beach to find his family, but left, to the place his son had parked his car. If she hadn't hidden the keys in the first place . . . Go back to the rules of fair play—his promise was no longer good. All bets were off, and so forth.

He was fine. Fit as a fiddle. Ready to go.

~

Inside, the smell was new car, just unwrapped. It was a shiny black European sports sedan with an oversized engine. The indicator was on the wrong side, and the parking brake was a small flick of a switch near the automatic gears. When he started to reverse a picture of the car parked behind him came up on a small TV screen in the centre of the dash, and as he drew closer to it, there was a beep that quickened.

'I can see that, thank you,' Martin replied to the beep, edging further back until it flatlined, not unlike an ECG when the heart stops, though in this instance, mercifully, the sound was a prelude only, last chance; there were still a good few inches in it. He wondered if there was a different sound for impact. A siren perhaps.

He shoved the gear into drive and pulled out a little too fast—in a rush to silence the beep, and to avoid being spotted behind the wheel of his son's car ... *Yes, alright. Tut-tut, bad Martin.*

The brakes were jerky too. All that money and the car bucked like a bull.

'Come on, baby,' he whispered, trying to smooth the ride with a lighter foot. That is what car people called their cars—*baby*—but out of his mouth it didn't sound bona fide. He wasn't a car man like his son, no point in pretending. He had listened to Ethan talk about cars over the years, curious (as one is in the face of anything a child has learnt in the parent's absence) that he had accrued and stored both the knowledge and funds to support his interest; as for the subject itself, he was an A to B man, and what took him there was an eight-year-old Nissan. Sometimes he liked to get his speed up on the freeway so he could feel free the way he was meant to—but his rejection of the material world in the seventies had left its mark in a disdain for expensive machines (all except watches; since the Rolex from chambers when he took silk, for watches he'd made an exception). Ethan laughed at his driving, said he was the only Supreme Court judge in the country driving a car you couldn't sell for ten grand. Ethan called him Mr Magoo. (Try as he might, Martin couldn't bring himself to find that funny.)

What lay in front of him now, as he reached the main intersection, was a closed-down internet cafe on the corner, and in the centre of the road a line of palm trees. He flicked the windscreen wipers on and off, and, without indicating, turned left, gently, gently. Not bad, though perhaps a little slow.

A car pulled up alongside him.

'Yes, yes,' Martin said, waving a hand to the driver, who now held his speed and leaning forward, chest to steering wheel, jerked his head in a sideways scowl. Martin could see he was a bald man in a black T-shirt, and out of the corner of his eye—for all the while he kept a steadfast gaze on the road ahead—Martin could see the open-mouthed, pumped-up prick stab his furious middle finger into the air.

All that was left was to watch him tear away in triumph and disappear into the distance, during which time Martin endeavoured to smother his own flicker of rage and focus on what the man would have done had Martin returned in kind the scowl and the finger, eye for an eye. He knew the type; they were the ones who got out of their cars at traffic lights and pulled tyre levers from their boots to smash heads or windscreens, and on it went, depending on the particular type of personality disorder—the particular type of scum. Only an idiot would take them on; that was an irrefutable fact, but just as irrefutable was that this man was now foot to the metal on a different road, feeling stronger for what had just happened, fuelled by each act of intimidation, each finger stabbed into the air, because on the street, outside a courtroom, there was nothing to stop him . . . nothing to stop him but another angry man.

It brought to mind the carjacking matter, the next of the judgments to be written. That was where it had started, the exact same place: a man sitting at traffic lights and minding his own business.

Martin was lagging behind, of course, with writing up these last judgments. He never used to keep anyone waiting, knowing that once you did that, the talk would begin, the whispers. Ever since old Bruce Jones copped twenty-three complaints and faced the judicial firing squad: it isn't that we want to eat our own, but aren't we always just a little bit peckish? Already (only a month after the hearing), Stephens had asked about the carjacking judgment (a month, six weeks . . .)—how he was 'travelling with it'—and it was not in the nature of a passing question, more a pointed reminder. Perhaps a little missive from above; perhaps there was talk, whispers.

At two in the morning last Wednesday (the same day as Stephens' quip), he had sat down at his own computer and found reasons to dismiss the appeal. The facts were these: a man and his daughter waiting at traffic lights on their way to a movie, the car doors opened on both sides by two strange men, one of whom waved a knife at the daughter and ordered them from the car. The trial judge had refused to exclude evidence of identification in circumstances where the victim had only a 'few seconds' to observe his attacker—for the most part having kept his eyes on the knife that had been held at the ten-year-old's throat. Later that day, in the police station, he had identified one of the offenders from a series of photographs. The arguments on both sides were ones Martin had heard many times before. The victim had claimed certainty, 'a hundred and ten per cent'; the defence had tripped him up on the colour of the attacker's T-shirt and framed a ten-point argument that his honest but mistaken belief would unfairly sway the jury. As Martin reread the transcripts, he couldn't help but wonder if maybe the father had got it wrong. It was, as they said, lineball. The jury listened to him tell his story about the sound of the banging on the doors, his daughter's screams, the way the blade touched her skin. (This was not a case of the scowling pricks or lever-wielding scumbags. This was not maladaption, but premeditation.) The man who opened his daughter's door was the man in the photograph with the number nine in the bottom left-hand corner; he was certain of it, would indeed bet his daughter's life on it—that was the term he'd used. The next morning, then, the judge warned the jury about relying on the evidence, all the reasons why the witness might be wrong—his state of fear, the fact he had seen the man for only a matter of seconds. Of course there was some force in the argument that no words could counter the power of the evidence of a frightened father, as much as the defence had tried: 'Think of the mistakes we make every day—we think we see some fellow but it turns out it was someone else,' the barrister had submitted, citing studies on the fallibility of the human memory. But the jury trusted its victim. They wanted to trust him. He was one of them and they didn't want to let him down. True enough. Depending on the twelve you got, that was what you were up against. Their loyalty lay not with the law, but with each other.

But those, of course, were Martin's private musings. He was a judge and, as the Crown argued, the system provided for warnings. There was other circumstantial evidence. The verdict was safe and satisfactory. To find otherwise would likely land the matter in the High Court, where the gods would put his judgment under a microscope and pick at his bones. Why leave himself open to that?

'How are you travelling with it?' Stephens had asked.

What had his answer been? Something vague but reassuring, nothing to let on what was happening at home at night when he sat at his computer, the mental fatigue. Where once it slowly crept, now it pounced from nowhere, decimating whole formations of thought and leaving a flattened landscape, a post-apocalyptic silence.

'Just finalising it now.' Or words to that effect.

And then for ninety minutes at two in the morning Martin found reasons to dismiss the appeal. They appeared on his page in a cogent and logical sequence. A final edit and the judgment would be complete, his pile smaller by one, and Stephens could shut the hell up. Getting back into bed, Martin tried to content himself with that, and with the thought it was only a matter of time before he would wake to hear it again: the whispered tune, the delicate machinations of a functioning legal mind. Still, floating into the fog of sleep, it already felt like a long-lost love.

Eighty in a sixty zone.

No silly prick could tell him he was too slow.

'Come on, baby.' It sounded better this time. Leaning back in his seat, the voice belonged in the world on the other side of the windscreen, high definition and picture perfect: luminous white paint on black tar, Hollywood palms and neglected shopfronts against a silver sky. A woman in a pale blue hijab waited at a bus stop outside the fish and tackle shop, staring up the street at a cemetery of angels and tilting headstones. And the beast had power in her, alright; Ethan wasn't wrong about that. This one, this baby, she was a bit of a beast—hadn't his son said that? He talked about them like girls, big ones, fast ones . . .

At the red light, he slowed to a stop and asked himself, *What comes next?* How to keep it moving . . .

There it was, an empty left lane.

Swerve in, Martin. Creep up nice and slow, and when the cross-street light turns orange, the second it does . . . Martin took off out of the gate rodeo-style, ahead of the rest into a clear stretch, two lanes free of traffic, free from obstruction. Nudging ninety-five, this engine could roar. The power surged like a demon through the black A-grade leather seat into his legs and his lungs.

'Hah!' Out here with the beast and the white sky.

He cranked the volume and got a squealing pop star. Where was the dial? No dial, just buttons; he pushed one and the pop star stopped. He pushed again; still no music. He pushed other buttons, tried to decipher the little symbols, then wondered what it was he was trying to find.

And what happened to the trees? He had been following the line of trees but now there were none ahead, and none in his rear view. Suddenly there was a haze around what came before and where to next. A street up ahead on the right, that would do it. He knew this road. Big gates into a chapel and a cemetery and a crematorium—he had been here to see off a couple of friends, to be present for their burning. The last was Jack, Annie's husband. Annie was Maggie's oldest friend; she and Jack had bought the gallery that first showed Maggie's work. Over the years Jack and Martin had formed a bond over fishing and single malt. When it came to funeral plans (the doctors had been blunt), Jack had told them all over a dinner at which he drank too much and barely ate a bite that he didn't want any fuss, directing Annie to get it all done in the one place, no moving about. She relayed the story in the eulogy: he had dismissed her suggestion that they scatter the ashes at sea, saying he didn't want the fish to get the last laugh. It was good funeral humour, Martin thought. And Jack was right, it ran like clockwork, to schedule—a well-managed business, like the colour-coded crates in the industrial site next to it: everything got moved, labelled, stacked, in place and on time—the way it should, none of this bloody lagging, nothing misplaced or forgotten, nothing slipping through the cracks.

The tumour in Jack's descending colon ended up being a secondary. The primary was in his brain. They said six months but he only lasted five.

'I always thought there'd be a little voice in my head,' Jack said on Martin's last visit. 'You know, a voice telling me it had started. But all these years . . . well, bliss and ignorance and all that; I suppose I should be grateful.'

The road ended at wire gates. There were just trucks now looking to offload, no place for Martin and the baby beast. His U-turn edged a little wide and the tyre mounted the footpath with a scrape of rubber on concrete, a jolt, but nothing to worry his head about—his head, his brain. But he *was* worried. If the brain were going then so should he. Crate on crate: shut down, pack up—all tidy and on schedule . . . Pills, he had always thought; pills would be easy, gentle. Gentle, not jerky . . .

Tomorrow he was back in court to hear more of the man who smuggled people in his boat—*Kids in leaking boats . . . This isn't the time to go soft.* He was suddenly weary at the thought of it. Ethan was only voicing what so many thought. But this was his son, his only son . . . And there, like the trees out the window flashing past, a bolt of memory: Ethan in the living room with his university friends after graduation, snippets of their conversation floating into Martin's study—some harmless stuff about a girl from the women's college (nothing worse than Friday drinks in his early years: how much better so-and-so would look without the wig and gown); then one of the boys started telling a story about the mardi gras, something about 'a truckload of fudge-packers'. Martin waited for his son to object, but there was just the sound of laughter—at best acquiescent, at worst conspiratorial.

When Ethan asked to live in at college ('You should hear the way the guys talk about it: these are years we'll never forget!'), Martin had thought Maggie was overstating the dangers of privilege and homogeny—straight from an all-boys private school to an all-boys university dorm: 'a few postcodes on a luxury liner'. But, of course, Maggie had been right. In any event they'd done their best to browbeat it out of him, and Laini had joined the fight. But still, sometimes, the mindless dregs . . .

He struggled now to recall what he'd fired back at his son over lunch, but what was clear and what he now wished to forget was the expression on Laini's face as he spoke, like there was a reason to be frightened of him. It brought back Maggie's words driving home after a God-awful cocktail party a few years back: she'd laughed and said that all night she'd felt like they were a couple of badly socialised dogs—when the other dogs sniffed around and lingered too long, the polite talk turned inevitably into a sort of teeth-baring, low-pitched growl. If today Ethan had been the mutt in search of a rumble, Martin had surely been the pit bull that ends up in the newspaper with a picture of a bloodied child.

But for now, the road in front of him, behind him the ground that stored Jack's ashes. He nodded to his friend in reply as it sounded again, the voice inside his head: *Ask yourself the question, Martin: has it begun?*

Had it begun without his knowing? Beneath the layers of his skin, the cells mutating in a wave of silent carnage. Was it already happening?

Would he feel nothing?

Back on the main road there was a golf club and a bus depot, the national park and the beach and the bay. Two Asian boys off the bus snapped pictures of the places in their guidebooks, skinny jeans and stripes of blue in their cropped black hair, snapping the park and the birds in the banksias.

There were things to remember here, bushwalks down to the beach with a small boy on his shoulders: Ethan—no, it was Finn . . . was it? The boy had left his thongs on the beach. He tried to dig it up, more of it, but the rest was forgotten—the place suddenly full of things he had forgotten: the face of the child, the name. Inside his brain, the space closed in. *This damn dissolving brain . . .*

Later he would not remember, but that was when it came back to him, the reason why he was driving: it was to find a place that had never left him, where he would not grapple and fail. Last time he had driven, last week (or last month?), that was where he was going: to that same known place, the place that had etched itself in his memory like a scar: the house, *her* house. *Her house.* The words jarred in his mind and fell into a hole as he turned the car around the loop at the tip of the bay, and by the time the loop was complete the space was filled with a picture of a tower in the middle of a lawn next to a sandstone building and, behind it, a hill.

There was a road out.

He was driving on that road in a car he didn't know.

It was not his car. It belonged to someone else. He had borrowed it, or rented it.

His breath drew short. The road ahead was familiar, but not remembered, this place of whispering shadows and fading faces that sniggered at the dying man.

Has it begun? Will I feel nothing? The cells mutating, the carnage—mutating, merciful. What was a man with a brain afloat? A man without a mind . . . what place for him? Where should his body go?

A main road, and a turn-off up the hill.

Up the hill it would go.

Ethan saw that his car was gone as soon as they crossed onto the footpath from the beach. Without a word he started running and by the time they reached him he had his mobile out, dialling the police.

Maggie put her hand over his. 'Not yet.'

Inside the house she checked the bedroom and the back garden. At the front door Ethan was smiling. 'He's taken it. The keys are gone.'

Even with Finn standing between them she let go of any pretence, cupping her face in her hands and repeating in no particular order: 'damn it', 'Christ!', 'the fool'.

'Mum, what is it? What's he done?'

'I should've told you not to leave them there,' she said. 'I have a hiding spot for ours.'

'What are you talking about? You hide the keys?'

And then Finn: 'Where's Grandie gone?'

When she saw the worry in his eyes, she crouched down on her knees and gave him a hug. She took a breath.

'He's gone for a drive, darling boy. He'll be back. You help Mum get the cake ready.' And when they had gone, she began to explain. 'We agreed he wouldn't drive for a while. He's lost a lot of points. He only has one left.'

'Speeding?'

She shook her head. 'Red lights and stop signs. The cameras get him.' It was almost enough to answer his questions, but not quite.

'So you hide the keys?'

Maggie told him what had happened a couple of weeks ago: Martin had taken the car—afterwards he said he forgot he'd ever agreed he wouldn't. He was gone a couple of hours, then he called from a service station in Matraville. He couldn't remember how to get home. He'd left without his wallet or phone. Maggie drove and got him.

'Was he drunk?'

'No, he'd had a couple. Finny, darling . . .' The boy had crept back in. 'Go back to Mum.'

But Finn stood firm. 'Why are you all worried for?'

'Grandie just didn't tell us he was going, that's all,' Ethan explained. 'He'll be home soon, buddy.'

As soon as the boy left the room again Ethan's smile dropped. 'Matraville? That's only ten minutes away . . . Why don't you tell me this stuff?'

She hesitated, trying to stop the tears welling in her eyes. 'Because I don't have any answers. He is going to see a doctor.'

Because I can't bear to hear myself say the words.

Ethan started pressing in the number on his phone, but she shook her head, pointed to Martin's mobile on the kitchen bench.

'He never leaves his phone,' Ethan said.

'He does now.'

'So where would he go?'

'I don't know, Ethan. He might have just gone up to the shops.'

'How much wine did he drink today? This is a fucking nightmare. What if something happens? The minute the police get involved . . . Jesus Christ!'

'Ethan, please! You think I haven't thought of that? You reacting like this doesn't help.'

'I'm sorry, Mum. You're right, you're right . . .'

Laini appeared behind them and took hold of Ethan's arm. 'Come on, let's give it some time. I'll make some tea.'

In the kitchen Maggie pulled Finn in for a cuddle. 'Why don't we have a piece of cake now and then you can watch some TV.'

But with all the solemnity a seven-year-old could muster, Finn shook his head. 'No,' he said. 'We have to wait for Grandie to come home.'

A suburban street: houses of horrid speckled brick. Ionic columns formed arched porticos and matching urns straddled swirly-glass doors.

But across the intersection and a little further up the hill—a little further, but not so very far away—the street was a different one: pitch-roofed public housing, the buildings small and same and side by side. Card houses, he thought. Finny had built a row of them that went all the way from the couch to the wall.

On the left was a building with a sign that read COMMUNITY HAVEN—ALL WELCOME, and loitering around it a group of dark-skinned boys with folded arms and hooded tops. Martin drove by them without turning his head and, once a safe distance past, he slowed the car alongside a row of houses differentiated only by the colour of the shutters and the state of repair. There was furniture in the garden of the last one: wooden stools and tables and a blue-striped couch, the cushions muddy and torn.

That was it; that was the house. *Her house.*

Ask yourself the question, Martin.

'Look, Grandie!' Finn had said. 'Look at my houses.' Then he kicked them down and jumped on the cards.

Why are you here?

~

Out the car window he looked down over the trees and clotheslines to the water. Others were scared of this place, these people. They were scared of the overgrown gardens. They were scared because nobody tended them and nature took its course, and boys stole wallets and grew up to carry knives into bottle shops and shake hands with their uncles in prison. Martin wasn't one of them. He wasn't scared, but he knew well enough that there was a lay to this land, and that he was sitting in a shiny parked car in a place where he did not belong.

Standing now on the corner across the street was an Aboriginal man with a ponytail of silver hair and legs poking like sticks from cut-off tracksuit pants. Straight and still, he appeared to be somehow rooted to the earth. Even when he turned his head ever so slightly and gave a single nod, he otherwise remained as he was, but staring now, as if waiting for some sort of assurance—a signal that the man in the car was alright, or that he would bugger off and move on. Not sure which, Martin nodded in reply, and the man gave a second nod, a movement that felt in part like an act of welcome—an act of kindness that, in the circumstances, was not warranted.

As a lawyer Martin had acted for only a handful of Aboriginal people, all men, and found them by and large to be hopeless criminals and hopelessly unpersuasive liars. Later, as a judge, he had determined their guilt and their sentence. He could comfort himself that as far as penalties went he had done his best to be lenient. There was always a reason to go easy: poverty, abuse, mental illness. And in the back of his mind the sorry beginnings, those too, the dispossession and the stolen children, starting all the way back. There was that fellow he sentenced when he was still sitting in the District Court, the one with the terrible story about his stepfather, things no child should see; his mother gave evidence and had to stop three times to drink water and wipe her eyes. It was no small crime Martin was dealing with, but he'd let the man walk, and it had held on appeal. And there were others. In his own small way, shaving off a year here, a few months there, Martin tried to do his bit, to make amends.

Maybe after eleven years on the bench he was starting to tire of the same stories, the same hopeless addict spouting the same reasons why it was someone else's fault; maybe he was tired of reading letters scribbled in prison cells telling him they were sorry for what they'd done to their victims, that this time, next time, would be different. Maggie accused him of losing his empathy with age, but it wasn't that. Over the years he had seen the evidence, and what he had learnt was that, more often than not, 'the next time' turned out to be in all respects the same as this one—that people's behaviour changed not because of any decision to desist, but because the environment in which it had thrived was transformed in some way, be it randomly or through orchestration.

'I just don't want to be that person anymore,' an offender might say. And that was all very well, but what was different now? *Tell me, what is it that will allow you to change?*

As to the wider issue, around dinner tables he would agree the government and the nation should be ashamed. Once he had helped to raise money for books for a community in Cape York and then privately wondered whether they would ever be read. Last year, when the third black man for the year hanged himself in a prison cell, a small part of him felt consoled that it might not have been a life worth living—and as for the reason why the life was not worth living, he was saddened by that, the miasma of abuse and neglect. At the end of the day, though, he was a member of the judiciary, and better that it was somebody else's cause. Maggie took it on, donated paints to artists and money to fund scholarships in private schools; Maggie took it on because as a girl living in a migrant camp she had seen it up close, what it was like to live on the fringe, to look in from the outside. There was always something to volunteer for—a refuge or hostel, the youth centre; Maggie held a poster saying SORRY and marched across the Harbour Bridge. And Martin watched it on TV, secure in the knowledge that things were being done by people making a better job of it than he ever could.

Martin looked back at the house at the end of the row with the couch in the garden.

Again he had come this far and in the pit of his stomach the same questions stirred: What were the chances that she would still be here, in her house with the leaking ceiling and the patched door? All these years later, would she even recognise him? And again, sure enough, brick by brick, the wall was built. Martin shook his head. He would turn around.

In the end, after all, hadn't she got the better of him?

Turn the key, Martin; drive away.

In the end, doesn't everyone get what they want?

But this time he didn't drive.

The sensation was familiar, welcome—the leaden weight of inertia. He let his eyes close to the warm, rolling light and the memory downloaded without him pressing any buttons. It wasn't the girl who lived in the street, but Maggie—not as she was now, but as she was the day she arrived in the loft: a girl at his front door with long brown hair and pupils wired with caffeine. The picture was there in the third eye, centre screen. While others faded, she formed and re-formed, and the memory of the day he met her played again, immune to the ravages of time. He had heard himself retelling it, repeating it just as the memory repeated, as though the girl was at his door again, on his kitchen bench, in the garden between the tenements . . .

Then the sound of a dog barking, and Martin opened his eyes. Just as quickly as he'd left, he now returned. It was the same place but somehow he was lost again.

Had he slept? No, just closed his eyes, *and in the blink of an eye* . . . There had been a man on the corner, but he was gone. Martin scanned the street, bothered that there was no sign of him. He turned the key in the ignition, pulled away from the kerb and drove up to the end of the block. On the footpath a dog lay asleep on a pile of newspapers, and inside the front window of the house—the one with the couch in the garden—a curtain hung, tied in a knot. A faint dread crept into his breath, but only faint, blunt. Things look so different in the dark.

His eyes reached the front door. There at eye level were four timber boards nailed over a broken pane of glass—the pane of glass on the yellow painted door that after all these years had never been repaired.

Ask yourself the question, Martin . . .

His foot pressed down on the accelerator, gently so as to be quiet. Better to go back the way he came. The car crawled into a turning circle. Too small for a single turn, he reversed.

On the screen on the dashboard the camera caught the rear view: an old woman in her garden wearing a Hawaiian shirt.

What did I do here?

The houses all the same: the old mission. When he shifted into drive, he saw another, younger woman sitting on the front step smoking a cigarette, and a child hanging from a broken swing, all staring at the white man in the car staring back at them. Gently, he told himself, quietly. But there was a shout, the old woman cupping her hands over her mouth, shouting across the street to someone behind him. He saw it flash in front of the car, the dog that slept on the newspapers. He hit the brake. Where was the dog? Then the sound of barking, and he saw the animal out his window as it strutted onwards, tail wagging. All was well, if he could just keep moving. He had no place here. It was strange to him, all of it: the dog, the faces, the street, the car. Get out of the car, walk away, a voice told him, but he didn't know if he was allowed to do that, just to get out and leave. He changed the gears again. Later, he would not be able to say why; there were possibilities but no evidence to support them, no memory and no record, no way to know if he was trying to move backwards, or whether he had mistaken forward and reverse. Later he would ask about it only once before the incident was buried along with so many others.

The people on the street were staring still, the younger woman getting to her feet, eyes filled with suspicion. And a man came out of a gate, a man with a silver ponytail and a face Martin knew. He walked behind the woman. They were not smiling. They were hostile. He mustn't let them reach him, he thought, as he pressed down on the accelerator. But the car did not move forwards. The beep quickened, flatlined. In the middle of the screen on the dashboard he saw a parked car and a boy on a red bike.

He slammed his foot on the brake.

But this time, it was too late. This time, there was a bang and the screen went black.

That was the noise it made on impact, not a siren, but a scream.

And after that, silence. He watched the screen to see what would happen next but it stayed blank, black. He pushed the gearstick into park but kept his foot on the brake to be sure it wouldn't move again. Then there was shouting, and a man approaching the passenger window. And he knew he would be trapped, and that he had to get out of the car. He opened the door, emerged. The boy from the bike was on his knees. Still there was shouting. The young woman charged at him like she wasn't going to stop. He tried to step back but stumbled and fell so that she towered over him, cursing, the inside of her mouth full of red-pink hate.

Martin clambered to his feet. 'I am sorry,' he said. 'I didn't see it.'

At the sound of his voice, the woman froze. Her gaze softened into a question. 'What are you doing here?'

She had olive skin and pale lips and for a moment it felt as though they were alone. The man with the ponytail had run into a house and the old woman was on the ground with the boy, and in the cradle of the boy's arms was the head of the dog. The boy was quiet.

Martin shook his head in reply to her question because he didn't know the answer. She spoke but he couldn't hear her. He turned away ... The man turned away as the dog with the crushed heart kept one eye open, as if to make sure the last thing he would see was the face of the tender boy who held him.

There was shouting again, but Martin couldn't make out what was being said, the footsteps behind just the patter of a drum. Walking past a house, he looked into the dark window and saw a curtain tied in a knot and next to the curtain, reflected in the glass, an ageing man who did not belong here. He was familiar, but not remembered. Something was happening to him; that was his thought as the wave of warm blood rushed into his chest. For a moment he felt light, suspended, the air around him like liquid. But next came the assault, the clamp of cold tendrils around the left side of his body. It was brutal, but not painful. It was a takeover, and he was willing to let go. He looked up at the man in the window. The face was a gargoyle; he raised his hand to it, and fell to his knees, the same question in his eyes, only now he knew the answer.

It had begun.

Part Two

The girl is standing in the doorway.

Martin holds his head in his hands and asks the question: 'Where's the fire?'

Even before he hears the accent, he knows who it is. 'Sorry, God, shit,' she says. 'I was banging away. I've woken you up.' He waits for her to complete the thought: I'll go, and come back later, or not; I'll go and I'll never see you again. But she doesn't move.

'You are Maggie,' he says.

The moment is fixed, a still shot: Maggie stands in the doorway, and pushing and pulling in the three-foot space between them are all the reasons he wants her to go, and the fact the longer he looks at her the more he wouldn't mind if she stayed. She was right; she woke him up and he hadn't got in until four.

'I did call,' she says. 'I left messages.'

He knows that; he has heard them all: 'Martin, this is Maggie Varga. I'm in New York'; 'Maggie again. It would be great to meet up . . .' Then a note under the door: she'd dropped by because she didn't have a number he could phone her back on. Dave waved it around and called her the Aussie stalker girl, then stood on a chair when Martin tried to snatch it back. Sure, he didn't want to see her—he didn't want anyone taking a status report home right now—but he didn't want to turn her into the butt of any joke . . . He'd thought if he just ignored the first message, she would stop.

But now bang, bang and stalker girl is here at his door.

'I know. I got the messages. It's just been crazy around here. Mad, you know . . .'

'Oh sure,' she says, and she smiles. This time it isn't polite or nervous. It absolves him and permits him to admire, and when he does, when he lets himself take a good look at the girl who is standing there, he is reminded of when he was a kid and he dreamt of opening the front door to find a labrador puppy in a basket with a bow tied around its fluffy little neck.

'Your mum said I should call you,' she says again, which he already knew. It had come at the tail end of his mother's last phone call.

'What is happening over there? What do you mean you're taking a break? You shouldn't be out of work too long. It won't look good . . .'

'To who?' he asked. She knew the plan: he was going to be a barrister when he got back and that meant no employer; he would be his own boss. What his mother was worried about was not having an impressive update for her friends.

'Are you trying to find yourself or something?' she asked, and behind her he could hear his dad: 'He's almost thirty years old, for Christ's sake! He'd better hurry up. The world won't wait.' That was the way they thought, like he was stepping off the planet somehow and not tapping into the inner core, the centre of the universe . . . Sydney, the Lower

North Shore, dinner parties with the same pent-up people in the same decked-out houses every weekend: that was stepping off. If anyone was ignoring the predicament, letting the world slip by . . . But he didn't put up an argument. He said he was thinking about taking the bar exams in a few months.

Then: 'Maggie Varga will call when she is in town, such a nice girl. You remember her mother, Lili—she used to cook those dinners at the house; she's become a dear friend to me.' He remembered the mother; she was a cool woman, some kind of chef, wrote ethnic cookbooks. But he wasn't in New York to babysit her daughter, and with how things had been going in the loft, he'd only be doing everyone a favour by ignoring her calls.

Except now here she is, Maggie Varga, at his door, and all her good bits are giving him a hard-on. Without looking down at his shorts he tells her to come in, says he'll just grab some jeans.

When he gets back the girl is perched on the edge of the bathtub that sits in the middle of the kitchen.

'There's a bath in your kitchen,' she says.

'That is observant of you.'

'How cool!' She turns the tap, seems startled when it spurts water out.

He explains that somehow it was the only place it would work with the plumbing. 'You can have one if you want. I won't look. Promise.'

She smiles and tells him she hasn't had a bath in six months. 'But I'm going home tomorrow. I can make do with showers one more day.'

All the more reason to relax: she is going home tomorrow. 'You want a coffee?'

She screws up her face, says she's been on a bottomless cup of coffee all morning. 'I sort of forgot to budget for the last day.'

It's then he notices she is eyeing the loaf of bread. So he makes her toast and she sits up on the kitchen bench and when she finishes he asks if she wants more. By the time she is onto her third piece he is smoking a cigarette and watching the crumb in the corner of her mouth, wondering to himself, *How did she get in here?* and already he doesn't just mean his loft, he means his life, at least this day in his life. Already there is something about Maggie Varga that has smothered the last remaining urge to get her out.

He catches himself staring, asks her how old she is. Twenty-one, she says, as she slides off the bench and sits down on the beanbag to look around at the walls of the loft. At the kitchen end is Dave's mural then Linda's scrawled poetry, on the other side a wall of Martin's photos, and the rest an art brut collaboration of friends and strangers who have come and got high and channelled Dubuffet in the dark. Once or twice when no one had been over the night before, Dave and Linda stood in the morning looking at a new painting on the wall, trying to remember how it got there. *The mystery man was here.* That was the best of it, they agreed: the stuff that got there by itself.

'This is so amazing,' she says. 'I can't believe you live here.'

He doesn't reply to that. The truth is, he still feels like a tourist himself, an observer. But hearing the girl gush, seeing it through her eyes, makes his place here feel legitimate. She makes him feel like this is home. 'I mean, you must love it. Do you love it?'

Yes, he loves it; he loves the grid of bars on the fifteen-foot ceilings and the chaos on the walls and the fact that every piece of furniture was found on the street. He loves that in the corner above his bed is a boarded-up window that bears his name; he loves that he left a one-bedroom apartment and a humdrum job and found a way to live on the other side of the world with people like Dave and Linda.

'It wasn't so amazing when Dave got it,' he says. 'It was pretty much condemned, like all the buildings around here. He fixed it up. Half the floorboards had to be pulled up and replaced. I helped out.' He points to a patchwork of boards and the gaps still in between. 'It isn't perfect, obviously. But it's livable. And now the fuckwit wants to charge us mad rent. Suddenly SoHo is hip . . .'

'Where did you get all the plants?'

'That's Dave. He's into his triffids . . . He reckons buildings should be covered in leaves and rooftops should be made into gardens.'

'That's cool.'

'Yeah. Dave is cool.'

'Are they his posters?' She is pointing to the *Gilligan's Island* posters that wallpaper the bathroom door.

'Yeah, he loves it.'

She looks around. 'You don't have a TV.'

Martin shrugs. 'I'm not sure he's ever actually watched an episode. He just likes the idea of it.'

'So how about you . . . You're a lawyer, right?'

'I'm not working as one right now. I was on a secondment, but I'm taking a break.'

'Lil said you're doing your bar exams.'

'You call your mother Lil?'

'Yeah, since I was little. It just stuck.'

'Yeah, well, the exams, that was the plan. Or I said that

was the plan. I'm working in a diner; I've been focusing on the photographs.'

She points at the wall. 'Did you take them?' He nods and she walks closer. 'Jesus, they're amazing. It's so wild that you just up and left and now all this. I mean, it's incredible!'

Apart from his mother's observations, it is the first commentary he has had outside his own head in twelve months, and though usually he'd object to the blast of adjectives, it is nice to hear something new.

'What about you, Maggie Varga? Where've you been?'

Back on the beanbag, plane by train she marks the map in the air with her finger. 'First I went to Hungary and found the house in Budapest where my mother was born . . .' When she gets to the art her eyes light up like a firecracker. She is busting to tell him the best of it: El Greco's house in Toledo; Goya's Black Paintings in Madrid. 'They are like my gods. Goya painted on the walls of his house, like you guys, like this, but no one was meant to see it except him. He couldn't hear anymore; he just had this ringing in his ears . . . Have you seen them, his paintings? The faces, the expressions—oh my God! That was what it was all about for Goya, these inner demons. And then he just got up and left it all there—he said if you couldn't extinguish the fire in a house you had to move away . . .' She stops there, her eyes lock on to his. 'That is good, isn't it? I thought about that a lot, about why he had to leave that place.' Shifting her lips around like she is weighing something up, she looks over his shoulder to his photos. 'Is that why you left?'

'A fire?' He shrugs. 'I'm going back. I'm here for a while, I don't know how long. There wasn't any fire. Maybe that was the problem.'

'You don't like being a lawyer?'

'I didn't like my job.'

'What sort of law?'

'Bit of this and that, commercial litigation. I was there four years. It was a place you go to die, if you know what I mean.'

'Sure, I mean it's a little dark, but yeah, I get it. You hated it. And you're going back to do it again?'

'Well, a lawyer, just a different type.'

She walks over to the photos again, stands up close to the wall and studies each image. He gets up and stands behind her, looking at them too, these pictures tacked and taped to the wall that link him to this place, this city. They are not in rows or in any sort of order; some overlap, some stand apart: a montage in black and white.

At the centre there are the boys in the subway.

The Scream.

He'd asked them if he could take their photo; they agreed, then, like he was attacking them, they started to scream . . .

There in the memory of Martin Field are the photographs on the wall of his loft in Hudson Street, New York City. There was another sequence from the subway, and from the tunnel, then up on the street, faces and fire escapes, skylines, bridges, body parts. Some of the faces had been drawn over in texta-colour tattoos, dragons on cheeks, hearts on foreheads. That wasn't him. That was Dave; on a couple he even stooped to John Lennon glasses and red-devil horns, then looked to Martin for a reaction. 'Don't get too precious,' he'd once said when Martin had framed a shot that he sold to the *SoHo Weekly News* for ten bucks. 'That'll just fuck everything up.'

When later Martin saw his first Goya at the Metropolitan, he didn't think of Maggie. The painting was of two old men.

The first, with a long white beard, was leaning on his staff in a gesture of contemplation. Hovering too close behind him was the second, with a face part-human, part-ghoul, the mouth stretched open at the first man's ear. He was shouting at him, or he was poised to devour. Martin had recognised him at once. It was Dave telling him not to be precious. It was his friend warning him not to care.

'This one, the one where the boy is holding his face, it's like *The Scream*; the graffiti is the red sky. Did you mean to do that?' And in reply to his blank look: 'The Munch painting, do you know the one?'

'I've heard of it.'

'So you are tapping into the great artistic unconscious . . .'

'Hah! I doubt that. I'm just messing around. I don't really know what the fuck I'm doing.'

But she's onto the next thing: 'I've gotta get a job when I get back,' she says. 'I am in crazy debt . . . But I'm going to do night classes to finish art school. That's what I'm going to do: I'm going to paint.'

She has turned away from the photos and is looking around at the other walls. There is a certainty in the way she announces her plans that rubs the wrong way; she is so comfortable in her own skin that it makes him want to wriggle out of his own, or at least find a way to make a dent in hers.

'So you're going to live with your mother?'

She nods, slowly, like she can see it coming.

'I'm just not sure I get it.'

'Get what?'

He hesitates.

She persists: 'What don't you get?'

'You go out and travel the world, and when you're done you go home to live with your mother and spend your nights at art class sitting in a room full of wankers. You know the type I'm talking about . . . It's a backward step, that's all I'm saying.' He falls down next to where she is sitting on the beanbag and faces her. 'If you are looking for any sort of freedom, I mean.'

The words slap, he sees that, but it passes. Leaning forwards, she narrows her eyes and cocks her head like she is giving the comment meaning-of-the-universe consideration, then she straightens back up to answer each part of it in turn. 'I am broke. I like my mother and I like living with her. And I need to learn. I don't know what sort of people will be in the class but I'm not there to make friends. I want to draw people. I want to paint.' At the end of the spiel, she nods, more to herself than to him. There is no doubt: he has made no dent.

'So draw, paint.' He stands up and walks over to the table by the kitchen, picks up a bowl filled with sticks of charcoal. He points at a spot on the wall. 'Draw.'

She doesn't move. 'I don't want to mess up your wall.'

'You kidding? Look at this shit. It'll be a masterpiece.'

So she stands up and takes a stick from the bowl.

'What should I draw?'

'You draw people? Draw me.'

At that she scrunches up her face then covers it with her hands. 'This is weird,' she says. When she takes her hands away and looks at him again she is still shaking her head in bemusement.

'What is so weird?'

'Sorry, nothing, no reason . . . I will draw you, Martin.'

'It's Marty here. People call me Marty.'

'Okay, Marty. So grab a stool.'

When he comes back she is staring at him, sheepish. 'I'm sorry,' she says, 'but I have to ask. Do you remember me? Do you remember me coming to your place when I was little?'

He nods. 'Sure I do, yeah.' Barely, but anyway . . .

'What do you remember?'

'I don't know,' he answers. 'I remember you were there in the kitchen with Lili, when she used to cook those dinners.'

She nods. 'I used to sit on the floor at the kitchen door.' She waits to see if that jogs a memory; when his face is a blank she continues, 'I saw you a few times.' She is studying him. 'Your face is so different now.'

'Come on, you really remember what my face looked like?'

She hesitates. 'We had a photo of you—of you and your mother. It was on our fridge.' Seeing he is perplexed, she explains that this was later, when their mothers had become friends. 'Lil has always been so grateful to your mum, for the catering jobs, and then for the friendship. She says there were women in your mum's circle who didn't approve.'

But he isn't interested in delving into family history. 'Okay,' he says, bringing it back to the here and now. 'So what has changed so much about my face?'

She tells him it is the shape. 'Shame, you were such a handsome boy.'

'Yeah, okay, I got it . . . So how do you want me to sit, funny girl? Clothes on or off?'

'Careful what you offer,' she says. 'Men are always disappointed with what ends up on the page.' Then she smiles that smile, and begins. As her eyes move down from his forehead to his chest and across his face from ear to ear, the smile fades. She blinks like she is taking a snapshot then turns to the smeared, off-white wall and draws an oval in a series of faint lines and through the middle, a vertical and a horizontal, scribbling and smudging as she goes. But still the angles are too strong. It is nothing like the shape of his face.

'I'm sensing you're more into the abstract school.'

She tells him to fuck off and shut up. 'You asked me to do this.'

He drops the smile, not wanting her to stop. He watches her brow furrow in concentration and feels the urge to reach out and touch it. Any which way, it is a beautiful face.

And the one on the wall: now the line of the nose, the nostrils . . . She is dividing it again just beneath the bottom lip. It looks too big to be his lip. It looks like a slug, and then another layer of slug on top. Better. They are good lips, just not his. And the chin is too big to start with, but then she smudges around the socket with the tip of her finger and it starts to make sense. There is something to recognise. It isn't bad. And she isn't squinting or screwing up her face anymore. She has zoned out, tuned in, her eyes a little ablaze but the rest of her face fixed, serene. She's done the ears and is onto the zigzag parting of his hair. Then she is scribbling; the neck and shoulders are on the wall in a few careless lines before she stops and stands back and squints again, shakes her head.

'Told you I'd make a mess,' she says. 'Now you know why I need art school.'

And, of course, it is no mess at all. Perhaps the eyes are a tad small, or close together—not quite generous enough in dimension (his eyes are neither small nor close together). But she's made up for it with a nice long neck and, overall, the image is to his liking, a fine fucking addition to their wall. It might be the best thing on it. He takes a fresh piece of green chalk from the floor and hands it to her.

'Sign it.'

~

Maggie signed it, and it stayed there after she was gone. She banged on the door and drew his picture on the wall.

Maggie V.

Fire in her eyes, but so serene.

Even if he wanted to he couldn't keep her.

It was Maggie Varga's voice again but she sounded scared now and she was asking him to come back to her. *Come back to me, darling man.* When he opened his eyes people rushed around in a mad, fluorescent fuss, Maggie V in the middle with her hair cut shoulder-length and streaked with grey. Next to her a doctor with his sleeves rolled up told him that he'd had a stroke, then pushed his sleeves even further and said it wasn't Martin's first stroke. The other man said nothing. 'You didn't feel it, the first stroke,' the speaker said. 'They call it a silent stroke. Maggie said you've been experiencing problems with your memory. Now we know why.'

He looked back to her again, this older Maggie with lines around her eyes—still beautiful. If anything, her body seemed stronger, her shoulders broader. She nodded her head now in time with the doctor like this whole hospital show was rehearsed, and they'd agreed on the final scene in his absence. He wondered how long they were going to hold back on the bottom line. When the doctor kept talking it was like someone had turned the volume down. Martin couldn't hear it all, but he didn't mind. He nodded like Maggie, in time. Like he was in on it too. After a while, though, they weren't nodding anymore and no one was speaking. They were just looking at him, waiting. It was the first time it had crossed his mind to speak.

'Sorry?' he said. Only it wasn't 'sorry'; it was 'thourry'.

Everyone tried to look pleased, but they hadn't rehearsed it well at all. Maggie smiled and held his hand while the doctor talked about speech therapy. He was glad he was tired again, not just weak, weary, but the kind of tired where he could feel himself disappearing and there wasn't anything he could do but slide down into the deep, dark one-man hole, the hospital room and all its lights safely behind him . . .

'So what are you going to do, Maggie Varga?' he asks.

When he stares, her cheeks flush pink beneath her grey-green eyes.

'You mean when I get home?'

He shrugs. 'When you get home,' he says. 'Or now, today. Whenever.'

Now, he means now, it is an invitation; what could it hurt? It was her last day; they'd spend a few hours together, and then they would say goodbye and one day he'd bump into her on a street in Sydney.

She smiles like she's inside his head, and when he asks the question he doesn't mind if she is.

'You want to go for a walk?'

The frizzy-haired nurse offered only momentary eye contact and a kind smile; gone were the chat and nursey cheer.

It was Martin's third day in hospital, and what the doctors had told them in terms of his recovery—his speech, his memory—was that anything was 'possible'. That was as far as they would go, reluctant to say 'probable', or 'likely'. Sometimes the brain repaired itself, sometimes another part of the brain stepped in to compensate, and sometimes the damage was done. A scan could tell them one thing, but the only real evidence would be in the coming days and weeks. So it was that the nurse's changed demeanour as she completed her tasks and left the room gave Maggie the sure feeling that the woman knew something she didn't, and that in the rooms where visitors were not permitted a whole different set of words was being used.

Later in the afternoon, around four o'clock, her suspicions were confirmed, though not at all in the way she had anticipated. Passing the staff tearoom, she heard the nurse's voice: '. . . It's that judge in room twenty-three, I told you the story. Look, I'm not laughing, I wouldn't—but you've got to see how they've cocked up the headline . . . So men in comas are driving cars now! We've got our very own killer zombie, eh?' And then there was indeed laughter, the kind you get after a bad joke.

Ethan had left the paper yesterday but she hadn't read it. There on page fifteen as she opened it now was a short column underneath two photos, Martin in his wig and gown, and an Aboriginal boy dressed in his footy clothes, eyes shining white against his brown skin. The headline read: JUDGE IN COMA RUNS OVER DOG.

Maggie nodded. *Our very own killer zombie.* She started to read:

> Supreme Court judge Martin Field is in a coma after suffering a stroke on Sunday in the streets of La Perouse . . .

The article went on to describe how Martin had reversed his car and hit the dog. The only quote in the article came from a witness who said that when the judge got out of the car he 'looked lost'. Maggie wondered who had called the paper, how the incident had become news—but the question was not a burning one, and when she came to imagine their friends who might not yet know turning to page fifteen, even then she felt strangely removed. At least this way, she told herself, she wouldn't have to make any calls.

What did it matter how people would read the headline?

She placed her hand on the side of Martin's face, rough and warm, and she held it there. Strange how all the days leading to this were stripped of consequence, how she lunged now into a future with no attachment to the world she had known. Already it seemed an artifice, that world—a stack of boxes behind a wall of windows. Her son and her grandchild, the paintings and empty canvases, the shelves of her studio crammed with the props of her craft, her friends, her home—all that she had treasured packed away in storage while the calamity played out. Strange again that there was a sense of relief in that, an unburdening. Ethan and Laini came and kept watch, Annie too—and there were dozens of messages. All of which belonged behind a window, in a box . . .

'Get on with it, my love,' she said to him as she began to rub the hand that was free of tubes and needles.

And somewhere between the wrist and the thumb came his delayed response, a lovely slurred whisper: 'Right you are.'

An hour later, as he sipped his soup, he asked the question: 'What happened?'

Maggie had asked the doctors if Martin would remember the events leading to his stroke, realising even as the words left her mouth they were a waste of breath. It was, they told her, *possible.*

'Do you remember anything?' she asked him.

There was no reply. He was waiting for her to go on.

'Do you remember driving? Do you remember going to La Perouse?'

At that he looked wary, shook his head.

'You reversed,' she told him. 'The car hit a dog.'

He nodded then, narrowing his right eye into a slit. The left remained open but lazy, and when the right corner of his mouth drooped into a quasi-scowl, the left corner held still, stubborn.

'But the dog is alright?' *Butha doge ith au-rye-at?* He shuddered at the sound of his words, as though they tasted sour. Saliva dribbled from the corner of his mouth. She dabbed it with a tissue.

It crossed her mind he needn't know that he had killed the dog, or at least he needn't know it yet—the doctor had warned of a risk of a further stroke in the first months in the event of undue stress. But no, she told herself, state it plainly now; speak the truth. Ignorance would only weaken him, push him further into the outer.

'It wasn't alright, darling. The dog was killed.'

His eyes filled with mistrust, then emptied of all recognition as though the speaker was not known to him. 'Why do you say that to me?' *Tawmay.*

Because it was true, she said. 'It wasn't anyone's fault. It was an accident.' But already he had turned away; already his eyes were closed.

~

Over the course of a week in hospital Martin's speech improved rapidly, remarkably—no more than the odd slurred word. As to his memory, it was quite normal that he didn't remember anything of the incident that had brought him here. That in itself, they were assured, was not indication of further deterioration. In a separate meeting alone with the doctor, discussing the memory problems that preceded the stroke—or, as it turned out, the *second* stroke—the doctor again could speak only in terms of the possibilities: it was a mild cognitive impairment, or it was the beginning of vascular dementia. Either was possible (not likely, not probable); they would have to wait and see.

Though the doctor was circumspect when he told them Martin could be home by the end of the week, Martin shook his hand and his eyes welled with tears of joy. It was a happy day, of course it was. He had done so well, in so little time. But inside Maggie there was a small voice prodding her to test him. She sat down next to him on the bed, and held up the newspaper article for him to see. 'You saw this?'

He squinted at the page. 'I did. Terrible photo. I look a hundred.'

She smiled; it was true, and it was a relief to get a glimpse of the old vanity. 'You remember nothing?'

He shook his head, but she persisted, and when she did he looked away. She took his hand in hers. 'You don't remember driving there? Did you know that place, that street?' She held up the newspaper again and showed him the picture of the boy. 'He was there, this boy . . . do you remember him?'

Silence. His hand began to shake. She caught herself and squeezed it tight. 'Let's talk about this later,' she said.

Already as she released his hand she could feel that it was steady again, and as he spoke he smiled. 'Thank you,' he said. 'I think that would be best. What is next?'

The last words he uttered as though he were in court presiding over a list of matters to be heard in sequential order. *Accident. Hospital. Home.* Maggie did not reply, and he did not repeat the question. Swinging her legs up next to his and leaning back on the cold metal bedhead, she reminded herself that the method was not new. By no means was it the first time that Martin had constructed his reality, cutting and pasting to a point where the image was acceptable. He would have them believe now it was a lapse of memory or an inability to process, but even then, sitting on the hospital bed by his side, she suspected that Martin was at work. There would be no explanation as to why the judge drove into the street and shifted his car into reverse, not for Maggie, and not for the boy in the football jersey who had lost his dog. There would be no explanation because Martin would never dig to find it. Another bone would be buried, another secret preserved . . . *Drive. Run over dog. Forget.*

She could cast her mind back and find other such sequences, ending with a scuttling of the aftermath, but for now she looked down at the page in her hand, to the smiling eyes of the brown-skinned boy, still in her mind Martin's unanswered question: *What is next?* Never more than now did the future seem so uncertain, so precarious, and never more than now did it seem so inexorably linked to the past. A simple truth turned in her mind: she could not answer 'What is next?' before she knew what it was that had come before.

~

The ambulance officer's name was Peter. He didn't seem at all surprised that Maggie had made contact with him. 'You see he doesn't remember anything about it, my husband, and I just felt—' But he stopped her there and, in a voice that hinted at relief, said it was a good idea that they meet. It seemed that the man had a story to tell.

They sat down at a small table in the middle of the hospital coffee shop. His smile was curt, his voice firm.

'It was no easy task for starters,' he said, without waiting for a question. 'There was a bit of a crowd.'

'A crowd?'

'Well, by the time we got there, half a dozen or so . . .' He paused. 'There were seven.'

As he described the events it was evident to Maggie that he was taking care to give an accurate account, as though the details mattered. As Peter and his co-worker Gerry drove into the street they saw Martin lying on the road. Squatting next to him was an Aboriginal man who had put Martin onto his side, and behind the man was a semicircle of onlookers, among them a woman who had stepped closer 'to get a good look-see'. And further down the street, they could see the dog lying on the road.

'There was a boy there, kneeling over the dog, and an old lady with her arms around the boy. He had the dog's head in his lap; he was sort of cradling it, and rocking. And there was this noise—at first I thought it was the dog howling, then I realised it was the boy, this God-awful wail, like he was figuring to call the animal back to life.

'The old bloke with your husband had done a good job—told us he'd checked the pulse and his breathing, a bit of a citizen, I'd say . . . who'd have guessed that? Anyhow, things got tricky pretty quick. First the boy runs up; he's got the dog's blood on his hands, and it's smeared on his cheek and his forehead. It was something to see . . . like warrior paint—you know, like in those tribal dances? He asks if we can help with the dog, see if it's alive. We're getting your husband into the van and I'm trying to tell him we can't do that, we can't help a dog, we've got to get to the hospital. So he starts pleading: "Please help him," he's saying over and over, and he's stepping in my way and I'm pushing past him to get from the back of the van to my door, so I didn't hear it, what Gerry said, but it set her right off . . .'

'Sorry.' Maggie stopped him. 'I'm getting lost. Set who off?'

'The woman, the one who was at the front looking down at the judge. I'm guessing it was the boy's mother.'

'And Gerry said something to her?'

'Something about the police coming, not to touch the car. I didn't hear it exactly, but there wasn't much more to it than that. There wasn't any delay, mind you, and your husband was stable, no question. This all happened at once, you know, like in a couple of seconds. Twenty seconds, tops. I might have been checking the straps, and Gerry's sizing it all up, looking at the fancy car that's sitting there in the middle of the road—door open and keys in the ignition and a bunch of blackfellas—and I guess he joined the dots: goodbye, car. We'd be sending the police and he wanted to make sure they knew that. Anyhow, whatever he said, maybe he shouldn't have said it, I grant you that. But she went off, that woman, like I've never seen. One minute she's staring down at the judge like she's seen some kind of ghost, the next she's charged up, cursing us every which way, mostly our white skin—effing white c's and what have you. We just took off. We had to.' Peter paused before going on, looking at Maggie as though waiting for her approval.

'Of course you did,' she said quickly.

He looked down at his untouched coffee then back at her. 'I had to push the boy away.'

'You pushed him.'

'I had to. He grabbed my arm. I said that—'

'Sorry, I thought you just said he got in your way.'

'No, he grabbed me; I think he was trying to pull me down the street, to the dog. I had to get him off me to get into the van.'

And again, he waited.

Maggie nodded. 'You had to get to the hospital.'

When he spoke again, the corners of his mouth quivered. 'And as we drove away, I looked in the rear-view, and there she was, kicking the car, the boy too.' Shaking his head at the memory, he picked up the saltcellar and rolled it in the palm of his hands. Then he stopped, looked at Maggie. 'I saw the thing in the paper, one of them must have called. I thought there might be some kind of complaint, I don't know what about, but you know, you just nod your head the wrong way these days and it's racist.' And when she didn't respond, he persisted. 'You know what I mean?'

Maggie shrugged. 'It sounds like an awful situation to be in, for you, for them. And you did your best, I'm sure.'

'I don't know if there was any damage, was there?'

'Damage?'

'To the car?'

'No,' she said, 'I don't think so. Just at the back where he reversed.' But she wasn't thinking about the car; she was thinking about the boy with the blood on his face. 'How old was he, do you think—the boy?'

'I'd guess eleven or twelve. And if that was his mum, you have to wonder what his chances are. Gerry didn't mean anything by it, I know he didn't. And there she had him pegged as the friggin' Ku Klux Klan.'

'Yes, but I mean, she was upset, the dog had been killed.'

'But that wasn't—'

'Of course that wasn't your fault—I am just saying, they were upset, the boy—'

'Sure, sure. I get that. But they don't do themselves any favours with that sort of carry-on. There they were, laying into the car like they've got a God-given right. I've got a son not much younger, and I'll tell you now if I saw him kick a car . . . It shouldn't be any different for that young fella, black skin or white skin, dead dog or no dead dog.'

'Yes, of course.' Even as the words left her mouth she recoiled from her assent. 'I don't suppose you know which house he lived in?'

The ambulance officer looked wary then. 'You want to find him?'

She nodded. 'I do.'

'Why would you want to do that?'

Even in her own mind she needed a moment to find the answer to his question, relieved at the sense of clarity when she did: 'I want to say sorry for what happened. And to ask if he would like me to buy him another dog.'

~

On the morning he was to be released, Martin was showered and dressed when Maggie arrived—showered and dressed and smiling, like a child who had got up early all by himself to be ready for the first day of school.

'Hallelujah, get me out of here,' he said. 'What's for dinner?'

She laughed. 'We have to wait to see the doctor yet. For dinner, my veal bake. Ethan and Laini are coming. Finnegan has made you chocolate brownies.'

'And dumplings with the veal?' he asked.

'Yes,' she said. 'Dumplings.' They were his favourite.

She checked the bathroom to make sure that nothing had been forgotten. There in the bin on the floor was the newspaper story about Martin and his stroke, the boy and his dog. Apart from that, nothing had been left behind.

So this was what was next.

Hospital. Home. Dumplings.

Next they are walking out onto the street, the sun overhead. The loft was sepia, but there is nothing muted once they step outside. The colour is a wave of scarves, sky, spray-paint. The fire escapes crawl with life—people pegging clothes or bodies flopped on mattresses left out overnight. To look up at them Maggie holds her hat with one hand, and can't go more than a block before she has to stop again and poke her head down basement steps or read some writing on the wall. Her hat is blue canvas, wide-rimmed.

No one is in a hurry. It is Saturday in downtown Manhattan, the end of summer.

'I wish I'd come down here earlier,' Maggie says. She has spent six days uptown burning the last of her money, getting lost in the park, bumping into people on the sidewalk and ticking off a long list of museums. 'It's not that I haven't loved it; I just always feel like I want to get up onto the rooftops.' She leans back into a lamppost, haloed by the bishop's crook, Maggie in her big hat and little skirt staring up at the sky and telling him where she wants to be.

'We'll go to the garden and meet Dave,' he says. 'I'll show you something better than the rooftops.'

Sometimes it hovered there, at the image of Maggie and the lamppost, behind them the streets of SoHo. There is the feeling that he had something to give her, this girl he had known for just a couple of hours, and with that, an unburdening of a loneliness he didn't even know he'd been carrying . . . The man on the street in a striped shirt staring at the girl leaning against the lamppost, ahead of them the whole day, and in that day, the seed that will later form the basis of his better decisions.

In the background there is noise—a curtain drawn, the sound of steps in another time and place but close by, in the next room, or the same room. It stirs him into limbo, a foot in past and present, but the effort is to remain where he is, on the street at the lamppost . . . then and not now. The smell is sweat and garbage—that is what keeps it: steam rising from the baking tar.

So they head to the garden. And first—on the way—there is Mrs Bess; first there is the pigeon lady.

They walk. He lets her stop, just tells her which turns to take. At the corner of Broome and Thompson she starts scribbling in her little notebook then puts the book away to follow men in boxer shorts and bowler hats carrying a coffin down Spring. That takes them to a pop-up market, the street closed to cars, streamers hanging from fire escapes and sidewalks buried in art and books. Garbage sweats in black plastic bags and squatters on stoops ignore the smell.

When Maggie twists her hair and ties it up into a knot, he watches like it is a magic act, and he watches her wipe away the bubbles of sweat above her lip and laugh when the guy on West Broadway wrenches the cap off the hydrant. A kid sits on top and dangles his legs to block the full force. Even on the other side of the street it sprays their feet. She looks down. The tiny hairs on her neck, he can see them in the sun.

Near the corner of Mercer and Houston she has stopped at a storefront window. Pinned to the glass in rows are paintings on pages of newspaper: bamboo and cherry blossom trees in black ink.

'What is this place?' she asks.

'It's the pigeon lady's studio. Check it out, to your left.'

She steps past the window into the entrance, peers inside and yanks her head back. 'Oh, Christ!' Perched on stools against the side wall on any given day are half a dozen pigeons.

'Rats of the sky,' he says.

'What are all the pictures?'

'She teaches people.'

It is then that a small voice sounds from inside. 'Please,' it says. 'Come in.'

Maggie looks at Martin. 'Come on . . .'

He shakes his head. 'Let's not.' He has walked past the place with the pigeons a hundred times.

'You're just scared of the birds.'

She smiles, he follows. It can't hurt to take a look.

He has seen the birds, but he has never seen the lady herself. From the back corner of the cluttered room, she emerges, a tiny woman in a jade kimono, glittering in the dim light as she shuffles towards them across the stone floor. Her neck remains perfectly still, like she's balancing the bun of black hair on top of her head. Close up he can see the hair is streaked with silver, but there isn't a line on her face.

'What can I do for you?' she asks, still holding Maggie's hand. 'Are you here for lessons?'

'Oh no,' Maggie says. 'I'm going home tomorrow . . . We were just looking at the paintings. The ink is beautiful.'

The pigeon lady nods. 'And where is home?'

'Australia.'

She is staring now, screwing up her eyes. 'But your parents?'

'They're from Hungary.'

Her eyes light up. 'That is why the perfect forehead . . .'

Maggie cocks her head, listening to the music playing. 'That's strange . . . This music, it's my mother's favourite.'

'Not strange,' the woman says. 'I like your mother.' She closes her eyes. 'When we do birds or branches it is good for the students . . . the violin flutters and flaps as the lark ascends, you hear that now?' Her hand rises in the air and comes down before she opens her eyes again. 'Sit down, please. Call me Mrs Bess. And I will get you tea.'

She doesn't wait for them to accept the offer, and is back in a minute with two little bowls. Marty knows pieces of the pigeon lady's story. She has been in SoHo for a couple of years, and already has a pile of students coming to her to learn the art of brush painting. Linda has a friend who went, said she made him draw bamboo for a year until he graduated to blossoms. Within minutes Maggie has extracted the rest of the story; it is the same as back in the loft—her eyes stay fixed and she listens like she's making a recording in her mind. It opens you up, he thinks, makes you feel like you are being discovered—like you are gold.

Mrs Bess migrated from Japan when she was a child and

grew up in Arizona. She learnt the art from a master when she was interned in a camp in the Utah desert during the war.

'I thought everything was taken. But I was wrong. That is what he taught me. I had lost nothing that mattered.' She studies Maggie's face. 'You know what I am saying.' It is not a question. 'You were born in Australia?'

'No, my parents migrated after the war, when I was five.'

She nods. 'You are an exile. Did they put you in a camp?'

'Yes, a migrant camp—for the first year or so.'

'And did your parents ever go back home?'

'No. My father died when I was twelve. My mother's still in Sydney.'

'So you will go back to her.'

'Tomorrow. I leave tomorrow.'

Mrs Bess nods with resignation. 'I never went back to Phoenix. Over the years I made my way here. And here I will stay, in my shop, feeding my pigeons and watching Americans pass by.' She looks at Martin. 'I know what you are thinking. And the answer is no, they have never shat in my shop.' A qualification comes with an impish smile: 'Not the pigeons.'

Maggie asks about the paintings pinned up around them. Mrs Bess tells her it is the beginners' work. They start on newspaper. 'Not worth wasting paper yet.'

Maggie smiles. 'I used to draw on newspaper when I was a little girl. That's why I stopped here, when I saw the drawings in the window. Please, can I see something you have done?'

Mrs Bess lets her eyes settle on Maggie's face again as though she is measuring it. 'Why not?' She shuffles into a back room no bigger than a closet. A door opens into a third room, on the floor of which is a mattress. Mrs Bess points to one of a number of brush paintings pinned to a board on the wall. The image is of rocks at the foot of an escarpment. 'I call it *The Lost Cat*,' she says. 'Find it.'

Maggie studies the picture, steps up to the wall and traces her finger around an outcrop of rocks that look to Martin like nothing more than that. Mrs Bess takes her arm. 'You have the eye,' she says. 'That is the first step.' She takes the painting down from the wall and signs the bottom of the page. *For Maggie.* And she rolls it up and ties it with a piece of string. 'Will you send me something? Something you draw for me in Australia?' she asks.

Maggie promises she will.

'Worry about the soul,' Mrs Bess says. 'None of the rest.' And to Martin: 'Even fear can be a gift. You just have to know how to unwrap it.' She claps her hands as though to release herself from the thought.

As they go to leave, she presses Martin's arm. 'This one is special,' she says.

Martin shrugs. 'We just met.'

'Still,' she says. 'You will follow her home.'

The words jar; he doesn't respond and he doesn't wait for more. Out on the street he breathes more easily again as he waits for Maggie. She has leant down and has her arms around Mrs Bess. A couple of pigeons come out first, fly straight out the door and up to a roof across the street. Then comes Maggie, all smiles.

'What a great woman!'

'Sure.'

'What do you mean, "sure"?'

'I mean, sure: great woman.'

'You don't mean that.'

'Okay, you tell me what I mean.'

'You are cynical.'

'Of what? The haiku bullshit? No, I love that stuff . . .'

'Ah, so easy to judge, close yourself off . . . but you heard her.' She is smiling, and with a skip in her step she stares him in the eye as Mrs Bess had done: 'This fear of yours, it is a gift . . .'

'Oh, get fucked!'

Now she's in front and has turned around to face him. 'You just have to unwrap it.'

So they are laughing and she is walking backwards past the kitchen sinks on Lafayette and he reaches out like he is going to strangle her, hoping she'll trip so he can pick her up and smother her with his bare hands. They keep the pace across the Bowery, then she slows up, looks around her. More and more of the shops are vacant; a Chinese grocery store peeks out from beneath the layers of graffiti. An old black man on a beanbag asks a girl walking the street in her underwear if she can spare any change. When they turn the corner onto Elridge, smoke is spewing from the blackened window of a tenement. There is the sound of sirens.

'Should we be here?' she asks. He listens for it but there is no fear in her voice.

He stops. 'This is it,' he says. She looks around her—the sidewalk strewn with broken bricks, cigarette butts floating in stagnant puddles. At the end of the street there is a man sweeping. Martin points to a plywood door in a crumbling wall. 'Behind here.'

The door needs to be yanked up and shouldered in.

Stepping through it, he keeps a watch on her face, fresh eyes marvelling at what is inside, the garden in the rubble. They are standing on the outer ring of a series of garden beds, each planted with vines and flowers and fledgling trees. Amid the dots of colour there is a patchwork of green—mint and moss, grass and lime. The rubble that remains is at the back of the enormous block: timber and piping and sheets of metal. And towering over both rubble and garden are the grey, muddied walls of the neighbouring tenements, the windows that had been bricked up or cemented over now being cleared again to let the light in.

Halfway around the path there is a link to a circle inside it, and another, until they are in the centre, at a Chinese Empress tree. Around them the garden beds burst with asparagus plants and creeping cucumber vines and a ground cover of strawberries and parsley.

'Whose place is this?' she asks.

'No one's. A friend of Dave's was living behind it when the tenements got pulled down. He's a poet, an artist, pretty radical. The whole thing was a stack of rubble. He started clearing it then began planting and put the paths down. He designed it all first; Dave will tell you about it . . .'

She follows him back to the outer ring and down a central path to the back of the block, where it is still what it was before—chipped, broken, shattered. There are weeds sprouting through the concrete and dirt, and in the middle of it all an American flag has been pitched, as big as a sheet and waving in the breeze. A few kids, black and Latino, are jumping on a mattress, half the springs laid bare like a wire skeleton, and behind them a little boy climbs to the top of an abandoned scaffold. On the other side of the rubble, sitting on a burnt-out refrigerator in yellow gumboots and smoking a joint, is Dave.

When he sees them he gets to his feet, his pale legs poking out between the boots and the hem of his shorts, a torn singlet scooped below his left nipple, but his chest is cut with muscle and his grey eyes are almost black, so even with the boots the overall effect is more menacing than comical.

'Greetings.' He isn't looking at Martin. 'My name is Dave. You are . . . ?'

'She's from Australia.'

'About fucking time. We've been waiting for his friends to come. You want some?' He hands Maggie the joint. She takes a puff and hands it to Martin.

'So you guys old friends?'

Martin hesitates. 'This is Maggie.'

Dave ponders the name. The light goes on. 'Maggie! Stalker girl!' Martin tries to cut in, but to no avail. Dave has his hand on Maggie's shoulder. 'His words,' he says. 'I told him he was a rude prick for not tracking you down. Here you were in the big city, and now all the time we've wasted . . . Has he shown you around the garden?'

'Sort of, just quickly,' Maggie says. 'It's amazing, awesome—I mean, what you've done.'

'Well, no, not me, I'm just a soldier, and this is just the start. Marty, take this.' Dave hands him a shovel. 'Follow me.' He picks up the handles of a wheelbarrow filled with horse dung and pushes it up the path to the outer circle and weaves his way back to the centre. He drops the barrow, stands before them and draws with his hands: 'You get how it works, see: the yin and yang . . . At the centre there is balance, and everything grows from there until the circles bump into buildings and the buildings come down. It's gonna keep growing, the circle, waves of energy will seep through the city, through the whole fucking world.' He pauses, hands mid-air, shakes his head in wonderment at the words leaving his mouth. 'It is incredible if you think about it, if you follow it through. It is food. It is art. It is everything. You feel that?'

'Sure,' Maggie says. 'Can anyone come in here?'

'You bet. Kids still play in that shit.' He points back to the rubble. 'But then they come here. You want some gloves? You can give me a hand.'

Maggie and Martin hammer in bamboo stakes for the sweet pea to climb while Dave spreads the dung. Over his shoulder he throws the question: 'You wanna weed this patch, Marty?'

Martin ignores it. There aren't any weeds. Then comes the follow-up: 'You staying with us tonight, Maggie?'

'I've got my stuff over in the hostel.'

'So we go get it.' He stops shovelling, studies her face with a view to purchase.

'Hands off, Dave. She knows my mum.'

'Well, I don't know your mom, Marty. I don't give a fuck about your mom. Do you give a fuck about his mom, Maggie?'

She is blushing and squirming but smiling all at once, like this was part of the tourist experience and Dave here was the Empire State.

'I don't think they'll give my money back,' Maggie says. 'I paid already.'

Dave gives it up, or parks it for later. 'And when do you go home?'

'Tomorrow. Tomorrow morning.'

Dave shakes his head at Marty, marvelling at the hit-and-run opportunity of a lifetime. 'So what are the plans? You want to come to a party, Maggie?'

Behind them kids are on the ground in the dirt, scavenging the last of the black raspberries. One of them has got the flag and they are marching in time. Dave starts reeling off options, but all of a sudden it's like a voice in a jar. Because now there is a louder one . . .

'Dad? Hey, Dad? You awake?'

The face was like the fair-haired man on the street.

'Sorry, I just wanted to make sure you were okay. You okay, Dad?'

He nodded his head. 'Fine, thanks.' He practised it now the way the speech therapist told him. A breath before the 'th' pushed the word out so it didn't get stuck in his mouth.

'Great. You look great.' Ethan's complexion was grey and the corners of his eyes were red because he rubbed them too much. He sat waiting, as though expecting direction. Martin obliged by reaching over and putting his hand on his son's arm.

'You look like shit. But nice suit.'

Now Ethan smiled, loosened his tie. Better.

'How was your day?' Martin asked. 'Tell me something . . .' It was harder when 'th' was in the middle of a word; his tongue flopped around it and turned the word to blubber.

Work was alright, Ethan told him, but the situation with the partners wasn't getting any better. He got up and opened the curtains. From the bed Martin could see the ocean, grey and distant in the fading light. 'I'm not good dealing with them . . . The politics of the place, it's just bullshit.' Sitting down again, he looked back at the door, a reluctant witness waiting to be excused. 'Here, I bought you some of those mints you like.' This time he rubbed his whole face up and down with his open hands.

It was like the face on the street in New York, but it was not that face. It was older—the eyes were worn—and it bore a load that the face on the street was yet to bear, one that Martin now recognised: it was the weight of guilt. Had he seen it there before? He couldn't remember; he didn't know.

'Grandie!' The child at the door. And behind him his mother.

'There you two are!' To let Finn get close Ethan stepped back towards his wife, took her face in his hands and kissed it. As the child related tales of his day, Martin could hear Ethan whisper, 'I missed you,' in his voice a resolve that the day, everything in it, was behind him. It was, as Martin himself well understood, the only way forwards.

'And Mum said when you're better we can fish off the beach. Can we do that, Grandie?'

Outside it had started to rain and there was a plane passing overhead in the sky. The boy had asked a question, and behind him his mother talked about the crumble for dessert then opened her handbag and pulled out another packet of mints and put them down next to the others. Martin smiled, told the boy he could take the mints.

'You keep them, Grandie. They're your favourites.'

Yes, he remembered that. It was because they were chewy, and not hard. Still the boy was looking down at him like he was waiting for something. So Martin asked if he had told him about the garden, right there in the middle of the tenements, and around it all just rubble. 'The strawberries go first, then the tomatoes. It is quite a thing, quite a thing . . .'

'I'm sick of that story,' the boy said, wincing when his mother pinched his arm. 'Let's do *The Bear Hunt*, Grandie. I'll start: *We're going on a bear hunt, we're going to catch a big one* . . . Your turn, Grandie.'

The boy fixed him with a stare as he waited but it was the woman who spoke, in a lovely, fluid rhythm:

'Long wavy grass.
We can't go over it.
We can't go under it.
Oh no! We've got to go through it!'

The boy squeezed his arm and prompted Martin by repeating the last line, and there, finally, they came, the words unleashed in a warm and welcome wave, clumsily gushing forwards: 'Swishy, swashy, swishy, swashy, swishy, swashy.' They laughed, because it was still a bit funny the way he spoke, and again when they came to the river, the deep cold river: 'Splash, splosh, splash, splosh.'

When the story was finished and the family was tucked back into bed, Laini said it was time to go help Nana. Only Ethan remained. Like everyone else these days, he was waiting for something too. People would come and sit by his bed—in the hospital, and now here at home—and Martin would wonder what it was they were waiting for. It was like a little game, guessing what it was. Maggie called out that she was home, but it wasn't that. Ethan's phone made the sound of a car starting, then it stopped. And then Maggie came into the room. She said she wanted to talk about something.

'I went to see the ambulance officer last week, before you came home,' she said. 'The one who brought you to the hospital. I wanted to ask him about the dog, and the boy in the paper.' She waited, his worst kind of waiting, the one where he was meant to say something. When he didn't she looked at Ethan again and continued. 'He told me where they live, the house. I think I should go there, don't you? And apologise . . .'

Ethan looked worried. 'They'll want money,' he said. He asked questions about the accident and Maggie didn't really know the answers. She just looked down and held Martin's hand, but her eyes were elsewhere and her skin was cold.

Outside the window now it was dark; the ocean had disappeared and the rain had stopped.

'Let's let Grandie get ready for dinner,' Ethan said. His voice was kind.

Martin wanted to tell him there was nothing to worry about, but he couldn't. Even with a breath behind it he knew that the words would get stuck in his mouth.

The plate slipped out of Ethan's hand into the sink. He hadn't meant to drop it, but even if he had, Laini's question and the way it was hurled across the kitchen so early in the day felt like an entirely disproportionate response: 'What is making you so angry, Ethan?'

As it happened, within the hour he would be in a position to give the question an answer. *Let me give you a for instance . . .*

Forty minutes after handling his breakfast plate with insufficient care, Ethan was in the lift at work, in the middle of sending a text, when Brad Styles slipped through the closing door. Ethan didn't look up; he didn't know there was a rule that said you had to. All he knew was that so far that morning he had ticked every box—he'd run the labradoodle he never wanted to get, squeezed Finn's magic enzyme-enriched guava juice, apologised about the plate and now, with a potential client due in twenty minutes, he was sending a message to his wife to remind her about dinner with his dad—recent stroke victim now being forced into early retirement. Brad Styles stepping into the lift didn't register on his Richter; he didn't know the man was there—honest truth—and by the time Ethan was done with the message, Brad was tapping something of his own, head down, three levels up to twelve. The silence was mutual, that was a fair assumption, or not. It was only as Brad was walking away that Ethan heard him snarl: 'And good morning to you too, Ethan.'

Ethan halted, turned to see the slight swing of the hips and the slow shake of the head as Brad Styles strode down the corridor.

Good morning to you too?

With just five little words, it trickled into the frontal sinus behind his eye sockets.

Why am I so angry?

Take a step back, you fucking little moron.

Ethan closed his eyes, took a long breath; that was Laini's suggestion for moments like this, and in the exhalation he put his mind to the possibility he had in fact caused some offence—the man felt snubbed—and that he was at fault. But try as he might to ingest it, his breaths became short, shallow, the taste at the back of his throat faintly acidic. No, he could not swallow it, because that would be giving in; that would be jumping into the cesspit of bullshit adolescent insecurities, jumping in and putting his head all the way under. It seeped through the pores of this place, from the top to the bottom, or the bottom to the top; whichever way, there was some game being played out in a foreign language behind office doors, in tearooms, over Friday night drinks and nibbles. As far as he could tell, the stage-one objective was to remember as many details about other people's lives as you could: kids' schools and sports were a big tick, postcodes, holiday destinations past and planned, favourite restaurants, parents' ailments, mild, serious, life-threatening . . . Bingo for bringing something back to the table, the name of a naturopath or new tapas bar or mortgage broker, something that showed you paid attention and took it away. That would mean you were considerate, a good guy, one of the team, and that would take you into stage two. It wasn't that Ethan had never tried, and at first it seemed benign enough. A few drinks, a couple of sushi trains, then dinners with wives, a Sunday brunch with the kids. But somehow he and Laini and Finn always seemed to be sitting around a table with people who had already clicked, and they never did. Maybe it was Laini, the way she acted after a drink too many, maybe Finn was too quiet, serious . . . It didn't help that Ethan neither played golf nor watched rugby, and had—as a means of ditching his old uni mates ('culling the fuckwits', as Laini called it)—become actively averse to both. And it wasn't that they never got invited anymore. It was just that they didn't go. He had membership (albeit B-grade); he just didn't have a lot of use for it.

'Are you okay, Mr Field? Anything I can do?' A secretary. Jenna. Or Janna.

Ethan smiled, shook his head, and felt the welcome return of indifference. Brad Styles was a senior associate vying for partnership in corporate leasing. Brad Styles was not his problem, though maybe it was in part a rebuke to him that on the way to his office Ethan made an atypical effort to wish a good morning over the top of the blue-rimmed partitions to anyone whose name he could remember. He closed the office door behind him and set up his laptop on his desk, checked his email, and confirmed the morning agenda: a meet and greet, three teleconferences back-to-back, and a one o'clock with Max. When his coffee came—the first of four for the morning—and the door was closed again, Ethan left it on the desk and stood at the window that ran the length of the office. Closing his eyes, he put one hand on the back of his neck, held tight as he cupped his chin with the other, and cranked it over his left shoulder, all the way to crackle-pop. Once he had given himself a minute to savour the release, he moved on to the right. His chiropractor told him that cracking his neck was the worst thing he could do, but his chiropractor didn't know how it felt to have your head in a vice. The blood flowed warm and fuzzy from his shoulders into his head and whatever lay outside his office door floated momentarily at a safe distance, like it was all just make-believe.

Ethan sipped the warm soy latte and cast his eyes now out the window, down to the people walking the paths of Hyde Park. He looked for one at his usual starting position, the fountain at St James Road. *There we go*: a plumpish woman in a red coat. She paused at the fountain and moved her bag to the other shoulder, and then continued straight along the park's main path, disappearing under the fig trees. This was Ethan's morning ritual: to pick a brightly coloured stranger to follow along the path to the trees where he would lose sight of them. The game was to find them again. At this point—the point when they entered the trees—it was a matter of waiting. From the main path there were seven arteries; only three of them would give rise to any likelihood he would spot her again, though in his favour was always the fact that those three led to the CBD. In his experience his chances were better than three in seven, better than half. So big red female had been two, three minutes. He skipped from the first path to the second and kept a lookout at the other end; if she'd picked up her pace she could be through it soon—sometimes he managed a glimpse as they crossed Park Street for the southern section.

He sipped, waited. She might have stopped to make a call; he wasn't throwing it in yet. There was this one time a guy in a yellow jacket did a one-eighty and Ethan caught the sneaky fucker coming back out at the fountain. He checked his watch. Sipped. And there she was, the red woman on the third artery, phone to ear, taking her sweet time . . . *Spotto.*

A double buzz. 'Mrs McCarthy is here.'

On the dot. 'Give me a minute.' He brought up the email. The referral was a friend of Max, the managing partner. Mrs McCarthy had been polite about her first lawyer but not her first husband. There was a reason to fight, but Max didn't say how much of a reason.

Ethan closed the email, gazed across his desk. 'Morning, ya little maniac.' In a fish tank against the opposite wall, suckermouth to the glass, Bob the Bristlenose Catfish gazed back. This was one dog-ugly fish, whisker-like tentacles sticking out of its spotted head, inherited—along with a Bolivian Butterfly fish called Lady—from Brian, the partner who'd landed a gig in London. 'This guy's pretty special,' Brian had said in the handover, pointing at the catfish. 'He just keeps at it, sucks his way round the glass. You never have to clean the tank. I figured he'd keep you company.' It was sad to see Brian go. Brian was the one who brought Ethan in. He understood Ethan. He backed him up. He drank Drambuie. 'I get it, mate, you're not a social animal . . . but you've gotta pat a few backs around here.' These were his last words before he got stuck into instructions on the tank: food, light, filter, you name it. And the plants, he had a list of everything in there, all different kinds: moss, ivy, lilies. There was a schedule and a checklist. When Brian finally shook his hand and left, Ethan turned to Moira, his secretary, and handed her the papers. 'I hope you got all that.' She had. Moira was great—with the fish, with everything. Then Moira left. Now there is Mia, sending out the wrong affidavits, doing fuck knew what to the fish. About a month back he came in to find Lady open-mouthed at the surface with her eyes all clouded over. That was when Ethan told Mia to bring him the fish papers. He read up on it himself, tested the water and fixed the levels, surprised to find it all strangely therapeutic. That night he read more, even cleaned the rocks and bogwood.

Brian was right about Bob. He was the soldier ant of the fish tank: hard-working, loyal, all-round good company. Whenever Ethan was there, Bob's little goggle eyes stared back at him through the glass. Not Lady. Even after Ethan saved her life, Lady hadn't given him a single glance. The oblivious Bolivian Butterfly: like the woman in red now waiting with strangers on the street for the light to change, never for a moment in her day did Lady get the sense that she was being watched.

Ethan tapped Spirulina flakes into the tank and returned to his desk as she danced up to the surface.

'Give it a rest, buddy,' he said to the catfish that kept on cleaning. 'Have something to eat.'

And, leaning back in his chair as he gazed contentedly around at his own four walls, he buzzed Mia. 'If you could bring in Mrs McCarthy . . .'

Tina McCarthy wasn't ready to jump ship, Max had said; she just wasn't happy with the way things were going at Marks and Bennet. Ethan knew better, of course. She was here in his office, and that meant she was ready. This was his favourite part: the catch and grab.

New business was the first agenda item at every partners' meeting. While the rest of the groups in the firm had dipped or flatlined, family law had risen by forty per cent over the last two years. The law was a business. Ethan ran his well. He made good money, and five years ago he had made partner at the age of thirty-one.

Still, whatever the level of success, he knew the practice was underappreciated. It wasn't just his father. (Even when he made partner Martin had asked him if he was sure it was what he wanted to be doing.) Family lawyers ranked as bottom feeders. Spinning money out of misery, all that—though say what you like, there was an art to it only few possessed. Clients dredged up their muck and Ethan waded through it and determined in the shortest time what belonged on file and what didn't. Ethan's clients quickly learnt not to argue when he interrupted mid-sentence to tell them: 'I understand that this is important to you, but it is not important to me.'

What they needed was for him to sift and to simplify; they needed him to break it down in their favour. Ethan had drawn up his own little list. Marriage was a structure with basic rules for set-up and maintenance. The size of the tank determined the space in which to swim. Take out the pretty plants and rocks and your players were bored to death. Forget to change the water and they just floated right up to the surface. And needless to say, introducing new fish, particularly the fancy, striped ones, was a risky business.

Ten minutes in with Mrs McCarthy.

A lapsed interior designer—fleshy, early forties, pale-skinned, mouse-blonde streaked with ash-blonde, and a slight hook in the nose she never got fixed. He smells deodorant not perfume. Except for the watch she doesn't wear her wealth. Maybe she's a hoarder: all well-bought, well-kept pieces—the leather coat is vintage, but he suspects she was the one to buy it new. She has an eye and a brain, no question. She has come through the worst of the rage, but there is something still stuck between her teeth.

'You might have gathered from what I'm saying, Ethan . . . Sorry, I shouldn't presume to know what you've gathered. Perhaps I should stop prattling and you should tell me.'

'You don't prattle,' he said.

'Oh, I do. I know I do. Stewart used to say that. I know I can go on a bit.' When she smiled her shoulders lifted in a 'what can I do?' sort of way. 'I just didn't know it was such a big crime.'

She coughed. He caught a whiff of last night's wine and this morning's cigarette.

'I suppose in a way I just want a second opinion, a pair of fresh eyes,' she went on. 'I want someone to say that signing off on all this is the right thing to do. I mean, we have a three-year-old child. And I'm not saying this lawyer hasn't done a good job. I'm not saying that at all.' She stopped there, grimaced. 'You know what he does? He keeps congratulating me on my "retreat from animosity". I admit that is starting to sound a little patronising. I just got this sense I was getting pushed out the door so someone could press print on the final account . . . He gets his thirty grand for sending a few letters back and forth and Stewart gets on with his life, case closed. Painless. "Retreat from animosity." Tell me what the fuck that means when a man is leaving you with a three-year-old child?' More coughing. 'Sorry, I'm prattling.'

So far: Tina and Stewart—a fifty-five-year-old sports nut who owned a chain of startlingly profitable surf shops—had been together for five years, and had a three-year-old son. The relationship between Stewart and Tina had ended over arguments about having a second child. The first pregnancy was the result of the seventh IVF insemination. The hormone injections had played havoc with Tina's mental health, and in turn their relationship. After a year of swimming around in it, the tepid water turned toxic. When Stewart told her he wasn't prepared to do it again, she hurled a jade statue of Buddha across the kitchen and it carved a third eyebrow at the centre of his forehead. Stewart jumped; swim for your life . . .

Given the length of the relationship and the fact that his wealth had been accumulated prior to its commencement, the offer on the table was a generous one: she would keep the five-million-plus Mosman home and would receive 150K a year until the boy was twenty-one.

'Sure, I mean, I agreed with the lawyer, the offer was good; I admit I was surprised how good, how quickly it came—too quick, you know, not enough thought. He never cared about giving Timmy a brother or a sister; he said he did but it was like he ticked a box when Timmy was born, job done. I was a lonely child, I told him, it isn't easy, but he didn't listen. He pretended he did, but he didn't listen.'

And as long as that lingered, the dregs of what should have been, Tina wasn't keen to sign it away and set him free. She didn't want to cut the cord because it was all that was left to bind them.

'It is hard, you know, being at home just the two of us, me and this little thing . . .'

Fresh eyes, Mrs McCarthy said she wanted. The guy had made an offer, a reasonable one, the lawyer told her so. *Tut, tut, silly fellow . . . she can't make it that easy.* His message to her: rest assured, it doesn't have to end yet. For the moment, what his client needed was something fresh on which she could focus, something to fill up the blank screen and the empty house.

'You say that after Timmy was born, you tried again three times?'

'Yes.'

'And are there any eggs still left?'

She nodded. 'Two.'

And there he handed it to her on a plate. 'Has an agreement been reached about what to do with them?'

She shook her head.

'You tell me, Tina: what would you like to see happen with them?'

Ethan looked over at Bob the Bristlenose, ignoring his food, suckermouth to the glass. 'You need to think about that.' He paused again before he spoke his final words: 'I'm sure your lawyer told you as much.'

Mrs McCarthy, Tina, declined the opportunity to consider it any further; she signed first an authority to have her file transferred from Marks and Bennet, and second a cheque for ten thousand dollars to the trust account of Argyle, Abbot and Williams.

'I feel better about this,' she said, rising from her seat. 'I am a robust woman, Ethan, but this morning when I woke up and thought about signing those papers, all the strength went out of my legs. I had to sit on the floor of the bathroom. The only thing that got me up was knowing I was coming to see another lawyer, that by the end of the day I'd get another perspective.' And with that she gestured for him to remain where he was, and she left his office.

~

Mia buzzed. 'I've got Laini on the line.'

'Put her through.'

'Hey, it's me.'

'Hey, me.'

'Your mum called tonight off. Your dad isn't sleeping.'

'Why didn't she call me?'

'She did, you were in a meeting. She said not to worry, it was just a bad night. And he hasn't stopped with the New York stories . . . This morning she caught him telling the cleaner about how he snorted speed at the table at some bar.'

'Well, better the cleaner than Finn.' Ethan had shooed Finn away last week when Marty started on about the artist who swung upside down and naked from a rope in the middle of a room.

'Anyhow, it's nice though, huh? We can stay home, I'll cook. What do you feel like?'

'I'm easy. What's on the blog today?'

'Thigh or breast.'

'Perfect, either.'

Laini's blog had enjoyed a recent surge in readership. As far as Ethan could work out it was a virtual meeting place for the uberhomemaker or the frustrated housewife, depending on what sort of day you were having. She began each post with a question, sometimes bland—thigh or breast?—and sometimes not. During this last funk of hers, the question was whether the best way to pull herself out of it was to meditate or masturbate. Over the period of a week she had seven hundred and eighty responses from women expert in either or both—one claiming she could bring herself to climax while sitting in the lotus position, hands on knees, mind over matter. Sadly, that was about as graphic as it got. Browsing through them into the night, what surprised Ethan most—beyond the ability of respondents to discuss the subject without reference to their genitals—was that they could also discuss it without any sense of compunction. He had always been under the impression that for women masturbating was a guilty pleasure, that in their minds it was in essence an act of infidelity. The frank nature of the responses seemed to disprove that. Lying in bed in the early hours, Ethan pondered that for a while, the disturbing fact that he had got it so wrong, before letting it go—taking his cock in his cold hand and morphing the imagery into something tantalising, the unknown, the unknowable.

It took him four weeks to raise the subject with Laini, the role of masturbation in dealing with everyday challenges. She laughed, said, 'Sure, it helps sometimes—but . . .'

'But what?'

'You know when I like it best?'

Instantly a pool of saliva formed under his tongue. He shook his head.

'When we are in bed and you are asleep.'

He waited. This was the old Laini. 'And?'

'And I watch you and I start. I try not to move too much or make a sound. It's always best when there's a risk.'

Ethan thought that through before making the obvious request: 'Could you wake me up next time?'

She smiled, reached her hand under the table. 'That'd kill the fun.'

In any event, as far as the blog went, the readership surge brought an end to Laini's funk. One of the more progressive mothers at Ethan's school—for by now it was doing the rounds of the Lower North Shore—worked for a publisher and had an idea that Laini could turn it into a kind of self-help book. But even now he sensed something was still up.

'So everything okay?' he asked.

'Yeah, you?'

'Sure, I'm good. I'm fine.'

'I love you.'

'Yeah, me too.'

After he hung up the phone, Ethan typed up a file note on a request for particulars regarding Stewart McCarthy's position on the fate of the remaining fertilised eggs, a request that would drag it out just long enough—long enough for Tina to know she didn't make it too easy for him, and long enough to send the account into a fourth page and ensure a fat final fee. For that to happen something needed to emerge, a change in circumstance. When he got the files he would go through them and find a backup or two.

Ethan finished the note, and started scribbling numbers on a timeline as he processed in his mind how the matter would play out. By Christmas, he estimated, it would be settled. Until then Tina McCarthy needed to feel she wasn't in this alone, because today, right now, that was how she was feeling: all alone in her big house with her child—her 'little thing'; alone on the cold tiles of her bathroom floor. She had lost a piece of herself and she was looking for a way to get it back. It wouldn't be long before she would start to pour her soul across his desk; there were the beginnings of it already. Next time he would stop her. *I understand that this is important to you . . . but it is not important to me.* And she would stand up and brush herself off. The husband would come back with a better offer to finally be rid of it.

And Tina McCarthy would know then, finally, for better or for worse, that it was all over.

'It is private,' Maggie said, or, 'No one is interested.'

How could he make her understand? He told the story because this *was* the story. That was his response to Maggie. She didn't like that he was telling the cleaner, but when Maria came into his study to clear out the bin, that was where he was up to. What was next was Hannah Lee.

And in answer to Maggie: 'Nothing about Hannah Lee was ever very private.'

~

As the subway jolts into motion, Maggie holds on and tells Dave she is going home to finish art school and she wants to be a painter.

'You're a painter?' Linda says and turns to Dave. 'Then she should come with us to see Hannah Lee . . .'

When Maggie asks who that is, Dave smiles, says wait and see.

An hour later they are sitting in a performance space. In front of them is a raised stage, enclosed by three walls; the audience, on milk crates and stools, forms a fourth. The floor and walls of the room are white, and in the middle hangs a rope and at the end of the rope a harness. They sit there a while, Dave and Linda, Martin and Maggie, more than a while.

'Is this it?' Martin gibes. 'We watch the rope?'

Linda orders him to zip it (this is a serious crowd), and with that the room goes dark.

In silence a shadow crosses the stage to the harness. When the lights come back, there she is: a naked woman hanging upside down at the centre of the white enclosure, her dark curls mopping the floor as she starts to swing. In her hand is a paintbrush, and when she swings from side to side her head arches upwards, as she stretches her arm out to swipe the wall with her brush. And back she swings to the other side to swipe again. The only thing to emerge amid a bunch of random lines is the letter I, and when it does, members of the audience begin to clap, at which she slows to a stop, picks another brush from a tin on the floor and starts up again, this time with her eyes closed, arching her body towards the one wall like an acrobat, returning to it again and again so the lines form an orange maze. And so it continues on the remaining wall, blue then purple then orange again.

But Martin isn't really watching what is happening on the wall; he is working through the parts of her body as it arches and cartwheels from upside down to sideways—the bobbing breasts, the stretched navel, the muscles as they tense and release, the glorious glimpse of pink as her legs splay—until the artist swings no more and the rope is lowered to the floor where she spreads her limbs and reaches over to write something in one corner before rolling over to the next. The lights go out and the shadow crosses the floor again and disappears from the stage. A rogue in the audience whistles. Martin wonders whether or not to stand up. But when the light comes on she is there again, her face smudged with ink, this time clothed in a black bodysuit and tights.

When she starts to swing, Dave leans over and whispers: 'I think we've seen the best of it.'

To which Linda snipes: 'Go back to Princeton, you fucking jock.' But it is she who stands up, and they all follow her lead.

'Come on, baby,' Dave says. 'I would've stayed to the end.'

Without looking behind her: 'I doubt it. She goes like this for six hours.'

Next is the street and the bar, but the nighttime begins to blur as images float out of sequence—the upside-down artist, an outstretched Maggie on a mattress in a garden . . . Someone, something is tapping at Martin's chest. Tap. Tap-tap, double time. It takes hold of him, like a clamp, from the inside. Then and now; he is walking through a door, and in his memory there is an older man, an older man lost in his memory.

Martin sat upright, held his hand in the place where the pain had been, or the place he thought it had been. He moved it up to his throat and down to his stomach, in search of evidence that it had been there at all. Beside him, Maggie slept, one arm reaching up and over her head, her breaths long and deep and even.

The rhythm of it, his Maggie, as the curtains lifted away from the open window and fell back again.

Every night since his return from the hospital that was how he woke, to pain or panic, but then to this, the room still but for the curtain, quiet but for Maggie's breath, and in his mind, clarity. There were no judgments to write. There had been an accident and he had run over a dog. The stroke was his second. And it made him forget, like old Stan who lived next door to the house where Martin grew up. He remembered Stan wandering the streets and his wife Sal weeping at their kitchen table with Martin's mother holding her hand. Stan woke in the middle of the night too, not to this, but wet with terror; he thought he was back in Birkenau and that outside the bedroom door lay the corpses of his sisters. After that Sal put Stan in a home but the terror mustn't have stopped because one night he swallowed a bottle of pills and went to sleep forever. When his mother told him what happened, Martin could see that taking the pills was a sensible thing to do, if that was the place you went to in the middle of the night, a room with dead sisters waiting at the door.

Where else did Stan go? Martin now wondered. What was chosen for him? Which branches were cut from his mind, and which were left?

~

John had called and come to visit.

He had been the Chief Judge just a little over two years and today was the first time Martin had seen him look uncomfortable in the job. A year ahead of Martin at school, John Giles had been his head prefect and had studied law at the same university. On the day Martin was appointed to the Supreme Court, John brought him a bottle of single malt whisky and sat down across his desk to compare watches and help him make a dent in it, the beginning of a ritual that Martin would grow to cherish. Coming from a bustling barristers' chambers, he found life as a judge to be a secluded one. Among themselves, judges did not on any habitual basis sit down to offload and share war stories, let alone stories of a more personal nature. Gone were the days Martin would come home pink-faced after a long lunch or a session in a pub. During his years on the bench he could count on one hand the number of genuine friendships he had seen formed between judges, and he himself did nothing to bump up the number. John Giles was the closest he ever came. Two scotches straight up on a Thursday night—never Friday, John's golf day—and while the talk might begin with the law, it often ended with John (in his wonderful deadpan way) reciting best-of snippets of Peter Cook and Dudley Moore, something to sever the daily grind and leave them at the end of the day with smiles on their faces.

John sat at the table on the front porch and looked out at the view. 'It is a beautiful spot you have here, my friend.'

'Ah yes,' Martin said. 'God's country.'

'Remember how the southerlies used to scare people away from buying oceanfronts? Lord, look at these places going up around you now. You'd be sitting on a goldmine here.'

Martin didn't disagree, and after only a brief pause John went on to thank him for having the medical report sent through. 'We have to move pretty quickly on this sort of thing—you know what the media's like, and obviously it's a minefield for appeals. So I've directed those last ones with judgments outstanding be reheard.'

'I've drafted the Malouf judgment,' Martin interjected. Malouf was the carjacker appealing on the basis of the identification evidence. 'It's ready to go.'

John shook his head. 'It's a safer bet, Martin, you understand . . . You don't want appellants subpoenaing your medical records. An extended leave pending recovery. It'll give you and Maggie the chance to take that trip. Then we'll get you back the minute you are ready.'

Martin gestured that he needn't say any more. Poor John, it was an awkward thing, putting a friend out to pasture.

The two men finished their cake and tea and talked about flight routes to Morocco and the balance of power in the hung parliament but made no mention of the greatest comic duo of all time. In the corridors and the chambers of Phillip Street there would be whispers but no knives; already Martin had begun to receive sympathy cards, some quite touching. With a cup of tea and a spoonful of well-phrased words, Justice Martin Field would fade and go away . . . So this was it: an extended leave, pending recovery.

'On second thoughts, John, let's give it a date. In three months we'll see what these doctors say, and if it is more of the same, I will announce early retirement and we can have one of those flash dinners to send me off.'

At which John leant across and took a firm hold of his shoulder. 'You are a fine judge, Martin. We do this however you want to do it.'

Better that way, yes—*when one can, to control the flow of things . . .*

The pills, for instance. It would be sensible, just in case, to arrange a stock for a rainy day. He would need to write a list of these things when he remembered them, and tell Maggie so they were not forgotten. Like spring planting, and the boy crying over his dog . . . He climbed out of bed and found a pen and a pad and made the first entry. It was Maggie's suggestion but he could see the sense in it: buy dog.

All that was left for Martin was this new set of facts to consider. At least that was what Maggie wanted him to do. A man and a car, a boy and a dog: she wanted him to piece it together. If only he could, if only he could do what she wanted. It was a matter of controlling the flow, yes, but the trouble was the undercurrent; the trouble was that what occupies the mind is determined not by what we or others want . . .

When the doctor told him he could go home from hospital, Maggie had leant down and kissed him on the forehead, the kiss long and tender, like a mother's kiss, and she had told him that he was going to be fine.

'Does nothing scare you?' he asked.

She shook her head. 'Of course it does. This does.'

And later, when he woke from sleep, 'I'm sorry,' he said.

'It isn't your fault.'

She seemed so certain. But how could she be when she didn't know what it was he was sorry for? There were things to say, but she wouldn't listen; she didn't want him to talk about where it started.

It was different with Ethan. They sat on the back veranda after dinner and drank beer and when Martin talked about New York his son's eyes didn't glaze over. Ethan asked questions and he listened to the answers like they mattered to him, then he went to the fridge and got more beer. When Maggie came, he turned it into a whisper and leant in: 'She doesn't like it.'

But Ethan told her to let him talk; it was family history. 'And Christ knows I've never heard any of this before.'

He had told him about Maggie arriving at the loft, and the pigeon lady and the garden. So he was up to the nighttime. He was up to Hannah Lee.

But Ethan shook his head. 'You already told me that. Remember? I said you'd have to walk up some very dark stairs to see something like that these days.'

'Yes, so you did.'

'Tell me about Linda,' Ethan said.

'It was Linda who decided we had to take her to see Hannah Lee. She was Dave's girlfriend. I lived with them in the loft.'

'I know that. But after Mum left . . .'

Martin flinched, then his voice was firm. 'Please, I haven't finished the day yet.' And after a pause, when he felt assured the parameters had been accepted: 'She was quite famous in her day, Hannah Lee. Linda liked taking visitors to see her—until a cousin from Texas insisted one night they stay for the full duration . . .

'Then later,' Martin continued, 'we went to a bar.' It was Dave's favourite because it was the last place he saw the Velvet Underground and he'd been mourning their break-up ever since. 'So we sit down in our little booth and Dave shouts across the table: "So, Maggie, what do you think of New York? Ten best things you've seen . . ."'

~

The bar: a booth with red cushioned seats and a dirty tablecloth. Dave and Linda sit opposite Martin and Maggie. The vocals hover, Emmylou Harris in her hour of darkness.

'I saw Diane Arbus at MOMA,' Maggie says. 'You should go, it's incredible.'

Dave shrugs. 'I don't really go above Fourteenth . . . I mean downtown, best things downtown.'

Here Linda interjects: 'He means, "What do you think about me?"'

'Well, that'd be a start; I'd like to know what she thinks about me. I can tell you what I think about her . . .'

Linda leans close and whispers something in Dave's ear that wipes the smile from his face. Then she turns back to Maggie.

'Tell me, Maggie, art school. What is it you want to paint?'

'Portraits, I think.' And when she sees that Linda is waiting for more: 'But in a context or setting. I like the idea of showing people's affinity with objects.'

Linda stares back blankly. 'And did you like Hannah Lee?'

'Well, yeah, I saw that footage of Pollock. She extends that, the act of creating, to the whole body, but I think in a way she's renouncing the physical reality.'

Linda nods and pats her hand. 'Did you read that somewhere?'

'Sorry.' Maggie recoils. 'That sounded banal.'

'Bullshit it did.' Dave grasps Linda's hand. 'You're a patronising bitch.'

This is what they do to newcomers, Dave and Linda: they fuck around with the tone and tempo, keep moving the posts. It is sport, and they are champions. One minute you are king, the next the gum stuck to their shoes. The worst is when you disappear and they don't see you anymore. All of it makes you hungry to be king again, because when you are king, they are loyal and attentive and you are all that matters and everything you ever wanted to be. Like right now, Dave and Linda turn it around, start peeling away Maggie's story as though she is a present to unwrap: from backpacking in Athens all the way back to the place of her birth. When Linda hears that her first home in Australia was a migrant camp, her eyes light up.

'I knew you weren't silver spoon like Dave and your lawyer boy here. That is pretty cool. And you are pretty cool. I drink to you, to you and your mother.' Then: 'What about you, Davey? What did you think of the show?'

'Personally, I'm not sure what we were meant to get out of it apart from a good look at a nice bush.'

Linda doesn't bite straight away. The argument goes something like this:

Dave: 'Okay, so she is taking the piss out of Pollock . . .'

'Well, you assume it's derivative: it all has to come from the great white master.'

'Derivative, subversive . . . I'm on your side, remember.'

'You think you are. You want to be. Why don't you go fight the junta, baby?'

It is the argument Martin's heard before: Linda versus Dave; God save America versus Dave save the Sandinistas, or whoever, wherever. Linda's cause was always 'the deeply fucked-up shit' happening under her own nose—the energy crisis, the censorship bill . . . Dave didn't like giving priority to the back doorstep. 'Every day people are being massacred and you are talking about lining up for petrol. Perspective is all I am saying.'

'I am talking about going to jail for describing the act of fucking!'

In the middle of the batting back and forth, Martin can sense Maggie watching him. He turns around to her, expecting that she is leaning back against the booth because maybe she's out of her depth, maybe a bit in awe—maybe she wants him to explain some of the politics—but as she smiles back at him through the dim, smoky light, he sees that none of that is true. Her eyes are narrowed, fixed, and they are asking not what it all means but what he thinks of it. Where do *you* stand? Her quick glance at Dave and Linda is distant, curious, before she leans in to ask: 'Do you take sides?' And Marty is struck with the sense that to her, right now, the answer to this is all that matters. That was the moment—later he could point to it—the moment that with a fixed gaze and a few words she positioned him outside the fray, and she alongside him. Of course, at the time none of this formed, the words just a warm and invisible breath, the gestation of what would later become her gift. For many years the moment would be forgotten, or recast as a simple come-on, and then one day he would begin to remember it again, this and what came next. Martin would remember, and then, finally, it would be everything.

'Jesus, baby, I'm far too straight here,' Linda says as she starts beating the table like a drum. 'Let's get sorted and get out of this place. Let's take Maggie out to play.'

So Dave pushes the tablecloth to one side and is lining up right there in the booth. When they are done Linda crawls up and straddles him, part of the show. That's what it is to Linda . . . 'Linda Lou, I do love you.' Dave sings it like it's the chorus of a song. 'Yaouwww!' She throws her head back and spies Martin watching out of the corner of her eye and says it is time for the party.

That is next. New York, 11 August 1973.

~

'So it's true,' Ethan said. 'My parents snorted speed on a table in the middle of a bar in New York City.'

Martin smiled. 'That we did.'

'And Linda—that night I mean: you had a thing for Linda?'

The smile faded again but this time the question was answered. 'Ethan, any man that walked past Linda in those days had a thing for her.'

Martin got to his feet then and walked to the other side of the lawn. When he turned back, he did not move, but looked with uncertainty at the ground in front of him.

'Dad, you okay?'

'I suppose so, yes. Looks like I will be doing a bit of gardening, that's all.'

'Sorry?'

'Did your mother tell you? I have had my last day on the bench, Ethan. I have had my last day in court.'

'You don't know that.'

But he did know. He knew that what he said to his son was true, and now in the back garden it weighed on him like something that had fallen from the sky. It was farewell to feuding companies with ineptly drawn contracts, to carjackers and people smugglers, and to all the rest of them. It was farewell to a courtroom falling silent in his presence. Justice Martin Field would never be asked to deliver judgment again.

The quiet was broken by a call from inside for Ethan to carry the sleeping Finn to the car.

Martin followed to say goodnight. As he reached the car, the boy awoke and held out his arms. Martin leant down and kissed him through the open door.

'Next time we'll go fishing,' Martin whispered.

The boy squeezed his neck. 'And we'll do the Bear Hunt by heart, without reading any.'

'Ah yes, that damn river: splash, splosh . . . or hang on, was it swishy, swashy?'

The boy laughed. 'No, Grandie, that's the grass.'

In the middle of the night, when Martin awoke, he walked out to the back lawn and knelt down at the edge of the garden bed.

Tompkins Square Park en route to the party, the paths unlit: a big dark path. Maggie takes her shoes off and stands on the grass. Swishy swashy . . . A black guy tells her she better keep her shoes on. 'You want to get on, lady?'

Down the dark path, stumble trip. Stumble trip.

And into the subway tunnel where the low light flickers and a homeless woman lights a match and prays to the fire.

The night scrambles with the day like a dream. They are back in the loft, then the garden, stepping over rubble, splintered wood and scraps of metal. The eyes on the wall are windows and the windows are burnt-out holes. Boys' faces blur under the fluorescent light like ghosts.

His chest is tapping, the sky black and endless.

Move on, Martin. That is his thought. *Hurry up and get to the end of it.*

Maggie made a pot of tea and sat down with Martin and his newspaper at the kitchen table and they talked about the doctor's advice, about rest and exercise and vitamins. She then moved to the subject at the front of her mind.

'I thought I might go up to the street where you had your accident, to find the boy.'

Martin squinted into the steam rising from his tea. 'This is the boy with the dog . . .'

'Yes. The ambulance officer said the old woman who was with the boy went into a house a door back from the cross-street.'

Martin put his cup down. 'It isn't the sort of neighbourhood you doorknock until you find the right house.'

She nodded. Of course, she had thought of that herself. It was in part the reason she hadn't yet gone.

'These people lead difficult lives, Maggie. I dare say the least of their worries is losing that dog.'

When he saw that she was ready to argue he put up his hand. 'I'm not saying don't go, just leave it until a weekend when Ethan can go with you.'

It was a sensible suggestion, and reason enough to put it out of her mind and listen instead to his caustic commentary on the letters to the editor in the newspaper—today either lauding or lambasting the backroom deals to form government—and, as she listened, to dare to hope that if their life was to be housed within these walls, there was no reason it could not resemble what came before.

When only minutes later the tangled neurons in Martin's brain steered him through a door into a different place and time, there was little hint of it. Still he sipped his tea and turned the page, then stopped. In the Health and Science section there appeared an article on ways to beat cellulite, and above the article, a waist-down photograph of a woman in a swimsuit. Maggie was only half listening when she heard: 'Poor old Sonia.'

'Sorry?'

'Sonia Kirby. Arse like a bruised peach.'

Sonia Kirby was the wife of the judge who had his chambers next to Martin's. At tedious functions to welcome or farewell other judges, the four of them had gravitated to each other for a while before thinking better of it and gravitating away.

'What are you talking about?'

Martin looked up from the page and smiled—a smile of warm welcome, as though Maggie had just entered the room—then he turned his eyes back down to the photograph, and up again, waiting for an answer to come to him. When it did, it was this: 'She complained about it. Cellulite. She wanted to get it sucked out.'

'When on earth did she say that?'

Again a smile, though this one more wary, less welcoming. 'I don't remember. At one of those dreadful gatherings, I imagine.'

Maggie started to clear the cups, then put them down again. 'Sonia Kirby told you her arse looked like a bruised peach?'

'She was drunk, I suppose. I don't say she used those words exactly.' He pointed to the woman's bottom in the newspaper. 'It looks like a bruised peach, don't you think?'

Maggie did not look and did not respond, and for the rest of the day she endeavoured to put it to the back of her mind, another bulky item into an already crowded space.

The next morning Martin followed her across the road and down the path to the ocean pool, where he perched on a rock while she did her laps. When she was done he stood at the ladder holding her towel, handing it to her as though this was his habit. A small thing, but enough to remind her, however gently, that everything had changed.

'You could do laps with me,' she suggested. She had no wish for that, but was minded to see how far this would go.

'God no,' he said. 'I hate laps.'

'Yes, that's right. You do.' At least he remembered that. And then more: Martin asked her something about the commission she was working on; it was for the brother of a woman she had painted over a decade ago. Martin remembered the painting. 'She was the blue dragonfly.'

In each of Maggie's portraits there was a motif, an object or a combination of objects, a conduit between herself and the subject.

Maggie started. 'How extraordinary.'

He shrugged. 'Ask me another.'

'The doctor fellow, Benson.'

'Easy—that was the cross-section of the bird. You weren't sure if he was too pleased with it.'

'Mary-Ellen Dodds.'

'The map. Colour-coded. Beautiful.'

'That was twenty-five years ago!'

And on he went, without a moment's hesitation, the images locked in his mind. 'That is marvellous, darling.' And then: 'Strange, isn't it? It's like you can see them.'

He smiled. 'As clear as you standing before me now.'

As to the day of the accident itself, now more than a month ago, she had stopped asking him for an account. Since the stroke—the second as they now knew—his attention was more and more grounded in a distant past. 'Some patients regale listeners with stories of war,' his doctor had told her. 'A battle or a particular manoeuvre. A victory. The facts are malleable, of course. Many a hero was made in the retelling of a memory.' Martin, it had turned out, had his own story.

All signs of paralysis were gone, and his speech was back to normal. Martin's appearance remained that of a healthy sixty-five-year-old man who looked younger than his years, and a conversation, if kept brief, might not dispel the appearance. They had been out to an exhibition opening, and a couple of dinners. It was good to see their friends again, the inner circle trusted enough not to tread awkwardly around what had happened: Annie and the gallery girls, a few of Martin's barrister mates. At the dinners there was less wine, less shouting across a table. With others they didn't know as well, Martin would speak with the curiosity of a stranger, repeating names and moving on to make a comment on his immediate surrounds—the sunlit glass in a bay window, the sweetness of the duck broth, the shape of a woman's dress (on the taste of food and the shape of women he was more and more prone to comment). As to what happened when a conversation was allowed to continue, there were those who were naturally inclined to stop and listen, and those who did so under sufferance or were brave enough to cut him short. She did not condemn the latter, and was at times even tempted to encourage it as she saw in Martin's eyes that he was scrambling for a way to get back to New York City, 1973. All that was required was a break long enough to ask the speaker-soon-to-be-listener about their travels; he would nod his head as they took him to various cities around the globe, waiting to see if they'd alight in Manhattan, then after a few minutes or so he'd reroute them there himself, explaining that when he was twenty-eight he had gone there on a secondment, and it was there that on 11 August 1973 he had met his Maggie. Eyes glazing over like the lens of a projector, he would embark on his tour—into his loft or the pigeon lady's studio or the garden in between the tenements—the audience held captive until eventually a way was found to extricate themselves. Even those who had been happy to listen could listen for only so long.

To begin with Maggie had admonished him, at first gently ('It is longwinded, darling', 'I think they've heard that story'), then not so gently ('Martin, you are being a bore', 'Stop being a nitwit'). But at dinner last week at Annie's, when Maggie went to open her mouth she saw him cower like a dog when a hand is raised, and she resolved then to let him be, to let him go. No, she did not condemn them, any of them, but this was what he had left, the man who had forgotten when to stop; people could find their own way to sidestep around him. They did not need her help.

When they got back to the house one morning after her laps, the Chief Judge telephoned and asked if he could visit in the afternoon. 'Yes, John,' Maggie heard him say. 'We would love to see you.' They went to the shops to buy biscuits and cake and Martin ironed a shirt that had no need of ironing.

A few days after the visit, Maggie heard Martin in his study and went to see if he needed anything. 'No,' he said. 'I am almost done . . . The identification was too weak.'

'What identification?'

'He said the shirt was green. He got it wrong because he wasn't looking at the shirt. He was looking at the knife.'

She reminded him of John's visit and suggested they take a walk. Later in the week, he was back at his computer again, working on the same judgment, commenting on the same evidentiary point. She brought him a coffee and said nothing, knowing now that the only way for it to be over was to let him finish. When he did, his associate—on Maggie's request—thanked him and confirmed receipt.

Then there was last Friday. She had heard him get up early to go fishing, but when she went out she saw his fishing rod and knife and tackle box discarded on the lawn.

Martin was standing in the kitchen at the fridge, the jar of chutney in his hand again. 'Chutney?' she asked. 'Let me get the marmalade.'

He looked at the label, then placed it on the table next to the plate with the buttered toast.

'No, thank you,' he said. 'I prefer it.'

'You prefer chutney on your toast?'

A single nod.

'For breakfast?'

'Yes, I do.' The reply was formal, the judgment final: 'For breakfast, I prefer chutney on my toast.'

Maggie knew well enough this was not a leak that could be patched to protect the whole. Watching Martin as he ate his toast and chutney, a nod of approval after every mouthful, she considered each deviation and its consequence: the fishing gear on the lawn, the jar that held chutney and not marmalade—and the man sitting across from her, the man who was only in part the one she had met in New York thirty-seven years ago.

That was what he spoke of now, again: that day.

'You didn't like the show?'

'What show?'

'Hannah Lee.'

She thought a moment before answering him, no longer surprised at the frontal leap into the past. 'Actually, I did.'

'But you didn't like *them*.'

Them meant Dave and Linda. 'Come on, Martin, I liked them fine.'

As he began to recount some part of their conversation in the bar, Maggie shook her head in disbelief. 'God, how are you remembering all this? Do you know what I remember of that night? I remember it was hard to breathe for all the smoke. I remember Linda climbing on top of Dave and you squirming in your seat. And I remember my first and last amphetamine hit. That's it, nothing more.'

He listened attentively, as though waiting to see if she would offer up a piece of the puzzle he was putting together in his mind. 'And the party?'

She laughed. 'I may as well not have been there at all.'

He feigned a wounded look. 'The kiss.'

She shrugged. 'I know, you've said it before, but it's a blur up until the garden. I remember the garden.'

He reached across then to take her hand, and when he did, when their palms pressed together, his grip suddenly tightened. 'Let's go to bed,' he said. The look that flashed across his face was a breathless child begging to play, but what settled when their eyes remained locked, when he pulled her hand down to him, was an urgency of the adult kind. 'Second thoughts, let's not move. Let's stay right here, why don't we . . .'

Though they did their best of it up against the kitchen bench, they moved to the sofa, and ended in bed, where afterwards they slept. When they woke, they woke at the same time.

'This isn't what we'd expected, is it?' he said, the words gentle, free of fury or frustration.

She shook her head, held her smile, wanting to keep him in this place where he remembered what was happening to him. Sometimes he would leave it and return so quickly she doubted herself for thinking he had left at all, hoped there was reason to doubt, clinging to it as she clung now to his hand.

'It never is,' she answered, but they would make do. They would get up out of bed and she would tell him it was a good day to fix the gate and she would ask what he needed so that she could get it from the store. Of course, then he might say: 'I can *fucking* well get it myself,' or, 'That stupid little quack telling me I can't drive.' Or, depending on how the wires connected this morning, he might thank her and tell her he'd have a look in the toolbox in the morning. What she was learning was that whatever she said or did in response did not matter; there was no benefit in her being firm and consistent. He was not a child who could be taught—that would not work. This was not a process of learning, but of unlearning, the shedding of what it was that he had known, what he had been taught, what he was told yesterday. A strange scattering, as though a thief had been in their home, and they were still looking around for what had been taken, some insignificant items that they told themselves they could do without, then the things of value they tried to shrug off. And of course the thief returned again and again, night after night.

Maggie took each day as it came—as was her way—until one day, a Tuesday, when the nurse came to visit.

After the last consultation the doctor had recommended a home visit 'to arrange things around the house'. Annie had offered to be there—'I'll remember to ask all the right questions.' When Jack was sick and they were making the arrangements for his palliative care, Maggie had done the same for her. And Annie meant well, she always did—holding Maggie's face in her hands as she arrived and telling her she was going to book her in for a facial: 'I've never seen anyone more in need of it.' It was another way of telling her she had aged ten years, Maggie thought, saved from dwelling on it by another bang on the door. This time it was a stout woman who reminded her immediately of the nurse from the hospital—a cloudy tinge of pity in her eyes as though she were privy to something they were not. And, like in the hospital, it didn't take long for her to discover what it was. Together Maggie, Martin, Annie and the nurse moved from the fridge to the cupboard to the bathroom cabinet, writing labels for all the plastic containers and boxes and bottles as they chatted about the glycaemic index and the price of limes, and when they were done and Martin had left to take a shower, the nurse sighed and smiled and, putting her markers back into their plastic case, said softly: 'The earlier you label things, the more chance he'll have of finding them later . . . while the words still mean something.'

Maggie did not smile back. Annie and the nurse chattered on even after Annie had ticked off the last question on her list. Maggie could hear them walking out the front gate as she closed the door behind them and turned back to face the empty hallway. *While the words still mean something.* A minute passed as she formed a plan of what would constitute her next steps. When she moved again it was to find the newspaper, to open it to the page of the Sudoku puzzle and hand it to Martin with a pen, then to walk out the bedroom door, through the garden and into her studio. There, in the middle of the room, cast by a few careless words into a bleak and unknowable future, she fell to her knees and she wept. She wept first for Martin and for the loss of their life together, and then—as a woman who saved her tears for rare occasions such as this one—she sat on the floor and wept for other things that she had lost: most of all—still, most of all—the touch of her own mother's hand.

'You will manage fine,' the nurse had said today on leaving.

This was true, as she always had, and though the words had brought her little comfort as they were spoken, they now recalled to Maggie what it was her mother had said when people asked how she coped with the death of her husband. 'I manage his death,' she would say, and her friends would nod, translate her clumsy English: she copes with it; she is able to manage. But though it was not uncommon for Lili Varga to fumble a word, Maggie knew that the use of the active verb was deliberate; there was nothing passive in the way her mother wrestled with death. She managed it as she managed life. When she woke at dawn she prepared meals for the day and wiped the bench clean before leaving for her job in the hospital kitchen. When she came home she spoke to her husband's framed photo on the mantel and nodded at his stony silence, then checked Maggie's homework and lay down beside her on the couch that was her daughter's bed and listened to her read. And when Lili went to her own bed exhausted by the day, she thrashed beneath the sheets on the other side of the thin wall and used her pillow to smother the guttural roar of her grief. When she was done with that she got up and went to the basin, where she washed her face and applied her cold cream, then looked in the mirror and affirmed it was the end of another day.

A relentless ghost, since her death there was not a day that Lili did not enter her daughter's thoughts, as she did now, as Maggie wiped her face with her sleeve and propped herself up against the bookshelf, above which hung the first portrait she had ever painted of her mother—in the bottom left-hand corner, a botanical dissection of her beloved kiwifruit: 'the first thing I truly loved about Australia'.

Maggie could almost hear her speak now: 'For pity's sake, pick yourself up, Magda. The nurse is a blithering idiot. *Idióta!* Does she know what will happen tomorrow? Not a clue . . . These people do more harm than good.' And on she went, until Maggie had indeed picked herself up and got to her feet.

In the kitchen now, Martin was making tea, the newspaper and pen on the table, both the Sudoku and the crossword complete.

And Lili, of course, was right. The nurse did not know what would happen tomorrow.

For tomorrow, just as the leaden mass of unspent time began to press down—a cruel joke after all his years of work—there it was, like a gift. Maggie cursed herself for not thinking of it sooner.

All morning Martin had been talking about the photographs on the wall of the New York loft, recalling the images and the time and place they had been taken. In the afternoon when she returned, she found him sitting on the bed surrounded by all his equipment—two cameras, a tripod, boxes of ancient, unused and unusable film.

'Look what I found!' he said, beaming.

Just the Christmas before she had brought him an SLR, digital and very expensive, but when she suggested he use that instead of the old one his face screwed up with the bitter taste of new technology.

'Oh dear, no,' he said. 'It is never quite the same.' He held the camera up and looked at her through the lens, then brought it down again and smiled with the revelation: 'This is it, Maggie. This is what I do.'

And he said no more.

All this talk of New York, Maggie now wondered, had it been for this, to bring the camera back into his hand? There was good reason not to dwell on that day—the pain of what came after. Maggie had tolerated Martin dissecting it into chapters and telling it form and verse because it seemed to have become a beacon of clarity in his otherwise muddled mind. Perhaps now, she thought, it had another purpose, this dredging of the past; perhaps he had found buried there a way to navigate the present.

She went to help with the film, but he put his hand ever so gently on hers. 'I don't need any help, but thank you.'

He took to thanking her more and more, for the least little thing, but always and most fervently for taking his film and returning with his prints, which he would lay out in rows on the floor of his study and tag with yellow post-it notes.

At the end of the day he would guide her through them, each row containing a story, each image a reminder of where he had been—and proof that he was still there.

For Maggie—with Martin's time taken up more and more with his photographs—it enabled her to go back to a project of her own. Though she had set it aside, it was one that had been in her mind every day since he had left the hospital. For Maggie, Martin's new focus meant a return to plan. It meant that she would drive up the hill to find the street in La Perouse, and she would knock on its doors until she found the house and the boy who had lost his dog.

Martin recognised it for what it was: a tag team.

Maggie left for her shift at the youth centre, and minutes later Laini appeared at the door, 'dropping in to pick up Finny's skipping rope'. The boy had taken up skipping recently after tiring of tae kwon do, and no, Laini had assured him, skipping was not 'more of a girl's thing' and no, he wasn't just 'taking a stab at it'; it was now a recognised school sport and Finny was aiming to make the team. As for the 'dropping in', Martin well knew that Laini had no need to pick up the rope (there were another five at home), and that she had come instead to check up on him. These days, it seemed, there was a limit to how long he could be left alone.

When she suggested she make them a cup of something, he told her he'd had enough tea and it was too late for coffee. 'I am going to plant my basil,' he said. 'Spring will be over before I can blink.' And with that he left her in the kitchen. When he came back inside she was still there, now pouring oil over a tray of potatoes and red onions. 'Are you staying?' he asked. No, she was not staying; she was just making a start on dinner for Maggie.

'Still,' he said, looking at his watch, 'I'd better get you a glass of wine.'

Laini finished her progress report on Finn and let Martin pour them both a second glass, then she leant forward on her elbows, chin resting on clasped hands, and said: 'I bet the last thing you want is for everyone to tiptoe around this.'

He smiled back; the wine had taken the edge off the fact that he was being minded. 'Well, I don't suppose that is your plan: to tiptoe.'

She laughed. 'It's not in my DNA.'

What then began was the first conversation of any length outside of the hospital in which Martin was asked to describe what was happening to him when his mind left a room and wandered back into the past. Laini asked questions that Maggie and Ethan were scared to ask, not just for fear of the answers, but because they shared a belief, as did he (it ran in the family), that putting problems into words gave them life and set them on a trajectory of their own, the speck of control one had over them to start with forfeited forever. Laini, needless to say, was not of that mind. To verbalise was to release. Like Finn and his burps: better out than in. And today, as Martin sat with her at the kitchen table drinking their bottle of wine (still waiting as he was for one of these damn doctors to come out with a prognosis on the rest of his days), he could see that there was something sturdy and no-nonsense about her approach, something in the nature, indeed, of a raft to a drowning man.

'One minute I have turned on the tap to water the garden,' he said, 'the next I am standing in a pool of water and the seedlings are floating around my ankles. I am better in New York, somehow. I have a timeline there.'

Then she wanted to talk about that, like Ethan did. 'I love that you are telling the story, Martin. It is about time this family started saying it like it is. I mean, go ahead: "This is us!" You and Maggie are an amazing couple; if it all came from a wild one-night stand, so be it, that is your love story . . . I can't bear all this fucking pretending.'

There was a precedent for the frustration now in her voice: Martin remembered it as she spoke—the conversation at the dining table just after Finn was born. They had finished lunch and Laini was trying to settle the baby's reflux.

'God, was Ethan this bad?' She tried to get Finn on the breast but he spat out the nipple and screamed until his face started turning blue. Maggie took him, held him over her shoulder and patted his back as she walked up and down the hall. It worked.

Laini looked defeated. 'She has the touch.'

'Sometimes all it needs is another pair of arms,' Ethan said.

'Yep, anyone's but mine. I know he's just this tiny thing, but it feels deeply fucking personal.'

Martin shifted awkwardly in his chair, with the sense it was not a conversation to which he should be privy. Laini caught on to that and started with stories of how Finn lit up at the end of the day whenever Ethan walked through the door and other cheery parenting moments until she stopped to ask Martin if any of it was sounding familiar. 'What was Ethan like as a baby?'

Martin could remember the bungled silence in the moment that followed, the distant background of Maggie in the hallway humming 'Old Macdonald'. Laini, naturally enough, looked to Martin for an answer. In time, perhaps it was only a few seconds, Martin smiled, cleared his throat. 'I'm afraid I didn't have a lot to do with Ethan when he was a baby.'

'Well, that must have been more the norm back then. Still, you would've copped an earful at arsenic hour, I'm sure. You can't tell me he was the perfect baby.'

'Oh no, I couldn't tell you that. He had reflux too, from what I understand.'

At this point, Maggie appeared in the doorway with the sleeping baby in her arms, a look on her face of bemused concern. It wasn't until Ethan saw the way his mother was looking at him that he seemed to realise the fault was his, that there was an obligation on him to inform his wife of their family's history, and that in that obligation he had failed.

Laini, exasperated: 'It sounds like you never laid eyes on him!'

Martin smiled as he folded his arms. 'Well, that's not quite true. I saw a photo.' He turned to his son. 'Perhaps it is time to fill Laini in on some of this.'

She glared at him. 'Martin isn't your father!'

Martin shook his head. 'Oh, no, it's nothing as dramatic as that. Certainly not . . .' He rose from his chair, put his arm around Maggie's shoulders and they exited the room, leaving Laini and Ethan alone at the table.

And now: *This is us!* she says.

This is us, indeed. As he poured the last of the wine a number of different responses to what Laini had just said formed in his mind, none of which he gave voice to. Instead came Laini's question: 'Tell me something lovely, Martin. Tell me about the first kiss.'

'Hah! Well, I can tell you she has forgotten it.'

'But you haven't.'

'Lord, no.'

'So then . . . set me the scene.'

Martin smiled. 'That's just where I'm up to . . .' And without explaining what he meant, he launched into it, the party in the Spring Street loft . . .

From the bar to the park to the party: a massive space on the fifth floor. It was already past midnight as they wove a path through the crowd, girls in sequined leotards and leopard-skin underwear, a pair of twins with identical bare breasts and matching chiffon skirts, and men in pinstriped suits and ties and silk turbans and red berets.

'Maggie had never seen anything like it in her life.'

Of course Linda fitted right in; beneath her coat was a white sleeveless catsuit, her magnificent flesh bursting out of it for all to ogle, and there was Maggie, still in the clothes she'd worn all day, the clogs and the miniskirt. All she could do was tie her blouse in a knot at the front. Linda took hold of her then and shimmied her into the dance, pulled her in tight before launching into some kind of matador act with an invisible cape and Maggie as her bull.

'I lost her,' Martin said to Laini. 'I went to the bar to get us drinks and the crowd swallowed her up. Just as I thought I might never find her, there was this God-awful piercing shout in my ear: "Hey, you!" It was Sylvia, the hostess—a mad redhead who liked to wear an Indian headdress—shouting across the room: "Get the fuck off my painting!" Everyone spun around to look and there she was, Maggie, standing up on some kind of platform. As I pushed my way closer I saw that the surface of the thing was made of rubber and it was mottled, multi-coloured, and Maggie was standing smack-bang in the middle of it, looking around in a panic trying to figure out what the terrible shouting was all about, and mad old Sylvia launching forwards and shouting: "Get your fucking clogs out of my vomit!"

'Maggie looked down at her feet; the piece of shit Sylvia called art was an image of spewed-up food chunks and swirls of yellow bile. Thankfully, Maggie got it; she was standing in art, and this was a performance. Looking out again to the crowd she took a breath, and sprung off and onto the floor in one gracious leap. A couple of people clapped, and Sylvia bowed to stronger applause, graciously extending her arm to Maggie as cohort. Magnificent, I thought, how she'd managed to come out of it unscathed. It was my idea of hell and there she was curtseying to the crowd. I wanted to kiss her right there and then.'

'How wonderful,' Laini said. 'And did you?'

'Not then, not yet. Soon . . .'

He continued with the story: They moved out of the crowd, back to an empty stool against the wall. Maggie told him she'd never in all her life felt this good. It was the speed; she was buzzed. He told her that, and she made the sound. Bzzzz . . .

And with that, eyes closed and buzzing like a bee, she looks good enough to swallow whole.

Instead he leant in and kissed her, just kissed her, a taste, wet and salty.

As Martin was telling the story now, he stared straight ahead at the refrigerator as though its door was a screen playing the memory, but after the kiss, he looked back to Laini and smiled. 'I spilt the drink I was carrying all over my pants. Bourbon and dry. That was it, a messy end to a first kiss.'

His eyes widened. 'You know, she knew she was going to be a painter then; she knew it when she was seven years old. Amazing that, isn't it? The way she always knew.'

Then came a different voice: 'That she always knew what?' It was Maggie behind him. 'Sounds like I got here just in time.' And looking at the empty bottle: 'Or maybe not. Laini, darling, are you going to be right to drive?'

Some time later (had they had dinner?), he was alone in a bedroom.

It was after the kiss. And there were her words, pure and gushing: 'I love this; I love your life.'

It went like this: The kiss, the spilt drink, and then . . .

'I'm not kidding; it isn't just the drugs,' Maggie says, pulling back but staying close. 'I love this; I love your life.'

There is an unexpected certainty in what comes out of his mouth as he passes her the glass: 'This isn't my life.'

She downs what is left of the drink. 'Is that right? So whose is it then?'

He nods towards a couch, at Dave and Linda, who are waving them over. 'I'm just a visitor. They are the real thing.'

She shrugs as she starts to sway to Bob Marley and tells him he is whoever he wants to be. 'You said there are things you want to do . . . What are they?'

He shrugged. 'I don't know. Get more serious with the photographs.'

'That's great, Marty—you're in New York; you can do anything.'

He tries to tell her it's complicated, he's meant to be doing the bar exams, but she shakes her head and presses a finger to his lips. 'Remember what the pigeon lady said: fear is a gift . . .'

'Yeah,' he says, 'sure it is. So let's unwrap it. Let's get out of here.'

There is an urgency now. She has crawled under his skin

like an itch. It is the drugs maybe (or maybe not, maybe this is his way, his thing . . .), but whatever it is, he needs to scratch; he needs to get to the door and stumble down the five flights and take Maggie back to the loft. He needs to fuck her and say goodbye and get back to what he was doing before. But she isn't behind him; she has taken herself over to the couch and is sitting down, her shirt pulled off her left shoulder as Linda draws a heart on it and Dave hands her a spliff. And that is when he feels himself plunging, reeling . . . Something about the vignette tells him it could all slip away. All of a sudden he is questioning whether to walk back or just leave, because all of a sudden he is a pretender and this has to be what she always wanted, who she wanted to be with, Dave and Linda—just like he said: the real thing.

He is sweating, his heart racing.

He squats down on the floor in front of Maggie. She looks at the spliff and then at him like she has a question.

Dave answers it: 'Weed on speed. It'll warm you up, give you a sidestep.' His voice sounds like it is coming from another room.

She takes a couple of tokes and when she is done, Dave puts his arm around her and pulls her in close then yells: 'You gotta be straight with me, Marty: is this how they all look back home?' He gestures to Linda and Maggie, side by side. 'It is like I have died and gone to the island and here they are waiting for me: Ginger and Mary Ann. Fucking beautiful!'

Maggie takes hold of the fingertips resting just above her left breast and turns to kiss Dave's cheek, then she makes everything right and slides down onto the floor next to Martin. Her pupils are full moon, and rolling . . . He puts his hand against her face; she presses against it like a cat, and whispers: 'Let's go.'

~

Maybe visitor was the wrong word.

It stuck in his mind as the edges blurred and the scene closed. When his eyes opened he was sitting in bright light on a ledge by the pool, watching Maggie swim. In his hand was a camera. He had started again with the pictures.

He watched her laps. This was what he did sometimes. Perhaps it was every day.

'Do I come with you every day, Maggie?' Mid-lap, there was no answer. Just the splash of water in an ocean pool.

Observer was a better word.

It was enough, wasn't it? From the minute she knocked on his door . . . It was a call to action. But the truth of it was that the pigeon lady was wrong: you don't have to do anything. Fear unwraps all by itself.

'Let's go. Let's go back to the loft.'

On the street the night is warm and the smell is pungent, like the day has died and is rotting all around them. They have left the party. It is two a.m.

'Let's go to the loft. We can get your stuff in the morning.'

'No.' At first there is just the single word in reply, and a sinking moment when he thinks it is over. 'No,' she says, her head falling back in bleary worship of the night sky, 'not the loft. The garden. Let's go back to the garden.' And her eyes spin, a rush of blood on weed on speed. 'Let's explore it in the dark.'

~

Back in his study after her laps, Maggie had come and gone. She hadn't liked what he had said. He hadn't said it right.

'I'm going to the studio now to do some work.' Her hair was still wet from the water.

He nodded. 'On the wall.'

She started to walk out, but stopped. 'I am not painting on the wall, Martin.'

Of course. This one was paper. This was the one she sent to Mrs Bess. 'This is why I call you.'

'What are you talking about, Martin?'

He was talking about the painting in the window of the shop. Months after Maggie had left New York, he had seen the painting in the window. It was an ink wash. There he was! The likeness was unmistakable: Martin sitting on a chair in a corner of the loft like a man in a junkyard. He appeared dazed, his shadow forming part of the wall, his body another object amid the debris. After that night in the garden, Maggie had gone home and there had been no contact between them (though it was unsettling how much the girl was in his thoughts). And then the painting. Martin saw it, stopped in his tracks. He went in to speak to Mrs Bess, who told him Maggie had sent it all the way from Australia. She asked if Maggie had done it while she was in New York. 'No,' he had replied. 'She only drew one, on the wall in the loft.'

The pigeon lady seemed surprised, then suspicious, and went to bring the painting out from the window. When she returned she looked closely at his face then pointed to the page, to the faint crevice on the chin, the line of the cheekbone. 'She knows your face like she has known you all your life.' She stated it as a fact, shrugged. 'She is an artist, this one. She understands demons even when she has none of her own . . . I'll keep it in the window so you can see it when you come by.'

As he walked home he remembered what Maggie had said that morning in the loft, how as a girl her mother had his photograph on the fridge. He wondered if Maggie had kept it and looked at it again when she had painted this last portrait.

'It was months after you'd gone,' he said to Maggie, who was still standing at the door of the study. 'I walked past her shop and there it was, the drawing you sent her. She kept it in the window so I could see it. That is why I called you.'

That was wrong. The chronology was wrong. She shook her head in anger.

'You didn't call, Martin,' she said. 'I called you.'

What he did not tell her, what he meant to tell her before she rushed off, was that years later he went back to see the pigeon lady. On his last visit to Dave, he had gone back to try to buy the painting. But Mrs Bess wasn't there anymore; the school wasn't there. All that was left was a shopfront and, above the doorway, a pair of shitting pigeons.

It was only later that night, dripping ink around the edge of a canvas, that she could pinpoint what was still bothering her. It was not the skewed perspective on the pebbles in the corner of the painting (that was no worse than it was yesterday—no better, no worse). As the last ink drop swelled, what Martin had said that morning in the study continued to replay—this idea he had seen the painting she sent Mrs Bess and, because of that, had called her.

As she often did when she was stuck on something, Maggie turned away from the painting and towards the objects on the shelves behind her. She would pick one—the plaster hand or the peacock feather, the dried acacia branch or one of the skulls (human, bat, unknown). Today it was the small canvas, a woman in a plain, pale dress sitting on a front doorstep; the backdrop was the brickwork of the building. It was a painting by an unknown artist that her father had rolled up and carried around a continent. Over time it had been damaged, a watermark on the lower step, and on the right side a clumsy attempt at restoration—the section of the overpaint contrasting with the subtler blend of the surrounding bricks. Maggie had thought to test it with turpentine to see if she could remove the overpaint without damaging the original, but she never had, at first for fear that whatever lay underneath would be too fragile, and later because there was a reason to understand the endeavour and, in spite of the crude brushwork, to respect its intention.

I walked past her shop and there it was . . . That is why I called you.

Martin had not called her.

It was a mistake of fact and Maggie had corrected him. Her protest had sounded like adolescent pique—*I called you, you didn't call me*—when in truth the event was the initiation of the rest of their lives. Yes, Martin was forgetting; he was forgetting what food he liked for breakfast—some days he still forgot that there were no more judgments to write—but he was not forgetting what happened in New York. The repeated retelling of what happened all those years ago, what made it bearable, sometimes astounding, was the accuracy of it, the newfound power of recall—and then this morning in his study, such a fundamental error in the chronology.

What Maggie realised as she gave up on the portrait and went to wash her brushes was that it was the first time he had stepped beyond that day in New York, to what came next. It was the first time he had ever mentioned the painting she had sent to Mrs Bess, and the telephone call between them.

And as soon as he stepped past the day, that was when the lies began.

The chronology—the truth—was this:

The first phone call, three months after her return to Australia—November 1973 (*You have a choice, Maggie*, her friends said. *It is 1973!*). The script was off track from the start.

'Hello, Martin, it's me—Maggie.'

She hadn't meant to say 'me', just that it was Maggie. 'Me' presumed intimacy. The tone in his voice she was sure was a reaction against it—the same tone he used that night in the garden in New York after she'd said her final piece, after she'd said too much.

'Maggie! Maggie. I meant to . . . how are you?'

Her friends said they knew a doctor who would do it. Her life was just beginning; she didn't need to go through with this. For God's sake, it was 1973 . . .

'I'm great,' she said. 'Fantastic. I started art school, and I'm saving some money.'

What her friends did not understand was that since her return home, Martin was her first and last thought of the day, and the fly in her head all the hours in between. What her friends did not—could not—understand, was that on the other side of 'he loves me not' was the belief that the life inside her was a sign of a shared destiny. She began an ink wash portrait, working now from memory—the only photograph she had being the one of him as boy—and as she painted she carried on a mental dialogue, continuing all the conversations they had begun in New York and writing and rewriting the one they would have on the phone when he called.

And she sat behind the counter in the dress shop or in her art class and relived the night from every which way. His voice: 'Lie down . . .' It played over and over: the pinched skin as he pinned her arms above her head with the warm weight of his body. Sometimes the only way to stop it was to bite the palm of her hand; only that would bring her back to the suffocating tedium of the present, the nausea of her pregnancy, a customer browsing and not buying, a lecturer looking to her for the answer to a question she hadn't heard.

She waited three months, but the call never came. That was why she'd got the tone wrong; in the version she'd imagined, it was Martin who dialled the number—she didn't need to tell him who it was. When it came to picking up the phone herself, she hadn't thought to rewrite the introduction.

'And you, what's news?' As the question left her mouth, the fact loitering in the subterranea of her mind came steaming to the fore: that her relationship with Martin was for the most part of her own making, that it consisted of a single day, or—in the words of Erica Jong—a 'zipless fuck'.

'Well, you won't believe it, but I've enrolled to do the bar exams. Linda finally convinced me. I sit them in a few months. So I've become a total swot.'

Though her brain scrambled for a response to mask the demolition of her hopes, it produced nothing more than, 'Oh my gosh.'

'Well, you know, she's right: as a lawyer, there's so much I could do here—I mean there's some fucked-up shit going on.' (Hadn't she heard those words before? Weren't they Linda's words?) 'And she's got this contact in the public defender's office and they think I can get sponsored through the firm. So I could do a bit of criminal defence work . . . They need lawyers out in the boroughs. And it keeps the parents happy. They've even sent me some money to see me through.'

'And photography?'

There was silence for a second. 'I guess later, maybe.'

As Maggie continued her part in the conversation, a perfectly acceptable imitation of calm in her voice, the words

'I am pregnant' repeated in her mind as some kind of joke, pathetic and cruel, more cruel and pathetic than any joke she had ever heard.

She finished the painting, and sent it to Mrs Bess.

Four months later—when she knew he'd be done with his exams—she made the second call.

His voice choked. 'It's mine?'

There was fear in it, more terror than fear. It made her want to scream. Instead, what came out was something she had never planned to say, a lie she had never planned to tell: 'I think so. There was a guy in Paris.'

'Oh . . .' And in that small sound, some relief.

A guy in Paris. There it was, his out, and a way for her to end the conversation.

It took two days for Martin to call back and he opened with: 'I'm really sorry this is happening to you.'

She didn't have a response ready for that.

But he was ready: he would sort this out. He would be back for a visit once he could get the time. There were tests they could do, blood tests to determine the identity of the father. And he would send her money, for 'baby stuff'; his parents had sent him more than enough. 'And then, once we've sorted it, we'll go from there. I'm not walking away from this, Maggie. I don't want you to think that.'

Somehow, she diverted the conversation back to the everyday. He had got his results and had passed the bar, and in a week was starting his new job.

'How's Dave?'

'Not so good. He took off; the drug thing got pretty bad.'

'And Linda, how is Linda?'

'Great, she's good.' And then the question she didn't ask because she knew the answer to it and all the ones that followed: So it's just you two there now?

~

When Martin came back for that first promised visit, Ethan was twelve months old. For Maggie, there had been months of chronic reflux and breath-holding spells, months of watching the colour drain from his lips, and at some point of every day she had looked into her baby's eyes with the thought that Martin was not there to look into them too. There was no more art class (no 'room full of wankers'), and more often than not Lili still worked night and day, leaving Maggie alone in the flat with the baby and the stack of books a teacher had lent her. When Ethan slept she buried herself in them, art history and mystic theory, a favourite on the art of automatism, and though it was not the time to paint, there were days when it was all she wanted to do, and through the delirium of night she would keep at it, her body exhausted but her mind separate, frenetic, free.

When finally Martin did come back, it wasn't that her love for him had paled, it had just changed colour.

She walked him into the room; the baby was sitting on the floor. 'There is no need for a test, Martin.' This was all she said. 'There was no man in Paris. This is Ethan, your son.'

Ethan started crying again. She picked him up and handed him to his father. The crying stopped.

She didn't know what she had expected of this first meeting, but not what played out, not this simple, quiet exchange. They sat on the square rug. Martin watched in gentle awe as Ethan rattled the plastic keys. 'He is amazing.'

'He looks like you.' The blond hair, olive skin.

'He doesn't have my eyes.' More grey than blue.

'No, you're right. He doesn't. They are my father's eyes.'

And later, in bed, when it came to that:

'The guy in Paris,' he said. 'Why did you tell me that?'

'Come on, you didn't really believe it.'

He shrugged. 'I did. Maybe I'm an idiot, but I did.'

'I said it because you were staying . . . because you were with Linda.'

There was no denial, of course not, only: 'But that's not to say . . .'

'That's not to say what?'

He stared at her. 'Jesus, this is weird. I'm not sure what's happening here. I mean, Maggie, I want to be a part of this. Do you want me to be?'

How could she blame him, she thought, when he had to ask the question?

And so it began, the stops and starts and the stalling in between, the muddled attempts to link arms across an ocean. News came that Dave was sick, in hospital. Linda called him at all hours. They didn't know what it was; that was what Martin said. He had to go.

And Maggie told him not to come back. 'Not until you're ready,' she said. 'Not until it's finished.'

When he did come back—at Christmas and the next July—her mother arranged visits with Ethan. Maggie had been picked up by a gallery where her friend Annie was assistant curator, and after a slow opening her first exhibition was a sellout. She went out for six months with her old tutor, and then for three with a banker she met in a library. On Martin's visit for Ethan's fourth birthday, he insisted on seeing her, told her that he needed to talk about Ethan.

They met for a drink.

When he said the words, there were a million reasons not to believe them, but she did. When he leant over and took her hands in his, she began to cry, and she couldn't stop. In the car she let him kiss her. She let him move them into his apartment and hang her paintings on the walls; she let it be true, and before the year was out, it more or less was.

That was the chronology of how a family was formed—perhaps with one addendum. A few weeks after they moved in, they were rehashing an old argument as Maggie set up her workspace: why Martin had stopped taking photographs.

'You're lucky,' he said.

'Why is that?'

'It was easier for you.'

'Sure it was. Mind-numbing job. Art school at night. Raising a baby without a father.'

'Come on, you've said it yourself: the perks of being a fringe-dweller. No one expected you to go to law school; no one watched over your shoulder to see if you got into chambers in Martin Place.'

She put the box down and turned to face him. 'Are you still playing that one? You're not where you want to be?'

And Martin's retort: 'I'm here, aren't I?'

She had her father's temper, Lili always said. So rarely lit, but then decimating . . . Later Martin would use the word 'launched' but it was enough to say she *stepped* towards him, leaving not an arm's length between them—'I could feel your spit on my face!'

'I will not be grateful for you being here. This is your

choice. We've done fine without you, and can do so again. I need you to understand that, Martin.'

Later, he woke her in the middle of the night. 'Marry me, Maggie.'

She sat up. 'I won't marry you,' she said, taking his hand. 'I don't want anything to oblige you to stay but for this, for us.'

He pulled her in close. 'Listen to me. That day in New York, I didn't understand it then. You know who you are, Maggie, like no one I've ever met. I'm in awe of that. And I'm in love with you. That's why I'll stay.'

Martin was a man with a clinical mind—in a courtroom or around a dinner table, he would slash and discard any matters extraneous and move in to dissect the question at hand. 'Yes,' he would say, 'but what is the gravamen?' Clinical, even brutal . . . It was only now that Maggie was beginning to see the deterioration in his memory in that same context.

This mental microscope on a single day, it gave Martin a story to tell and brought the camera back into his hands, yes, but it did something more than that. By shining a light on the day it cast a shadow over what came after.

By looking to the beginning when he sensed he was nearing the end, a giant step was made over all the days in between.

Part Three

She stood silent at the open door.

Come, Maggie, she told herself. *You've made it this far . . .*

She had driven up the hill to find the street and had walked up the front steps of the only house showing signs of life, a few doors back from the cross-street. Now all she had to do was knock. She raised her hand, held it in the air, and let it fall again to her side.

Inside on the floor were a pile of toys and a blue plastic crate, and, on top of the crate, a bowl of Weet-Bix still soggy with milk. The walls were a mural of crayon cars and butterflies and stick figures with miniature bodies and humungous heads. Maggie looked back, to the swing without a seat and to her car parked outside the house with the couch in the garden. But for a child sitting on a fence in a hooded top, today the street was empty of people: no dogs or boys on bicycles, no accidents waiting to happen. Luck in life, she thought, was so often a matter of timing.

A child's cough broke the silence.

'Hello?' She spoke softly. 'Is anyone there?'

Inside there was a noise, a step. It was only then, as she gasped for air, that Maggie became aware of the depth of her fear.

Come, Maggie, she said to herself. *What is the worst it could be?*

'Is anyone there?' she repeated, again in not much more than a whisper.

As she began to rummage through her bag for a pen to leave a note, there was the sound of footsteps, and Maggie looked up to see a woman standing at the end of the hallway, an Aboriginal woman in a green tracksuit—in her late twenties, maybe a little older, and as thin as a bird, her wild and wiry hair matted into a ponytail at the side of her head. At the sight of Maggie at the door, she flashed her startled, sunken eyes and flew past her like a gust of wind, the smell of cigarette smoke lingering as she raced out the gate and down the street.

Maggie stood in her wake, found her pen and hurriedly started to scribble her note, leaning the scrap of paper against her handbag. She was interrupted by a voice: 'You from the department?' Looking up, she saw another woman shuffling towards her down the hall—a larger, older woman with short white hair and skin the colour of muddy water. She wore an orange Hawaiian shirt, short-sleeved and collared, patterned in sunsets and palm trees, and a long floral skirt in pinks and reds. Her feet were bare.

Without waiting for an answer, the woman went on, 'Well, she ain't here.'

Behind her now the sound of a child's voice: 'Nana!'

'No, I'm not from the department,' Maggie said, stepping back. 'My name is Maggie Varga. I'm here about an accident in the street about six weeks ago.'

'I don't know nothing about any accident, and none of mine know nothing and none of mine done nothing, so you're best to shove off.'

Though there was an attraction in following the order, Maggie stood firm. *You have come this far* . . . 'Please,' she said. 'The dog was killed. My husband was the man in the car. I came to say sorry to the boy.'

The woman's neck, until now invisible, extended from the collar of her shirt. 'You ain't from the department?'

Maggie shook her head.

The woman looked her up and down. Maggie was wearing black woollen trousers with a white shirt and a navy blazer—a little makeup, and no jewellery. 'You look like you are.'

So she had got it wrong, after all, Maggie thought. The outfit was a last-minute change out of the jeans and grey cardigan and her favourite silver beaded necklace. Standing in front of the mirror to check herself before she left, she had suddenly decided: No, that would not do. It was one thing to fit in with the locals, but today surely it was more important to show that an effort had been made. As for the beads, they were buried in the glove box along with her watch. Better not to sparkle, she had thought as she pulled up at the kerb. Martin was right: this was not a street where you went around knocking on doors.

Maggie stuttered in reply, uncertain how to prove herself. She had seen the boy in the paper, she explained, or tried to explain before the shriek of the child blasted down the hall.

'Naaannnna!'

And as the woman turned back inside, she called out over her shoulder: 'People don't knock much around here. Mostly just barge right on in . . . You might as well do the same.'

The hall led into a family room and a kitchen where there was an open door to a paved brick courtyard. In the doorway, wearing a pair of purple underpants and a string of matching beads, stood a girl of two or three pointing to a green texta lid lodged in her right nostril. The old woman swooped the child up to the kitchen bench, cradling and admonishing all at once.

'Now don't ya move,' she said, as she pulled a pair of tweezers from the top drawer and with expert hand pincered the lid from the nostril. The child slipped down from the bench and ran outside to a low plastic table where she picked up a texta and continued with her picture.

'I can't tell ya how many times lately these things have come in handy,' the woman said, dropping the lid into the bin and the tweezers in the sink. While around them the floor was covered in books and toys, the kitchen itself was immaculate. Even so, the woman picked up a tea towel and rubbed in circles as she spoke. 'Sorry, so let me get this: your bloke is the judge who ended up in the ambulance?'

'Yes, that's right.'

'And how did it turn out for him?'

Maggie told her that Martin had had a stroke and was now at home recovering.

'Well, that is good to know. We thought we had ourselves two corpses in the street until that ambulance came. Then we saw it in the paper he was in the coma. Didn't hear anything since then. I'm glad to hear he's on the mend.'

On the mend . . . It was a soft-sounding, simple phrase; if only it were apt, Maggie thought, noticing then the woman peering back at her as though she was trying to add something up.

'I didn't recognise him,' she finally said. 'Only Kayla did, me son's missus.'

Maggie started. 'Sorry, you say she recognised him?'

'She sure did.'

'You mean she'd seen him in the papers before?'

'Yeah, I guess so. There was that murder case a few years back when he copped the flak, but it wasn't for that she recognised him—and it wasn't for that I remembered him once I'd seen the name in the paper. Your judge was my son's first decent lawyer. That's what he was to me.' And when she saw the bafflement spring to Maggie's face: 'That'd be news to you, is it? Well, ya wouldn't figure it, for sure. Here he is, the man that represented my boy all those years back, collapsing in front of me on my street.'

Maggie hesitated, as one on the precipice of discovery. The questions began to form: why Martin had come, the reasons to keep it secret . . . 'So he was here to see you?'

But the woman shook her head. 'Lord, no, I don't say that. What on earth would he come see me for? He hit the dog, that's all, so this was the place he stopped.'

'And you're sure that Martin represented your son?'

'Same one, no word of a lie: your judge—before he was a judge, of course. I met him in the flesh, at the courthouse down in Redfern. It was a hell of a business, Roddy's first lagging. A bunch of 'em held up a sports store, syringes and knives and what have you, bloody mugs all hooked on that filthy shit. Your judge was a fancy QC and got him bail and a plea deal and he done alright, got a couple of years but he could've got more. It's a long time ago now, no reason he'd remember us . . . But I can say he was a decent fella, so I'm glad to hear he's back home with you, you tell him that from us. He's doing alright then?'

'Yes, he is, but his memory . . . He can't remember the day,' Maggie said. 'He can't remember why he was driving up here.' Their eyes locked, Maggie in search of an answer, the older woman understanding now there was another reason why Maggie was here, like she was expecting it all along.

'I can't help you there, love. We hadn't laid eyes on him in that long. And Rodney's back inside, been there since Christmas. Plenty of people pass through this street. There's the community centre and the clinic around the corner, it gets a lot of visitors, and people like to drive up the hill to get a look down at the bay. Maybe he got himself lost. It seemed that way, by the look of him. I don't think he knew where he was.'

Maggie nodded, back to the beginning. The woman had offered up an answer, and for now, Maggie would accept it, in part relieved the subject was exhausted and that the only reason she had left to be here was the stated one, the better one—to apologise to the boy.

The old woman smiled and ripples appeared across her broad forehead. Her eyes were deep-set and dark against her silver-white eyebrows, which she raised now as she asked her visitor: 'You wanna cuppa?' There was a chink in the spine of her nose and a thick, furrowed midline across its flattened bridge. Though her chin was short, the jut was stubborn. There was barely a face that went by in a given day that Maggie didn't think of drawing, but a face like this was a rare find—a face some would say carried in it the motto of the soul.

Maggie agreed and took a seat at the bench. 'My name is Maggie,' she said.

'Lord, there am I too busy trying to push you out the door . . . Pleased to meet you, Maggie. I'm Iris.'

As Iris passed the tea, Maggie asked if she knew the boy who owned the dog. A look of pride flashed across the woman's face. 'He's me grandson, Tyson. That's Roddy's boy.'

'Does he live here?'

'Sometimes he does. He goes between me and his mother in Redfern. Right now that's where you'll find him, on the Block down there . . . You might want me to pass him the message. I'll let him know you came by, I'll do that, but listen, Maggie: I saw the paper and I'll tell you now—it wasn't really Tyson's dog. It was the street dog. We all fed him when he needed a feed and he hung about. All the kids played with him, Tyson especially. He loved the dog, he was the one that pulled them ticks out—with all this bush around the dog got plenty of 'em—but it wasn't his or nothing. You don't owe Tyson anything. And like I said, your judge was decent to us. He kept on his feet and arguing in that courtroom for my Rodney, and afterwards he came to me and asked if there was any message that he could take down to him in the cells. He showed us a respect I ain't seen from any lawyer since. I can tell Tyson you were here, Maggie, that you came to say sorry, and that'd be plenty.'

Maggie offered no argument, sipped her tea and asked about the little girl.

'She's my niece's daughter from Dubbo,' Iris said, 'but my niece is doing it tough—seems that's the way with the whole mob out there right now.'

And with the kitchen bench between them the old woman proceeded to tell Maggie all the ways in which the Dubbo mob had done it tough—the girl Lana's baby 'launched stillborn' a day before her cousin Buddy went inside, leaving her niece Shayleen to look after the kids 'when she can't brush her own teeth'.

'So I've got this one a while,' she said. 'Just until things turn around. Good times are due in Dubbo, there isn't any doubt there.'

The talk moved to places, towns, where other cousins lived. 'I've been living here on this hill all my life,' Iris said. 'Some days I feel like I'm turning into one of them rocks looking down over the ocean.'

The little girl tottered into the room with her finished picture of a pink and purple sun. She held it up to Maggie for praise and ran out to do another one for her to take home.

'You know, I remember I came here to La Perouse as a child,' Maggie said. 'We went down to the Loop to see the snake man. We caught the tram.'

'You did? Well, that must have been in my time—me and my mother used to sell the boxes with the shells on 'em, all different shapes . . .'

'I remember them! The Harbour Bridges!'

'Well there you go. Mighta been me selling 'em.'

Maggie looked at the woman perched across the bench with the cup of tea in her hand, and remembered the day she and her parents caught the tram to the tip of the Loop at La Perouse to see the man in the pit who let a snake bite his ear. There were some lizards too (their necks frilled up if you poked them with a stick), and things for sale, stalls of boomerangs and artworks set up by the Aborigines from the reserve up on the hill. Maggie held her mother's hand looking down at the cross-legged, brown-skinned girls with nothing but a cotton dress between them and the hot, tarred road. Lined up there in front of them were shell-covered boxes in the shape of hearts and flowers and, best of all, big Harbour Bridges with the bases painted red so they looked to Maggie like upside down smiles, the shells like little white teeth.

'There was a bunch of us back then,' Iris went on. 'We used to do all different ones, different shapes, and sell 'em to the tourists. The bridges, and the little baby boots.'

'God, I must have been nine or ten. I remember the boxes, the treasure boxes. I begged my mother to buy one!'

The smile that settled on the woman's face was the smile of someone you'd known all your life; it made Maggie want to reach across the table and take her hand. 'I still make 'em, the boxes,' Iris continued. 'I'm the only one who still does. The kids get the shells for me down on the beach and bring 'em up here.'

She put her mug down on the bench, stood up from her stool and started walking out of the kitchen, turning around only when she reached the doorway. 'You want to see?'

Maggie followed Iris into the hall and up the stairs, to a room above the kitchen. There was a single bed and a chest of drawers. Tubs of shells sorted into different types and sizes lined the wall, and next to them on sheets of newspaper were the boxes—painted crimson and sky blue and covered in shells forming intricate patterns, just as Maggie remembered them. 'Oh, Iris, they're beautiful.'

'There were lots of us doing it back then, like I said.'

'And now just you?'

'That I know of.'

'Do you sell them? Can I buy one from you?'

'Take one. A present from me.'

'Oh no, I wouldn't do that. I'll pay you.'

'Pick one,' she said.

Maggie leant down and held a box in her hands, and holding it there, recalled that she had her own story about going down to the Loop that day—a story she hadn't told for as long as she could remember. Suddenly, it felt only right to share it.

'Do you remember the kids that used to jump off the jetty and catch the coins?'

Iris nodded. 'Sure I do.'

'That day we came, after I watched the snake man, I saw the crowd and went over there, to the jetty.'

Right up at the end of the jetty, she told Iris, was a group of Aboriginal children in shorts and nothing else, and with them a tall moustachioed man. He dug his hand into his pocket and pulled out a coin and he threw it high into the air and into the water. As newcomers pushed forwards to get closer to the edge, the biggest boy dived in after the coin. Everyone waited. As the seconds passed, Maggie started counting them. Twenty-one, twenty-two, twenty-three . . . The man who threw the coin was leaning out from the jetty trying to get a look and Maggie began to wonder if the boy was ever coming back up. She got all the way to fifty, fifty-one, and like a leaping fish the boy shot out of the water to a gasping crowd and, letting his head sink beneath the surface, he held up two empty hands. It was a show, alright. Once he pulled himself up and stood tall on the jetty, he opened his mouth and there, between his glistening white teeth, was the coin. The crowd burst into applause, and the boy took his bow.

'And you know what I did?' Maggie went on. 'I watched for a while, thinking to myself I could do it just as well as they did. Then I did it. I dived in, dress and all.'

Iris let out a laugh. 'I bet you're the only white kid who ever did it.'

'I could state it for a fact,' Maggie said, cringing at the next part of the memory. 'When I came out with my coin, a woman came storming out of the crowd and dragged me off the jetty.'

Iris shook her head, a slow downturn in her lips. 'She did that, eh? Shame on her for laying a hand on you.'

And more shame, more shame for what she said, Maggie thought, but didn't go on.

'And you gone jumped right in yourself! That is beautiful, that is . . . I knew there was a reason I let you into my house, Maggie. And your judge on our street!' Iris nodded. 'There are lines between us, you and me.'

And with that came the call from downstairs: 'Naaanaaa!'

Iris pushed herself up off the floor and walked from the room. Again Maggie followed in her slow steps, down to the bottom of the stairs where the little girl was waiting, holding her arms in the air. Iris scooped her up and kept walking to the front door.

Maggie reached into her bag for her wallet, but Iris shook her head. It was stern. 'I'll just get cranky if you do that. Accept it from me. They don't get much appreciation these days. I'll pass on your message to young Tyson.'

'I'd still like to see him,' Maggie said.

'Then you'll have to come back and see me too.'

Iris reached out with her one free arm and enclosed Maggie's hand in hers. Maggie nodded, having accepted a gift instead of giving one: in part absolved, she thought as she walked down the front steps into the street, and in part more indebted than when she came.

At home, sitting at the desk in her studio, the gift grew heavy in Maggie's hands, as though it were made not of shell-covered plywood but of solid stone.

Of the moments in life that form us, be careful not to blink too long: that was what her father had once warned. 'Pay attention, Magda. They don't put their hand up and tell you what they are.' More than half a century later, she understood something of how it worked. As it occurs, the event furls and twists its way around the organs—an invisible cord, a silent asp—around the stomach, the lungs, the heart, so that later when a button is pressed and the synapse is triggered, it tugs, causing a contraction. For the response is surely physiological—nausea or shortness of breath, even pain in the chest. As there it was now, sitting at her desk as she opened the box and ran the tip of her finger over the varnished inlay: the tug, the trigger, and when Maggie caught her breath she was still that girl, the dripping girl being dragged from the jetty . . . There are those events, and this was one.

What she remembered of it now was what happened after that first boy retrieved his coin. As Maggie tried to make her way to the front of the crowd to get a better look, another man pushed through right to the edge of the jetty and, muttering something under his breath, he gestured to the next boy waiting, then raised his arm and threw a coin as far as he could out into the water. As it disappeared in the distance, the boy shook his head, and the man laughed, a laugh as big as his button-bursting belly.

Maggie remembered watching the laughing man, and thinking of the poster that hung on the wall of the migrant reception centre, and what her mother had said. Waiting in the queue, Lili had wondered out loud why they couldn't have filled in all the forms sometime during the thirty days they had been at sea, and tried to distract Maggie with the picture on the posters that said the same thing as the leaflet on the bunk on the boat: that they had arrived in the land of tomorrow. The picture was of a house on a farm with a pink roof.

'You know your colours, Magda,' Lili had said.

'Yes, Mama.'

'*Rózsasín*, Magda. Pink.'

In green fields around the house, sheep grazed and a man laughed on a spotted horse.

'*Zöld*, Magda. Green.'

Behind the house was a purple mountain with patches of yellow flowers and, atop, a blue windmill.

'Green,' Maggie said.

But arriving the next morning at the migrant camp, it was not green or yellow or blue. Once an army barracks, it was a place of corrugated sheds and sun-dried earth, the shrubs that Maggie pointed to drained of colour. The only resemblance that life in this place had to the picture on the wall was the laughing man. Men in this country were quick to laugh. Too quick, Lili thought. 'They are laughing at us,' she said to Frederick, but he shook his head. Humour across cultures, he explained, is just difficult to translate.

'What is absurd, it is different here,' he said, 'just like the hour of the day. It is upside down.'

Standing on the jetty and listening to the man laughing at his irretrievable coin, Maggie had cocked her head as far as she could to one side, though could find no angle that would help her understand what the man found so funny. Eventually, he was gone and more coins were thrown, a handful at a time, the smaller children jumping into the water all at once.

Then it came to her turn.

When she climbed back onto the jetty she didn't hear anyone clap. The only one to pay her any attention at all was this one lady, with a face frilled up like one of the snake man's lizards, who pushed through what was left of the crowd and started sucking in breaths like there wasn't enough air. Dripping in her dress, Maggie tried to look somewhere else but the woman grabbed her by the arm and began to drag her off the jetty. Maggie yanked back but not before the woman said what she wanted to say. It was hard to understand because she was talking so fast and she started and finished every sentence with: 'You hear me!' At first it sounded like she was worried Maggie might drown. 'You have to be more careful,' she was saying. But then her words made it plain. She wasn't worried about drowning.

'You hear me! You don't swim in that same water, you hear me . . .'

She slowed down for that bit so Maggie didn't have any trouble hearing. Then she took hold of Maggie's arm and started pulling her down the jetty, telling her to find her parents, who'd give her a flogging if they were any kind of decent God-fearing people. 'What would they say if they'd seen you swimming in that filthy water?'

There wasn't anything wrong with the water, but Maggie couldn't find the words to say that. The only thing she could do was jump down on the woman's foot as hard as she could, and run.

Afterwards, when her parents saw her wet clothes, she told them she'd swum off the jetty with the other children. She didn't tell them about the coins, or about the lady. She was in trouble, but mostly because she had lost her hat and Lili was so terrified of the Australian sun ('These idiots who lie down to worship it!'). And though on the tram on the way home she was still shaken, there was a strange comfort in the feeling that she was beginning to understand how it worked; she was beginning to see an order to things. The people in the camp, the ones who'd just got here, they were right down at the bottom. Once you got out of there and lived somewhere with just you and your family, like they did now that they'd moved to their flat in Bondi, you stepped up a rung and felt sorry for the ones stuck back in the camp—not because it was that bad, just because it was rock bottom. Sitting on the tram leaving the Loop behind her that day, it came to her, how the rest of the order worked. No one had come to help as she was dragged off the jetty by a stranger, no one had told the woman to stop. The water wasn't filthy; it was clear and blue. There was another rung that she never knew about. Inside her something stirred—part shame, part relief. Even when she'd been back at the camp, she wasn't at the bottom after all.

Later, when her mother talked to her friend Sandra at the library about coming to Australia and life in the camp, Sandra shook her head from side to side then up and down, like she was making a cross, and said she couldn't imagine what it was like. 'It must have been so very hard for you.'

Maggie listened to her mother telling stories about the camp, about the sand and the dirt and the shacks made of tin. At first Maggie wanted to speak up because it sounded like a year of nothing good. She had her own bad feelings, but it wasn't about the dirt or the shacks. She wanted to tell Sandra about the friends she'd made and the toys in the dinner room, about Kristina, who brought them the floury apples, or Eva's mum, who fed her most days after school, but after a while of listening she heard Sandra say that it was all safely behind them, *safely behind them*, and it felt good to hear that. The woman on the jetty was still dragging herself up in Maggie's dreams. Maggie hadn't known what to do to stop it; she hadn't known how to make her go away. And here was Sandra making it sound so easy. 'You move on,' that was what she said. Maggie pondered that a long time, the appeal of a future unmuddied by the past, and then made the mistake that children so often make—in believing the word of an adult.

Now she placed the shell-covered box on the small rosewood table next to the desk in her studio. The table was cluttered with old family photographs and trinkets that had been given to her as a child by her father. This was a table of treasured keepsakes—the silver-framed images, the little statues of Hindu gods her father had bought in Colombo and hidden in the palm of his hand . . . The box, like the statues and the photos, was there on the table to hold a piece of history. It sat next to a photo of her mother and father, Frederick and Lili, and between them Levi, the grandfather she'd never met. The photograph was taken at a train station in Budapest before she was born, in a time and a place she had always considered to be the beginning of her story: not her arrival in Australia or her birth on a kitchen floor in Lisbon, but a farewell at a train station, because a story begins with its reason for being, her father had said, and for that he told her she should look always to this day, to this time and this place.

The day in La Perouse: after her father's death she'd wished she had told him what had happened, what the lady had said about the filthy water, how she had shouted and dragged her from the jetty. Though she'd told herself that in her heart she believed the woman was wrong, why was she so careful at home in her bath to scrub herself clean?

In the photograph her grandfather was wearing a dark grey suit and a hat. He was smiling, but not Frederick. Levi was not as tall as his son, but seemed to be the one holding them up. So many times she had stared into their eyes, wondering what was said between them and what was not.

She had stood in her dripping clothes looking up at her

father. 'And you think they will let you on the tram like that?' That had been his question, but his voice had been soft.

'I went back today, to La Perouse,' she said now, looking at the picture. 'And I met a woman who I think you would have liked.'

Ethan's secretary buzzed. 'Max will see you in five. His office.'

Max was the managing partner, and he was calling the meeting early. That wasn't like him, not his style; most times Max just strolled in your door around meeting time. As Ethan started to wonder what was up, his mobile phone rang. It was Laini.

'Hey, babe, how's things?'

'Okay.' Silence. 'Not okay. I don't know . . . What am I doing?'

He checked his watch. 'Come on, babe, we've done this . . . You should do some more work on the blog, think about the book thing.'

'I already posted today,' she said. 'What time will you be home?'

'Early. We've got Mum and Dad's, yeah?'

'I'll be packed and ready. I pretty much already am.'

'Okay, so maybe the gym or something, yeah? I really gotta go.'

'So go.'

'You okay?'

'Yep.'

'Love ya.'

'Yep.' And then a click.

He held the receiver in his hand for a moment before putting it down. It was something she'd only just started doing, hanging up before a goodbye, and like the other times, it left a build-up of phlegm at the back of this throat. It wasn't like Laini to take out her problems on him. If anything, when things weren't going great for her she would throw more at their relationship—buy him little gifts, spend hours on best-ever dishes, hit the lingerie stores . . . She was right: she had too much time to overthink, find fault, and that didn't suit her. Ethan was starting to wonder where the old Laini had gone; the old Laini would never hang up like that. She was on his side; she knew what he needed, what he liked. She wasn't one of those skin-and-bone women who messed with your head. She was the kind with the big heart, safe hands.

Meeting Laini had been a game-changer, no question. Over the years his school friends had scattered and had never really been replaced, and most of the friends he made at college were better left behind. They were the guys for whom money was a fix for everything: whatever the nature of the problem (a parent's smashed-up boat, a ten-thousand-word contracts assignment due in three days), a price could always be worked out. They were the guys who at high school had their birthday parties in Aspen and now spent summers heli-skiing in Canada. For some reason Ethan had made it into their sanctum, and sure, it was a blast—the time of their lives and all that—but the truth was too many uni days were spent trying to forget what he'd done the night before: what cocktail of drugs and drink, what prank gone too far, which girl, which girls ... trying to forget, and hoping that nothing would come back to bite. It culminated in a night before graduation, in Ben Parker's room, the lights off, a girl; she didn't say no, but she didn't say much at all. The biggest lesson Ethan learnt at university was how to separate himself from nights like that, how to purge himself of guilt, which left him at the end of five years as pretty much an empty vessel. And then this place, the firm. He had been dating Laini less than a month when he realised he needed her more than anything he'd ever needed before. Laini let him like himself again. She let him play grunge up loud and check out caryards on weekends (the one thing from college that had stuck: driving around in his mates' cars made it hard to go back from there).

Laini was life-giving. He was the centre of her world, end of story. Even having Finnegan didn't change things. Sure, she stopped with the hair colours and their world became a chemical-free zone, and she threw herself into parenthood, of course, they both did, but none of it ever meant he got neglected. He heard how it worked in other families—about those women who went all crazy-mama once they had a kid—but that wasn't the way Laini ticked. Big heart, safe hands ...

So what the fuck was going on with her now?

Maybe it had something to do with the argument a few weeks back. That was a possibility ... She was upset because the first she had heard about his work issues was at lunch with his parents the day of his dad's stroke. It dredged up an old wound.

'This isn't even about keeping secrets; that's not what's happening here. It's that you can't be bothered to tell me, like you don't see any point in it. And it isn't because what you've got to say isn't important, it's that *I'm* not worth it. I'm not worth telling.'

'What are you talking about? My father's just had a fucking stroke! What do you want from me?'

As she'd considered the last question, her gaze held, then dropped to the floor when either she couldn't think of an answer, or didn't like the one she found.

Okay, so he knew what she was talking about. Old wounds. What he was starting to understand was that if you let them fester too long you risked metamorphosis. You risked a whole new problem, a whole new life-sucking beast.

It went back to the day of the lunch at his parents' after Finn was born. Martin and Maggie took the baby and left them alone at the table for Ethan to explain the story of his early years.

'The short version?'

'Is there a long one?'

'Not really, not that I know.'

'So go on.'

'Well, Martin is my dad. But I didn't know that till I was four.'

So began the explanation to the mother of his son of how his own mother had raised him on her own for the first four years of his life. 'They met in New York and had an affair. She came home and found out she was pregnant.'

'She didn't tell him?'

'Yes, she did. I mean, I think she was considering an abortion . . . There may never have been a *me*. Unwanted pregnancy, shock horror—but then it was a happy ending. Here I am.'

'So what happened? What changed her mind?'

'I don't know. I never asked her. Time started to run out, and she decided to keep it.'

'Keep *you*.'

'Yep, keep *me*. She told Martin. He sent money. I think he even said he'd come back, but Maggie thought it'd be for the wrong reasons, you know, obligation not love, blah blah . . . He came and saw me when I was a baby. I don't remember it, of course, but anyway it didn't work out and he went away and came back again a couple of times. Then we went on a holiday together to Coffs Harbour. That's when I first remember him. I got blisters on my nose from sunburn and Mum blamed him. When we got back we started staying over in his apartment, then by my fifth birthday we all moved into a house in Balmain with a garden. I had a tree to climb and we got a VCR and I went to a school where I had to wear a stupid boater. And he was my dad. Only he was Marty, stayed Marty until I was ten, then I started calling him Dad.'

Ethan stopped, but Laini kept shaking her head, then nodding and making little noises like she was hearing it all over again in her mind. Later, when Martin and Maggie came back into the room with Finn, Ethan's effort to make light of it sank like a stone and took the whole table with it: 'Anyway, so I was just explaining the big hole in the family history.'

He could count on his hand the number of times since boyhood that he had seen his mother angry ('Careful,' Marty would say. 'That's a line you never want to cross'). Not one to shout, she released some kind of impulse, an ice-cold wave that pierced into the chest cavity of its target. He felt it even before she spoke.

'Please, Ethan, understand one thing.' She handed the baby to Martin and pressed a palm on the table as she turned to her son. 'There was no hole. In answer to your question, Laini, Ethan was a beautiful baby with a mop of blond hair and grey-blue eyes, but he had reflux, chronic reflux, and when he was six months he started holding his breath whenever his crying went on for more than a few seconds. His lips went blue and he fainted. The doctor said it wasn't serious, that it was relatively common, and that if I blew in his face he would come to, but still, every time it happened, every time he fainted, I thought to myself that this time he would not wake up.' With that she turned back to Ethan. 'Your father was not here, but there was no hole. I can tell you, those years with you, with just you and me, in many ways they were the most important years of my life.' At which point she leant down to kiss baby Finn on the forehead and left the room.

As Laini packed up their things in the kitchen, Martin finished off what little was left in his glass before filling it again. 'They tell you all is forgiven,' he said softly, staring into the wine. 'For God's sake, never believe them.'

It wasn't until they were pulling into their driveway that night that Laini asked the question. 'Why didn't you tell me?'

It was a quiet cul-de-sac in Cammeray, the hum of cicadas filling the mass of night sky. The house was what they could afford after they got married, the staged renovations funded with Ethan's annual bonuses. While Laini was generally prepared to 'make do', Ethan had a habit of spotting a tap or a window in someone else's house and thereafter hankering for the same or better in his own. So their front door was steel-framed glass and, later, the entrance ceiling lined in hoop pine, the kitchen bench a three-metre block of concrete poured in situ. If Laini objected to the expense, he'd hold her face in his hands and say: 'I like beautiful things.'

'I don't know,' he said to her that night, carrying Finn from the car. 'It doesn't matter anymore, I guess. Marty came back, he stayed. Like I said, happy ending.'

But it wasn't the right thing to say to her, the mother of a new baby. It made her frightened. In the middle of the night when she came back to bed after feeding Finn, he slid his arm around her and she turned to him with tears on her face.

'Don't tell me those things don't matter, Ethan. They matter. You didn't have a father, and then you did. I mean, can you remember how that felt?'

'Sure I can. It was like we were a real family. We even looked alike; people used to say it all the time—the spitting image, like father like son. I loved it when they said that.'

And so he had. There didn't seem to be any point in telling her the rest of it, that sometimes when Martin went to work, Maggie had to hold Ethan in her arms to calm him down. Yes, his father made them a family and in that way the ground had firmed, but then there were those days when the front door closed behind him or the car took off and the very same ground seemed to open up and swallow the little boy whole.

But Laini didn't prod. She didn't know there was a reason to. Instead, she asked him to tell her the story again about Nana Lil.

'Come on, hon . . .'

'Tell me.'

It was one of his first memories. They were baking in the kitchen, her cream puffs. He dropped a bag of flour on the floor and it exploded like a bomb. The memory was how it had scared him, that he went to cry, but that when Lili saw it, she'd started laughing, a big and spluttering laugh, and they laughed together making flour footprints on the floor.

'I loved it when you told me that,' Laini said. 'Everything matters, baby. Don't leave me out.'

She slid her arms around him and pulled in close for the first time since Finn was born.

'I won't, I won't . . .' he repeated again and again, in between every kiss. And though his body moved in complete accord, in his mind he reserved the right to disagree with the essence of what she had said. In the beginning, yes, it had seemed possible to be that man, the man who slowly releases the innermost pieces of himself—possible, and strangely rousing. But that was the beginning. That was before.

Max Green was the short and handsome managing partner who rode his bicycle to work and spent his four-week holiday every year snowboarding in Beaver Creek. Somehow he managed to keep the tan all year round as well as the bounce in his step. Everyone liked Max; everyone could talk to him, nothing too big or too small, et cetera. It wasn't that Ethan was trying to buck the trend, but the fact was Max wasn't really Ethan's kind of guy. For all his 'I'm here for you' touchy-feely crap, Ethan sensed a deeply held view on Max's part that he was better than the rest of them. Max Green ate amaranth for breakfast and quinoa for lunch; he lingered in front of mirrors to worship at his temple and repeated a secret personal mantra to himself every morning. Ethan knew the type, everyone did: Max Green thought his shit smelt like meatloaf.

'Here is Ethan!' Max said, waving him into his corner office. And when he sat down: 'How is Ethan?'

Uncertain as to how long he was going to persist in the third person and whether it required immediate discouragement,

Ethan limited his answer to 'Ethan is fine' rather than 'Ethan is fine, how is Max?'

'And the home front? The lovely Laini?'

'Never better.'

'And how is your dad recovering?'

'It's slow, but he's doing pretty well.'

'Terrible thing. Great man. That must be taking its toll—on you, I mean.'

Ethan nodded, shrugged. 'As these things do, sure.'

'And generally, there's a lot on your plate.'

'Of course, we're busy.'

Max nodded, thumbed his chin. 'That's my view of things.'

Even for Max, it was an odd turn of phrase.

'Are we here to talk about workload, Max?'

'Or whatever you want to talk about.'

'You called the meeting, Max. I thought you wanted to know how it was working out with Sally.' Sally was the new solicitor Ethan had hired to assist with the increasing workload.

'I do, I do. Tell me.'

'She is working on a third of my files. It's left me open to focus on new business, just like we planned.'

'I saw Tina McCarthy was on board, good to see. And I've only had good feedback on Sally.'

'She had four years under her belt. She knows what she's doing, no question about that. And she's putting in the hours.'

'Okay.' Max looked across the desk now, hands in prayer position. 'So what are we here to talk about? You want to get to it?'

Ethan shrugged. 'I guess . . . Though I'm getting the sense you're about to tell me the sky is falling down.'

And without correcting him: 'There has been another one

of those complaints, Ethan,' Max began. 'About your attitude, the way you interact with staff.'

'Is this about the IT guy again? I apologised for that.'

The IT guy was a Mr Fix-it on level nine who was paid a six-figure sum to deal with glitches in the computer network. A month ago, Ethan was working on an urgent deed of settlement when the document froze on his screen. He called down to IT; he called all three numbers on his sheet and no one picked up. Ethan had been in the office since five a.m. It was now ten, the deed was due by midday, and the client was a fucking arsehole. After trying the phones a third time, Ethan went down to level nine, and when he walked into the office there was Peter, sitting back in his chair with his legs on the desk and a game of Scrabble on his screen.

'I sent a written apology. And no one's even asked him why he wasn't picking up the phone, or why the fuck he didn't see the messages. I'll tell you why: he was working out how to get his J on the triple-letter score. Am I not entitled to get a little angry?'

'He said he felt threatened, Ethan, that you physically threatened him.'

'That is bullshit. It was an expression. Anyway, I apologised, what else can I do?'

'Nothing. We're sorting that out. If it were an isolated incident you wouldn't be here. But there is more.'

Ethan looked across the desk at little Max in his big chair and tried to lengthen the inhalation; instead he choked on his breath, coughed to clear it, and as he coughed, the muscle seized in his neck.

When Max continued, it was more a background noise: 'So the other complaint . . .'

Ethan raised his hand in the air, then reached over his shoulder to the back of his neck. With the other hand he cupped his chin.

'Ethan, what are you doing?'

He closed his eyes.

'Ethan?'

And he cranked it. Crackle, pop . . . pop, pop . . . less than perfect, but a substantial release.

When he opened his eyes, Max was looking away, shaking his head. 'You know how bad that is for your spine?'

Ethan shrugged. 'I find it helps.'

'You should see my chiropractor.'

'You were telling me about another complaint.'

'Yes, I was. Plural actually. If you get the word-processing girls to stay back, a simple thank you is all it takes. And last week in the lift . . . Brad Styles is a nice young bloke, Ethan—you could just say hello. Ethan?' The voice was getting louder. 'Ethan? Are you listening to this?'

He nodded. 'I am.'

'And?'

Sifting through the responses forming in his mind, he settled on the least offensive. 'I don't know whether to laugh or cry.'

'Well, I've got a third option that I want you to consider.' Max seemed to hesitate. That was unlike Max. 'I want you to see a counsellor.'

'Sorry?'

'Come on, Ethan, you know as well as I do this has been going on for a long time. A counsellor will help, a qualified psychologist. Someone who can get you through this—get you to the other side.'

Ethan made an effort to swallow but gave up midway. Rising from his seat, he walked to Max's window to assess the view of the park from a fresh perspective. The fountain was too distant to be a starting point. He would have to pick someone entering from either Elizabeth Street or the southern steps. The same game in reverse. 'Thanks for the suggestion, Max,' he said, turning to walk towards the door. 'I'll think about it.'

Max stood up, then reconsidered and sat down again. He felt taller from his chair. 'I called it a third option, Ethan. The other senior partners canvassed a fourth—but I didn't think you'd want to hear it.'

Ethan stopped at the door, waited.

'A fifteen per cent cut in your equity.'

Without turning around: 'You can't do that, not with what I'm bringing in.'

'Read the partnership agreement. Three strikes, remember? You know as well as I do the pile's been building. Counselling is a good option. I had to fight for it, Ethan. I'm on your side in this. And I should tell you, out of friendship, I'm the only one who is.'

The handle on the door was surprisingly cold to touch.

'Get back to me in a couple of days, okay? This is just about jumping through a couple of hoops. That is all it has to be.'

Back in his office, Bob was working the far end of the tank. Strands of Spirulina had started to sink to the bottom. Once they reached it they just formed part of the gunk. Maybe he was doing something wrong, Ethan mused; maybe he had to cut back on the food. At the window he picked a guy down in the park in an orange baseball cap but lost him as soon as he got past the second lamppost. His mind wasn't on it, or the guy took off his hat.

Maybe Bob was on a hunger strike.

He picked up the phone to call Laini. But what was he going to say? He'd never told her about what happened with IT. It wasn't going to make sense in a vacuum: I didn't say hello to a solicitor in the elevator so they want to take my money. Or worse: I am going to see a counsellor. Fuck it, this was some sick joke. There was only one thing to do: put it out of his head, business as usual. The McKenzie arbitration at three p.m. Dinner with the parents. He'd see the counsellor. No one needed to know. Then he'd spend a Sunday afternoon with his partnership agreement and a fine-tooth comb and work out how the hell he was going to get out of this place . . . That was when he'd talk to Laini, when he'd had a chance to package it.

The phone still in his hand, he pressed an internal line. 'Hi,' he said. 'Have you got a second? I need you in here.'

Sally Rigg brought in the file for tomorrow morning's mediation and took him through her summary and bottom line, sensible and within reach, exactly as he had asked.

'Done and dusted, I should think,' Ethan concluded after skimming the document a second time.

'Do you want me to be there?'

'Yes,' he said.

Today she was wearing a grey pencil skirt and white blouse with a high frilled collar. His eyes went all the way up and down. 'You playing dress-ups?'

Deadpan, Sally leant back in her chair and crossed her legs the other way. 'I love this shirt.'

'I hate it.'

'Then stop looking at it.'

He leant forwards so that he could see down again to the skirt that covered her knees.

'Where is the skin?'

She held up her hands, her palms facing him.

'What good are those?'

Her eyes widened, just a bit.

'Sorry, I like your hands. I worship your hands.'

She undid the top button of the blouse. A glimpse of clavicle.

'They want me to see a shrink.'

Her hands folded now on her lap, she tilted her head to one side and squinted, getting him from the right angle to consider the proposition. 'Anger management.' It was not a question.

He nodded.

'So see a shrink. I do.'

'What on earth for?'

'He's trying to work that out. I'll let you know when he does, if you like. Though that might take this to another level. I'm not sure you're ready for that.'

'No, you're right,' he said. 'Let's keep it straightforward.'

'Yes, let's keep it about Ethan.'

'God, you can be nasty.'

She shrugged.

'The door,' he said, starting to tap the side of the desk. 'Then I want you to come here . . . pull up the skirt, and bend down for me—' still tapping '—right here.'

'In your dreams. It isn't even closing time.'

He leant forwards again on his elbows. 'Alright then, let's do it your way. You close your eyes and I'll walk you through those dreams . . . but the skirt—be a good girl and show me some of that skin.'

On Maggie's second visit to Iris, children were climbing on the broken swing in the garden, and on a couch on the porch a young woman rolled cigarettes.

'Hello,' Maggie said, and without a smile the woman gave a single nod of her head.

'Is Iris here?' she asked.

The woman hesitated. 'Who should I say?'

'Maggie. I'm not . . . from the department.'

The woman licked the cigarette paper and rolled it down over her lip. 'Irrissss!' A trio of mynah birds burst out of the Christmas bush at the edge of the porch.

Iris appeared, smiled. 'Maggie, you back!'

'I thought I might try to catch Tyson,' she said, which only in small part was true.

'He ain't around, but never mind that. You sit down with Peggy here and I'll get us a cuppa. There.' She pointed to a chair next to the couch. 'I ain't leaving you standing this time.'

When Iris went inside, Peggy offered Maggie a rollie.

'Thanks, no,' Maggie said.

Peggy had come from Dubbo to stay with Aunty Iris and 'take a break from the place'. When Maggie said Iris had told her a bit about the troubles there, Peggy looked puzzled by the idea this white woman knew her business.

Iris returned with tea and Tim Tams and took her seat next to Peggy on the couch. The birds came back, more of them now, a couple jumping up the front steps.

'Bugger off!' Iris stamped her foot and the birds flew away. 'They'd waltz into the kitchen if I let 'em.'

Peggy took the bowl of biscuits. 'None for you, Aunty. I saw the pack next to your bed.'

'Oh hell, Peg, lay off.'

Peg didn't lay off because the biscuits would mess with the old woman's sugars and someone needed to tell her. 'Kids, come and get a cookie!' And to Maggie: 'Any left over and she'll sneak some for herself, you watch.'

'You just keep smoking them fags there, Peg, and you'll cark it 'fore I do,' Iris said as the children started running for the porch. 'Here, kids . . . Hey, ya greedy mugs—one apiece is plenty.'

Each face was a different shade of brown, each smudged with garden dirt. The younger ones flashed smiles of white teeth and darted off to play while the older girl lingered, eyed Maggie with uncertainty.

'Off you go now, love,' Iris said to her, and when she was gone, continued, 'Maggie here is wanting to catch up with Tyson. You remember, Peg, I told you about that judge who drove in here and had the accident? Well, Maggie is Mrs Judge. She wants to buy Tyson another dog.'

Peggy laughed. 'Last thing Tyson needs is a friggin' dog.'

'That's just what I said.'

'There's a list a mile long of things he needs before he gets a dog.' Though Iris raised a hand in protest, Peggy rode over the top of her. 'He could do with some new Nikes for a start, that'd get him off all our backs. Forget the dog, I say, and get him some decent bloody shoes.'

As Maggie started to say she'd be happy to get the boy shoes, Iris stamped her foot on the wooden porch. 'I am telling you now she's not buying him nothing! You listen to me, Maggie—' Iris held her gaze '—Tyson had plenty more to cry about that day. The dog getting hit was a blow, but it just broke the back of it. The truth of it is, those tears were a long time coming.'

Peggy reached a hand over to Iris's shoulder. She wasn't going to argue with that. 'He's a good boy, Tyson,' was all she said, and then to Maggie: 'Just so I get this straight in my head: you really came up here to say sorry and get him a dog? You came here to do that?'

Maggie nodded.

'Why don't you just leave some money?'

'Peggy! Shut the fuck up . . .'

'Yeah, right, okay,' Peggy said, putting her hands up in surrender and turning back to Maggie. 'You wanna say you're sorry? He should hear that. He doesn't hear it enough.'

The children in the garden had all climbed up to different branches of a tree. The littlest one called out that he was stuck.

'Lana, you help Billy down right now,' Peggy shrieked.

'No, Mum, you, you . . .' Billy shouted back. 'Lana gonna let me fall.'

And Lana: 'He won't let me touch him!'

Peggy jumped up from the couch, storming over like she was going to pull the tree out by the roots with her bare hands.

'How many are hers?' Maggie asked.

'None, technically,' Iris said. 'Peg's more an aunt, but two of them call her Mum.'

'She doesn't have her own?'

'Nah, but kin give her plenty.'

The little one had jumped onto her shoulders and Peggy was running around chasing the rest of them like a two-headed monster.

'You got kids?' Iris asked.

'A son.'

'Grandkids?'

'Yes, just one, a boy too.'

'I bet you spoil him like crazy.'

Maggie shrugged. 'And then, like they say, at the end of the day you hand them back.'

Iris shook her head, laughed. 'Not round here you don't . . .'

Before she finished the sentence a woman entered through the front gate. Her short red hair was a bolt of colour against her grey suit. 'Hello, Iris,' she said with a smile. 'You remember our appointment?'

'Well, I'm here,' came the reply, Iris's spine visibly arching in the woman's presence.

'And Tilly?'

'Asleep inside. You go on in and check yourself.'

With a sigh of frustration the woman looked at Maggie, clearly assuming that by virtue of the colour of their skin they were somehow on the same side. 'Iris, I'm just here to see how it's working out.'

Iris nodded, gave nothing more.

'And Tyson? Where'll I find him?'

'Visiting his mother.'

The woman's lips pursed a moment then her jaw moved

from side to side like she was loosening it for a fight. 'He stayed here last night?'

'Sure did.'

'He can't stay down there, Iris.'

'And I just told you he stayed here.'

'We had an appointment today.'

'I'm here, aren't I?'

'With Tyson too.'

'I can't keep up with who you want and when you want them.'

'He wasn't at school yesterday, Iris.'

'I know that. He got a sore belly. What you doing, anyway? He went every other day this week. You checking every day now?'

'No, I am not checking every day. I receive a report from the school. He is doing so well, Iris; he's a bright boy.'

'Don't I know it.'

'But he's been in Redfern again, with Kayla. You know as well as I do what that means.'

'He's looking after her, that's all he's doing,' Iris said, and hearing the words leave her mouth, raised a hand. 'I know, I know it ain't a job for a twelve-year-old boy.'

'You're right about that,' the woman said. 'Just get him back here, Iris. That's what you need to do.'

The words were spoken more as a plea than a directive, but still with the authority of an arbiter, implicit in them the threat that inaction would have consequences—all of which Iris bore in her ancient leaden eyes the way a packhorse bears extra weight: unflinching, more of the same, the same old load, the same road ahead.

'I'm going to have to sight Tilly,' the woman said—like the child was a set of accounts, Maggie thought, and this was some sort of audit.

'You know where the room is,' Iris told her. 'Don't wake

her up like you done last time. You don't need to shake 'em to tell if they're still breathing.'

'I know that, Iris. I just need to see if she's alright.'

With the last words there was a shift in Iris's face, a hardening. 'You ever seen a child under this roof that's not alright?'

'I'm only doing my job.'

'You go and do it then. Wake a sleeping child. Poke around my house. Then bugger off. Go on, Debbie, write that down . . .'

'Delvine,' the woman corrected her, and went inside.

'Whatever the fuck your name is,' Iris muttered when the woman was out of earshot. And then to Maggie: 'They're more worried about their paperwork than anything, that's what it's all about. You read about that boy that starved, the one they tied to the cot? That child was on their books, while they're ferreting around inside my place and waking up Tilly here . . . They had it all ticked off, of course, so no one was to blame.' Iris's voice trailed into a whisper as she stared at the ground, shaking her head. 'A child died in its own bed while they're ticking their boxes, but it's no one's damn fault.'

A minute later the woman returned. 'Sound asleep,' she said and smiled. And before she could finish the words came the sound of the child screaming out to her nan.

Iris pushed herself up off the couch.

'You done?' she asked.

Iris waited until the woman was out the gate before going to get Tilly from her cot.

'This is light on for Iris,' Peggy said to Maggie. 'Sometimes she's got three or four at one time. Lord knows how many she's had here over the years.' And in a low voice: 'She don't put up with questions like that about how the kids are looked after. She lost a baby daughter, Iris did, when they were still in the hospital. There ain't anyone that takes better care of these kids.' And as Iris returned with the little girl: 'How many you reckon, Iris? How many kids you had?'

'Tilly makes it eleven. Here you go, bubby . . .' Iris peeled a banana halfway down and broke it off. Tilly swiped it and mashed it into her mouth in three bites. Iris gave her the rest. 'That a girl . . . You still hungry? She got an appetite, this one.'

'What about you, Maggie?' Peggy asked. 'What do you do? For work, I mean.'

'I'm a painter.'

'What do you paint?' The question came from Iris.

'People mostly. Portraits.'

'And people buy them?' Peggy asked.

'Yes. Most of the time.'

'How much they buy them for?'

'Peg, shut up, would ya!'

'I'm just asking. I'm interested . . .'

'I don't mind,' Maggie said. 'It varies. Sometimes not so much . . .'

'What's the most you sold one for?'

Maggie hesitated. 'Well, one year I won a prize, so that one sold for quite a lot.'

'Like more than ten thousand?'

'A bit more.'

'So you're good then . . . Aunty won a prize for her boxes, you know that?'

'No, I did not!' Maggie answered. 'You said no one wants them anymore.'

'That's crap, Aunty. The galleries want 'em. Truth is she can't make 'em quick enough.' As she spoke, Peggy looked from Maggie to Iris and back again, and even before she asked the question, Maggie could see what was on her mind. 'You could paint Iris!'

'Oh, bloody hell, Peg, would ya shut up?! What the hell anyone want a painting of me for?'

'They make ones look exactly like you, just like a photo . . . Like that one they done of Uncle Gerry! You loved that, Aunty.'

Maggie interrupted to explain that hers were different, not so lifelike. 'I do brush painting, with ink. Mainly ink, and watercolours.'

Iris sat back in her chair. 'I bet they're real good.'

'Well, if she won a prize and she sells them for a bucketload, I bet they are too.' Peggy went quiet then, leant back on the couch with Iris as Maggie sipped the last of her cold tea.

'I'd love to paint you, Iris,' she said. 'If you'd like me to.' In a way, she realised, she had already started; ever since meeting her she had been sketching Iris's face in her mind.

Iris shook her head and cawed. The words came in a high pitch, as though she were mid-conversation. 'Here you gonna put some picture of my craggy old head up on a wall, people think I'm a loon . . .'

For a while the three women sat in silence, until finally Iris spoke. 'So how long'd I have to sit still for?'

Peggy clapped. And Tilly too.

As she was leaving Maggie had just one question for Iris, and it wasn't about painting her portrait.

'Your son,' she said. 'What is his name?'

Iris looked at her sideways.

'I want to ask Martin about him,' Maggie explained. 'To see if he can remember him.'

Iris looked at her a moment as though the offer contained a threat to her or to her son. Then she shook it off. 'I suppose there'd be no harm,' she said. 'My boy is Rodney. Rodney Keith Matthews.'

Cross-legged on the floor with his pictures: low tide, a small girl in striped swimmers squatting in the sand. The woman smiled but kept watch: old men don't take photos of little children, they shouldn't do. He knew, but yesterday he forgot.

Low tide was morning, snaked ripples in the sand. The girl poked them with a stick.

In the afternoon there were bluebottles, their tails wrapped up in seaweed.

The sting was there, all wrapped up.

Hiding.

Maggie had hung corkboards on the wall so he could pin up the pictures. Stick them with pins . . . Good thing Dave wasn't here to scribble horns or stab holes in the eyes. Once it was on the wall it was communal property, that was what Dave had said. Even the books on the shelves; Dave loved those books, then one day he put them in a box along with jars of Linda's beads and gave it all to the kids' art project in the Bronx. So Martin didn't make a thing of it when Dave drew on his photos. What were a few photos?

But it wasn't just the photos, was it? It wasn't just what hung on the walls—it was everything inside them. Dave wore other people's clothes and ate other people's food. He refused to pass judgment on art because that meant ascribing value and with value came yield and the need to control. 'It is what it is what it is what it is,' with a wave of the hand. And there was the rub: Linda so quick to laud or disparage. It played out in the end, the argument between them: Linda climbed her way to the Upper East Side as art buyer for Saks Fifth Avenue; Dave shared his life and his work. Dave shared a disease in a needle, shared the fate of so many others . . . They were both right, Dave and Linda, they always were. The art existed both inside and outside the mind; it was both real and unreal. It could all be abandoned, and yet nothing could.

There was an email from John, a courtesy. The judgment had been handed down in the people smuggler matter; because of the delay, it had been given priority. The court had allowed the fresh evidence but dismissed the appeal. The sentence would stand: prison and then deportation. That was that.

Martin turned away from the computer and looked back to the images in the prints on the floor: across at the pool, on the beach, inside this house and on the street. These were the days' events. Some were familiar, some were not. Sometimes the shutter had a mind all its own. He could not determine how long it would take for the light to pass, whether the image would be dim or exposed. Sometimes, more and more, the lag between scenes was unexplained, as though he was an actor in an avant-garde film, the narrative obscure, senseless: a man sitting on the floor with his prints, and now, next, the same man standing at a bus stop . . .

In a blink, there he was, in the glare of the street without glasses or a hat and next to him an empty bench and a yellow sign with a picture of a bus and a list of numbers and times.

Ask yourself, Martin. Ask yourself the questions.

How did you come to this bus stop?

When did you get here?

What are you doing here?

These were the questions he had to ask himself when a scene sneaked up on him unexplained, out of the blue, out of the terrible dark.

And then Maggie beside him: 'Stay here, Martin. Sit here and don't move, do you understand me? I will just be a minute.' She was cranky because he'd gone and bought tickets for Morocco ('We are not going to Morocco!'). She disappeared into the shop and he was sitting on a bench next to a woman with a lovely, scoop-necked T-shirt. The way she was sitting with her elbows on her knees, he could see her blue-striped bra and her bulging, honey-brown breasts: good enough to bury his face in, he thought, like big Barbara Lowry from chambers. When the bus came and the woman got on it, he followed her up the steps to the driver, but when Martin tried to give him money the driver wouldn't take it because they didn't sell tickets on buses anymore, only in the newsagents.

'Where are you going, mate?' the driver said and then, when Martin didn't answer, shook his head. 'Maybe you should just wait here at the bus stop. Are you with anyone?'

Martin smiled at his buxom young beauty, who stared back at him now with a strange defiance before she spoke: 'Bloody pervert.' To which Martin swung around suddenly and stumbled off the bus onto the footpath as Maggie came running. When she stopped, she looked up into the bus and saw the way the beauty was staring down at him.

'They won't sell you a ticket anymore,' he told her, but she wasn't listening because he was in trouble again.

Back in the car she was cross because the seats were hot, and even though he opened the window to let in the cool air, still her eyes glazed over like marbles and he knew he was making her tired and sad and he wished she wasn't, wished he didn't. He wished he hadn't pissed in the fireplace. 'I need someone to help me, Martin,' she said. 'Someone to be there for you when you don't remember, when you get confused.'

He didn't say anything to that. More and more he was uncertain when he was meant to speak and when he was meant to stay silent.

Sometimes, though, it was clear; it was clear that he was not there to observe or to be managed, but that he still had a part in it. It was as clear as the line between the cliffs and the sky.

He was fishing on the beach and Finnegan came running down.

'Grandie! Have you got a rod for me?'

He handed Finnegan his own rod to hold. It was heavier than the one the boy was used to, but it was all he had, and Finn was strong enough for it. He would make a good fisherman because he wasn't in a hurry and he listened to instructions. Martin watched him lift the line at the first tug, just gently, to trick the fish into thinking it was a prawn trying to wriggle away. The day Finnegan caught his first fish they were on the rocks and the boy slipped down into the water and scraped his leg but he didn't care; he strained his neck to see the graze—bubbles of blood, red raw skin—then nodded in recognition of the pain, determined to ignore it. They measured the fish and took a photograph, and before they threw it back

Finn christened it Kevin. Martin put the photo in a frame and gave it to Finnegan on his birthday.

'I don't mind fishing off the beach if that's what we have to do,' the boy said now.

Martin smiled. 'We'll catch some squid. And look at this . . .' When the wave washed back he pointed to the holes in the sand then dug his hand under it and pulled out a pipi. 'They make good eating. You ever try a pipi?'

Martin took the rod back and Finnegan found four more. No fish today, but five pipis. Next time they'd make it worthwhile and fill up his hat. For now Finnegan put them back in the sand.

'There is a girl on our street,' the boy said, 'who doesn't go to school. The teacher comes to her house. I wonder if I should do that.'

It was with the boy, that was when it was clearest: the time to be silent, the time to speak. Martin listened carefully to the words, tipping his head down to his shoulder to prise loose a snippet of something that had lodged itself there. 'There is a problem at your school.' Finnegan waited for him to say more. 'A problem with a particular boy, I recall. You don't tell your mum and dad because . . . ?'

'The school will call a meeting. And I'll cop it bad.'

'But you cop it already.'

The boy didn't argue with that. 'He weed on my bag. And in my water bottle.'

Martin reeled in the line. 'I've not heard that before.'

Finnegan shook his head. 'You just heard about the rock.'

'He threw a rock at you?'

'I told you that.'

'Yes, you did. Now we should tell someone else. The school will know what to do.'

'No, they won't. They'll call Mum and she'll have a fit . . . I'll tell her. I will. Just not now. I think we have to get back now, Grandie.'

Martin put the rod on the ground. He knelt down then and held his grandson by both arms. As clear as the day, as the line between the cliffs and the sky. 'This boy is a little criminal. And you are his victim. He has tricked you, Finnegan, into thinking you can't change that, but you can. You just have to be brave. Let's go and tell your parents. We can do it together.'

Finnegan listened, nodding his head. 'After dinner, Grandie,' he said. And then: 'I didn't drink it.'

'You didn't drink what?'

'Nothing . . .' For a moment the boy looked like he was expecting something to be said, then he smiled, the smile of someone older than his years, an incongruous mix of relief and regret. Just a flash and it was gone and they were packing away. 'Tell me about Nana again, about how she stepped on the painting of vomit,' the boy said. 'I like that bit best.'

As they walked up the hill, the sky tinged orange with the waning sun, a flock of cockatoos burst from the branches of the big conifer. The boy and his grandfather laughed at the flurry of movement and sound. Then the tree was empty again, and the boy and the birds were gone, nothing changeless: the surface of the water was still, but always beneath, Martin thought, the pull of the currents, and deep down in the sand, the edifice of a greater plan.

Maggie, it was Maggie, wasn't it, who led them back to the garden? It was Maggie who kept them under the night sky.

It was she who held the pencil in her hand.

'Let's go. Let's go back to the loft.'

'Not the loft,' she says. 'The garden . . .'

The rush of blood. Blood on weed, weed on speed.

'Let's see it in the dark.'

As though the dark is benign. As though the streets still rustling with their homeless ghosts have formed a single lane leading to a softer earth . . . They walk with clasped hands, past the lamppost where she had stopped to scribble in her notebook, the sidewalk now empty of art and books, the corner where the water had burst from the hydrant now dry underfoot, past the pigeon lady's window and across the Bowery, the old man still sitting in his beanbag, and outside the Chinese grocery store, different girls walking the same walk.

Between them is a mind tunnel, all the way nothing said. Then he stops, shoulders the door open, and they step inside.

When Maggie knocked, Iris came to the door.

'I was working on a box,' she said, then looking down to the satchel in Maggie's hand: 'You really here to do the painting?'

The house was quiet. Peggy and the children had gone back to Dubbo, so today it was just Iris and Tilly, and Tilly was sleeping.

Maggie nodded. 'Why don't we go back up? You can keep working and I can make a start.'

Upstairs, Iris's room was clean and spare. The bed was made with just a blue sheet and a single pillow and on the chest of drawers sat an empty vase. With its sloped roof and small windows, the room had the feeling of an attic.

Along the wall beneath the windows were the tubs of shells. The half-finished box was the shape of a leaf. 'There's a gallery in Canberra that's gonna take 'em,' Iris said. 'Reckon they want four by the end of the month. First they asked for bridges, but I told 'em I'm done with bridges. I am sticking with the leaves and bush flowers.'

She sat down cross-legged in the middle of the floor, wearing the same clothes she had worn on Maggie's first visit, the orange Hawaiian shirt with the long floral skirt, and again her brown feet were bare.

'Where you wanna sit, Maggie?'

Maggie got down on the floor against the wall and pulled out her sketchpad and pencil. 'This'll do fine.'

Iris did not make a move to start on her box, but sat watching Maggie, waiting. 'You want me to look at you or something?'

Shoulders hunched and head tilted down, the half-smile was that of a supplicant. Her hooded eyes gazed back with uncertainty, waiting to be guided. Maggie felt the weight of that trust, the privilege, and with it a deep and wrenching affection for this woman she had only recently come to know. Every day over the last week it had been in her thoughts, coming back here to paint Iris—a light at the end of a darkening haze.

'Why don't you just keep going with the box,' Maggie said, 'and I'll do a few sketches.'

The two women went to their work without speaking, the only sounds the call of the mynah birds clinging to the windblown branches outside the window and, inside the room, the graphite scribbles of Maggie's pencil. Iris painted glue on shells of different shades and shapes, pressing them lightly onto the surface of the box before letting go and moving on to the next. Her hands moved so quickly they seemed careless; it was only after Iris has almost finished the lid that the pattern emerged and Maggie could see the rhyme in it, the flow of movement and the interplay of shells with shadow and light.

As she worked, Maggie studied the woman's face, the wiry white of hair and the burnished brown skin of her forehead, the maze of lines etched at the corners of her upturned lips, the furrow between her eyes as deep as a crevice in a rock, and in the corner of her left eye socket a tiny fold of skin. Within a frame of pale, sinuous lines, Maggie sketched in matted scribbles as though the face were a landscape, rugged and untouched—untinted, unplucked; there was barely the trace of an eyelash but like an old stump the hair sprouting from the mole on her cheek remained. Maggie doubted the pores had ever been clogged with makeup or the wrinkles patted with cleansers and creams. Recalling the cloud of invisibility that had descended with the slight sagging of the skin on her neck, Maggie doubted whether the same sagging, the same irreversible process, had at any time caused Iris a moment's concern.

'Do people always like it?' Iris asked. 'How you paint 'em?'

'Mostly. I have to paint them as I see them. Sometimes they say: "I don't want anything disturbing," or, "I want to be able to hang it in the bedroom so it's got to be something that makes me happy when I wake up." I get in trouble with the motifs.' Maggie explained the motifs, how in the process of painting the object would come to her. 'The more people pay the more they think they can put an order in. There was a woman once, and in the corner of the painting there was a little Kachina, a doll. She didn't like it because she thought it looked as though the doll was laughing at her. She wanted me to overpaint it with a butterfly. She even told me the colours she wanted in the wings.'

Iris laughed. 'Like the bloke in Canberra telling me what shape to make my boxes. They say you create what you see when you close your eyes; well, I don't see the fucking Opera House, I can tell you that.'

The side of her box complete, Iris stopped, looked at Maggie with her watery eyes and that humblest of smiles.

'You ask him about Rodney?' she said. 'Did he remember him?'

Maggie put her pencil down to answer. 'Yes, I asked him, and he remembered. He said he'd thought Rodney wasn't a bad fellow but that he'd got himself mixed up with the wrong people.'

Maggie recalled the conversation she'd had with Martin. He had hesitated when she'd asked him the question, and answered her still looking down at the photo in his hands as though it contained the requisite information. They were his words, nothing more—not a bad fellow, just mixed up with the wrong people.

'And this woman Iris that you see, she is his mother?' Martin asked.

'Yes,' Maggie said. 'I wondered at first if that wasn't the reason you'd gone up there that day.'

When he looked at her then his eyes dimmed with a worn and bleary sadness—the sadness, Maggie thought, of having no answer and no way to find it. 'I don't know,' he said.

'I wondered if you hadn't seen him again, this man. Perhaps he'd come before you in court; he is in prison again and I thought . . .'

But Martin shook his head. 'No, that isn't it, Maggie. I've not seen him. If he'd come into court I would have had to recuse myself, and I'd remember it. That isn't right.'

'No, very well, and it doesn't matter anymore. You are here, and look at this, these photos—these are wonderful.'

After hearing what Maggie had said about her son, the sadness now in the eyes of Iris as she went about gluing shells to the side of the box was of a different kind: though old, it was not blunt with age but jagged and barbed like a broken bottle. She mouthed a word, but made no sound. Only minutes later did she nod and speak.

'He's right, your judge,' she said. 'About Rod being mixed up with the wrong people. But in his case it was just one, just her. He can shake off his idiot mates alright, but not Kayla. I remember back then, when he went inside that first time, I thought he'd come to his senses. Before that, he'd done a bit of thieving; that was the sum of it. Then he met her, Kayla, and she was greedy for the drugs, and soon enough he was hooked like she was, and they were as bad as each other. The only difference between them is that he wants to be free of it, in his heart I know he does. But not her, not Kayla. They had Tyson when they were just kids themselves, and she never stopped using, not for a second. To get that filthy shit she'd sell her soul if she could. I don't like to say that, she's kin, but it's hard to lose your boy like I done. It's hard when you can't even bring yourself to imagine the kind of life he's leading.' She stopped and picked up the box with both hands. 'I do that, though,' she said, her voice a low monotone. 'I sit here making my boxes, thinking what he's doing right now, in there, inside—with every shell, every day, like I'm sharing it.'

And Maggie could see in the old woman's eyes that for the short time she spoke of her son she had indeed left the safety of the room—brought back only by the sound of footsteps downstairs, and soon after the sound of a cupboard slamming.

'Just the boys coming for a feed,' she said, then sensing Maggie's anticipation: 'Not Tyson, love. He never goes straight to the kitchen. He always comes to see me first.'

A few minutes later, voices called up the stairs, 'Thanks, Nan,' and the house was quiet again.

'Do you get to see Rodney?' Maggie asked.

'I sure do.' As though anything could keep her from him. 'Every Sunday I take Tyson. He's at Windsor now so we can do it. When he was in Lithgow we only made it once a fortnight. They move 'em around so much, it's a bugger, I'll tell ya.'

With that Iris put the box down and stretched her arms out to the sides like she was waking to the day. It was enough sitting, enough talk. She pushed herself up off the floor before turning to ask the question: 'We done?'

And so they were.

~

When Maggie came back for the second sitting she brought a larger satchel of tools. Iris watched as she laid out a square mat and pulled from the bag an ink stick and a small stone bowl the colour of charcoal and, last, a case of brushes—the largest of which she dipped into a cup of water and blotted onto the centre of the bowl. With the ink stick she stirred the liquid for a number of minutes, Iris watching all the while, eyes alight with the spark of new discovery.

'What's it made of?' she asked.

'Soot and glue,' Maggie said. 'They make a dough then dry it and use it to make ink.'

'You don't just buy it?'

'You can. But this is better. Can you smell it?'

The smell was pine and sap, fresh peat. And after she had stirred it, the shining black liquid was the texture of melted butter.

Iris smiled. 'Aw, Maggie, that's lovely, that is, that's like the ochre . . . How'd you learn that?'

Maggie told her the story of Mrs Bess, the pigeon lady, and how they had continued writing letters and sending drawings to each other long after Maggie had come home.

Iris reached over and picked up the ink stick to smell it and feel its weight, dipped her finger into the bowl and ran it over a scrap of paper on the floor. She smiled and, when Maggie began painting, she sat back and looked away, down at her box. 'I don't want to see it until it's finished.'

Iris paid no mind to being watched, working again now as though she were alone, until she was done for the day and she pushed the box away, leaning back against the wall. 'Your people, Maggie,' she said, 'they ain't from here?'

'No, my parents were from Hungary. We came here when I was a little girl.'

'How often you go back to see your mob?'

'I've been twice.'

Iris cocked her head. 'Just the two times?'

'My parents both died here. They left Hungary before the war and I was born in Lisbon. I didn't remember my aunt or cousins. I went to Hungary when I was younger to find where my parents had lived, and again after my mother died. I met a cousin then who lived in London.' She stopped now too and looked at Iris. 'I envy you your family.'

It was an unlikely envy—both women thought it—but there it was, a fact.

'You just wanted the one, your boy?' Iris asked.

They had tried for more, Maggie said. 'But there was always a reason not to try harder.'

The old woman shrugged. 'You done what you did.' Then she leant in closer. 'I was thinking about you this morning, Maggie,' she began. 'I was thinking of that story you told about you diving off the jetty, and it reminded me of something I hadn't thought about since I was a kid on the mission here . . . There was this one girl: same as you did, her parents had come after the war and she was living in a migrant camp, but this one was here in La Perouse, over the hill at Frogs Hollow. It was full up with migrants like you that came after the war.

There was just one school for all of us, black and white—the kids from the mission and the migrant camps. So this little girl—I've been trying, but for the life of me I can't remember her name—this little girl made friends with me cousin Nell. She had skin so white looked like it had been painted on, and big blue eyes, and there she was runnin' round with grubby Nell and the rest of the little ones. There was a big fence around the mission; the game was to stay on it all the way around. It was so damn narrow they may as well have been balancing on a wire. I remember seeing her do it, this little one; she fell off and climbed right back on with her bleeding knee like nothing happened. But what I remember best—what I remembered this morning—is what she done the day the truck came for little Willy Madden. We saw it coming, and we all ran off and hid like we did every time we heard that truck, and the little girl, you know what she did? She came running too and hid among the trees along with the rest of us—like they'd take a white one just as well as a black. Like there wasn't no difference. Like you, jumping in that water. I'll say it again, Maggie: there's lines between us. I can feel 'em as sure as I can see you sitting here.'

It was the first of many stories that Iris would tell Maggie about her childhood on the mission, stories that flowed one into the next, about waiting in the dunes at dawn to watch for fish and digging pipis out of the sand and cooking them on fires on the beach, about the spirits in the trees that wailed in the wind, and about the grog-fuelled manager who barged into their shack at nighttime to line the kids up for inspection. Iris told stories and finished another side of a box as Maggie painted her picture.

They were almost done for the morning when the footsteps came charging up the stairs, and a boy in a football jersey appeared panting at the door—not the boy from the paper, not Tyson.

'Tom's done a fuckin' runner,' he cursed. 'You seen him, Nan?'

She hadn't, Iris said, not since last Tuesday when he slept over then buggered off in the morning with her spare change and her best coat. And, as quickly as he had arrived, the boy was gone. Not long after there was a man's voice calling from downstairs. Maggie followed Iris down to see two police officers standing in the open doorway.

'We just want to have a look at the room where he stayed, Iris,' one of them was saying. 'If you don't let us we'll go get us a warrant and come back.'

'You just go ahead and do that,' Iris hissed, closing the door and shuffling back down the hall. And when she reached the kitchen, all in a day: 'Cuppa, Maggie?'

Tom was Tyson's brother; different father, though, which made him no blood tie to Iris as far as Maggie could work out. But by then she knew better than to question ties. In the five weeks Maggie had known her, Iris had been to as many bedsides or funerals, two in Dubbo, back and forth by bus and train. Every Saturday she got herself to at least one of her grandsons' footy games and screamed loud enough at the ref last month to get a caution from the club. Sunday was the trip to Windsor, and through the week if she wasn't hauling one out of a pub at closing time she was enrolling them back in school or taking them up to the dentist. When there was no one at the house to watch Tilly, she took her along, pushed her in her stroller, pulled it in and out of buses. Maggie stopped asking her how she did it; there wasn't a logistical problem the woman couldn't steamroll.

She never made a note, not of a church service or a game venue or a bus route; she kept it all in her head. It wasn't just that her door was never shut or that she stocked her cupboards not knowing who she'd be feeding. It wasn't just that she was anchor and safety net to her urban clan. Iris was more than that. She was its memory.

'You remember all this, all these appointments you have to keep?' Maggie once asked.

Iris smiled, tapped the side of her head. 'If it's important, I remember it.'

~

The third and final sitting. It was a still, sunny day so they sat on the porch.

To the blotted ink and fine lines on the page, today Maggie added brushstrokes in muted tones of blue and brown.

'You almost done?' Iris asked.

'There's some more I need to do at home, but I don't need you to sit anymore. I have enough sketches.'

Iris came forward in her chair. 'What haven't you done yet?'

'The eyes. I leave them until last.'

And further forward still. 'Why do you do that?'

'Because once I finish the eyes,' Maggie said, 'the picture comes to life and you fly away.'

Iris smiled, nodded. 'I think I'm gonna like your picture.'

As Maggie put her brushes away, Iris leant across to touch her hand.

'You just missed him the last time you were here,' she said with a smile in her eyes. 'Tyson, I mean. I told him about you, and about your painting. You'll get to meet him now, Maggie. He's coming back to stay.'

Maggie gasped. 'Iris, that is wonderful.'

'Ain't it.' A broad smile spread across the width of her face. 'So I asked why he hadn't been visiting his nan much these days—you'll like this. You know what he said to me?' She paused, waited. Maggie shook her head. 'He said it was because the dog wasn't here anymore; he didn't have to worry about looking after that bloody dog. Would you believe that? So I've been thinking, and I reckon your idea about getting him another dog isn't so bad—not from you, love, from me. I'm gonna go to the pound, get one ready for him when he comes back.'

The talk had moved to when Tyson and Kayla were coming and why—'the tip she's been living in is being bulldozed'—when Iris pointed to a house across the street and down the block. 'She's going to go back to her place, that one there, but Tyson can stay here with me.'

The house she pointed at was the one Maggie had parked in front of the first day she came to the street, the one with the blue couch in the garden. Of all the houses it was the most neglected; perhaps in her mind she had made that observation, but it was only now that she really looked at it for the first time.

'That's Kayla's house?'

She felt a trickling unease before she had any sense of its cause.

Iris mistook the way she stared, embarrassed at the state of the place. 'She ain't lived there a while. I'm gonna get it cleaned up before they get back.'

The front gate lay broken at the foot of a tree and a gutter hung loose from the roof; from the garden a branch stretched to the door as though poised to knock on it.

'I didn't know she lived here,' Maggie said.

'Ever since they were together, she and Rodney. God knows how she's kept it all these years.' But when she saw the way

Maggie still stared down the street, her own eyes narrowed. 'What you looking at anyway, Maggie? What is it, love?'

Maggie turned away from the house to regard Iris, every line in the old woman's face now so familiar. 'Nothing,' Maggie said, giving voice to the word, but only voice.

After Iris went inside, Maggie walked down the street to her car, and then crossed over to the house where Kayla had lived. Standing on the footpath, she could see through the front window a curtain tied in a knot. The front door was painted yellow, and on the door a broken pane of glass had been nailed over with timber boards. When she stepped into the garden she saw that the lowest board had been prised loose, and wondered whether, if she walked up the steps and stood at the yellow door, she would be able to see inside. If she were to look through the gap, what would she see?

Driving home she took a wrong turn. An unknown street led her to roadworks, a standstill.

What would she see?

While her conscious mind had sidelined the question, its back rooms permitted it entry now with open arms, and there, sitting in an unmoving car and cursing the wrong turn, it began to fester and to agitate memories of a certain and like kind. When finally the traffic began its slow creep, she failed to indicate at her first turn and swore back at a cyclist who spat at her tyre, so that by the time she pulled up in the drive beneath the blackened clouds, the business was done: everything was out of place, not just the streets behind her, but the garbage bins and the front doormat and the tin for the teabags, and her husband, pottering on hands and knees with his Blu-Tack and his photographs, was more than a day further away.

Your judge was my son's first decent lawyer. That was what Iris had said on that first visit.

So he was here to see you?

No, she had said. *He hit the dog, that's all, so this was the place he stopped.*

Already the question had taken root: was it there that he had stopped, or was it at a different house, the one across the street and a block away?

~

In the studio she sat at her desk and stared at the painting like it was a blank page. When she looked out the cobwebbed window she saw Martin there now, kneeling down at the edge of the garden bed. She watched him as he dug holes in the dirt and filled the holes with snow pea seedlings, framed by the window as though she had painted the image herself.

When he was finished with the seedlings, he went inside, and Maggie got up from her desk to follow him. She found him back in his study, sitting on the floor with a single photograph in front of him. Still looking at the photograph, he pulled a cigarette from his pocket and lit it, and with the exhalation of smoke he closed his eyes, just as he used to . . . He had got the packet yesterday while she was buying the seedlings, and looked only mildly surprised when she told him it was the first packet of cigarettes he had bought in twenty years.

Maggie knelt down and picked up the photograph from the floor. On the border was the faded date: August 1979. It was a picture of a naked woman sitting on the edge of a bath in the middle of a kitchen. She was bent forward from the waist, her head dropping between her open legs. It was Linda in the loft. The light came in from the window and fell on the small of her back.

Martin's eyes followed the photograph in Maggie's hand. 'She was a beauty, wasn't she?' he said. 'I think it's the best one I've ever taken. Do you think?'

It was just months ago, Maggie thought, remembering that Sunday lunch, that she had allowed herself to believe the passage of time provided protection—that day by day there was a growing distance from whatever came before. Now, somehow, the reverse held true. With each day, they seemed to be moving backwards, she and Martin, in a creeping tide of time and space, ever closer to a past that was not the stuff of nostalgia or reminiscence but of potholes that had been sidestepped and never repaired.

And as it turned out, the road was not straight: at the end it formed a loop, forcing us all to turn back.

Ethan checked Laini was asleep before he sat down in the dark at his computer and opened her blog.

Over these last weeks it had become his habit, to scroll through the About Me section and the photos of Laini and the labradoodle, and to continue past the day's post to the Comments link.

Since the 'meditate or masturbate' conundrum had opened the floodgates, her readers' comments and Laini's responses to them had taken on the tone of a confessional. Here it was again, in response to yesterday's post, a frenzied flourish of virtual unburdening:

'I couldn't tell my therapist this but . . .'

'I am married to a woman who doesn't make me feel anything.'

'I am a serial home wrecker.' (That one from VeryYummy Mummy.)

And most startlingly of all: 'I would rather put my face in the fire than give my husband a head job.'

Laini did not suffer fools; she was quick to tell readers who stepped across the line to crawl back into the hole from whence they came. But the rest of her replies were all shades of the same wondrous colour: I am no one's moral compass. Nothing is unsayable. This is your space.

It reminded him of the old, life-giving Laini, and it reminded him (not without a tinge of resentment towards this sea of grasping strangers) what it felt like to share in her bounty. Then, just yesterday, he started to get a taste of it again. She was worried about him, his moods. (He'd slammed a door; the glass had cracked.) His mother had noticed it too. They had talked. Even when he was a boy, Maggie had said, there were problems when Martin came back from New York; it all escalated this one time when she and Martin were having some troubles and Martin had moved out.

'She said it sent you into a rage, baby. And it got me thinking about what's happening to Martin now, and I wonder if maybe that's what the anger is about.'

To this, Ethan's was a phased reaction. First, reflexively, he flinched. Laini wanted to trawl through all that paternal-rejection stuff and it wasn't easy to shut down. But with that, the shift in her focus, he was lifted (albeit briefly) by a sense of relief: the blog had sucked up the self-loathing and given her some headspace, which meant there was more Laini energy coming his way: briefly, because that in itself led to a reality check. It had worked okay in the early days, all her questions—'I want to know you. I want to know *all* of you.' He could answer and deflect; it was easy enough, but harder now, he realised, as over the years he'd accumulated more and more pieces he wasn't able to share.

And finally, maybe a little out of left field—as his thoughts meandered around the blog and looped back to Laini's digging—there formed in his mind a Venn diagram of marital knowledge, at its centre that portion which ought to be shared. What the blog offered in this picture was a fresh line of communication, a new and improved method of discovery. Forget for a minute what Laini wanted to know . . . After weeks of reading her answers and replies, Ethan had begun to form a question of his own, and though initially he had no intention of ever asking it, as time wore on, as he fell into the habit of sitting glued to a screen at night indulging in the mind-fuck that was his wife and then leaving for the office in the morning wondering what blouse Sally would be wearing when he arrived, the necessary adjunct was whether or not what he was doing would mean the end of his marriage. The fact that the question remained unanswered was beginning to threaten his ability to look his wife in the eye and hence function as any kind of husband, which led Ethan now to the view that one way or another, he needed to know.

What the blog offered was the gift of anonymity. And so it was that tonight, in the dark of his study, he clicked on what was for him a new box: Add Comment. (Mentally relabelled: Test the Waters.)

As FaithlessJohn, he wrote: 'I love my wife and I love having sex with other women. One feeds the other. Honestly, I am a better husband for it. Thoughts?'

Ethan reread what he had written three times, nodded to himself, and pressed Post.

It was the sight of the bats in the distance that had confused him.

Twilight, he had thought. Dinner. 'What time will dinner be?'

She looked frightened by the question and told him it was morning, and they were above him then, cockatoos not bats; he could see the yellow tails. It was morning, of course. The sun was rising and not falling. And with that knowledge, out of his shallowing breath, a cloud of dread descended again—not because of the fact that he was wrong, but the fact of a beginning.

Scrambling or still, always now the same answer, the same taunt: it had begun, and every day it began again.

Last night over dinner, barely a word: a man and a woman in a room, the connection between them one of circumstance. He thought to ask her what had made her go so quiet, but better to keep it vague.

'I am sorry,' he said.

And that was all.

Maggie waited until Martin went to bed to return to her studio. It was after midnight.

She opened the bottom drawer of her filing cabinet, and at the back of the drawer, from an unlabelled file, she pulled out an envelope.

She switched on her lamp and turned off the main light, then sat at her desk with the envelope in hand before putting it down in front of her. There it was, the faded handwriting: Martin's name and his work address. When she picked it up to hold it again, she could feel the power drain from her hands as it had done all those years ago when she had first found it tucked between the covers of a book. The book, she remembered still, was called the *The Book of Torts*.

It was 1982.

Martin had started in new chambers when she saw the book lying next to the box on the floor. The move had been hurried as he was trying to get set up before leaving on a trip to New York. Dave was in rapid decline. At first they were told it was pneumonia, then cancer, some form of leukaemia.

It was a virus that was attacking his immune system. They couldn't find a treatment. This was to be Martin's second trip that year to see him. When she saw that the letter was from Linda she assumed it would have the latest news on his condition, or that is what she told herself as she opened it, as she pulled the letter from the envelope.

'Our man is a hero unto the last . . .' it read. 'They want to bulldoze the garden on Eldridge Street and replace it with housing blocks, but he has managed to get ten thousand signatures on a petition so they've called a halt . . . Pyrrhic, maybe—saved to be bulldozed another day—but safe to say he will not be alive to see it happen. That is my news, darling Marty. Dave is going to die. And before he does he wants to give us his blessing for everything we have done and everything we are going to do—for our fucked-up love, as he calls it. Is it so fucked up? (A little mucked up, sure, but *fucked* up?)'

There was no past tense.

It had been four years since Martin had returned to live with them in Sydney. Ethan was now eight, almost nine.

What Maggie remembered now, sitting at her desk, was the feeling as she turned the letter over in her hand that deep down she had seen it all along, the same feeling she had today standing outside the house with the yellow door. Linda was not the end of it; there had been another side all along. Martin hadn't driven into Iris's street because he was lost, but because he had been there before.

I tried to end it, he had said when he came through the door and she showed him the letter; he had tried on his last visit.

Maggie put up her hand to stop him. 'But before that . . . every time you went back.' It was a statement, not requiring confirmation.

And then, from Martin: 'If it helps, even when we were living there together, I was never enough for her. There were always other men. We spent more time hating each other than anything else.'

If it helps . . .

Maggie did not understand then, nor did she now, how the information could in fact have helped. Did he expect it to arouse sympathy? Was the idea that he had been punished enough? Entrenched in his suggestion was a self-regard to which she had never found a way to respond.

She told him to leave and he stayed in a flat in Randwick for a month, and every night when she closed her eyes, it sucked the breath out of her: Linda in her white catsuit, her golden flesh and her acid tongue, and whatever it meant, however it played out: their *fucked-up love*—first the reunions in New York, and afterwards, with the distance between them, all the ways Linda had lived in his mind. She didn't need him to tell her that. More than anyone Maggie knew what distance did.

There was just the light from the desk lamp, the corners of the studio in darkness. On the desk was the painting of Iris, the eyes still blank. How to fill them, the eyes of the woman who as a girl had run from trucks for fear of being taken from her family, the mother who had cared for eleven children but was separated from her own.

And behind the light of the lamp, in between a statue of Ganesh and the framed ink drawing by Mrs Bess—a rocky outcrop, the Lost Cat—was the photograph of Lili and Frederick, and her grandfather Levi.

'He looks like you,' she had said to Martin as he sat with his son for the first time.

'He doesn't have my eyes.'

'No, you're right. He doesn't. They are my father's eyes.'

Maggie did not look their way, to the faces in the photo, but in the recesses of her mind they lingered—the fact that they had lived, the lives that they had led. Their eyes stared out, speaking of the horrors and miracles to come. That day it was a farewell they each knew in their hearts to be final. Three years later it was another: Frederick and Lili and their little daughter Maggie waving farewell to the families of strangers on board the *Fairsea*, bound for Sydney. They embraced one last time as they were ushered down onto separate decks, one for the men, one for women and children—big empty holds with triple-tiered bunks, each with a mattress and a blanket and a leaflet on the pillow. On the cover of the leaflet was a map of Australia, and in letters curved around its northern coastline, the promise: 'The Land of Tomorrow'. The *Fairsea* travelled towards it, across the Mediterranean to Egypt, through the Suez Canal to Yemen and out into the Red Sea, to Colombo and across the Indian ocean to Fremantle and to Sydney, and every evening of the month-long journey—dubbed their 'pleasure cruise' by Frederick—they would meet at the children's dining table on the mess deck, taking it in turns to trick their ashen-faced daughter into taking a mouthful, and to think of all the reasons under the sky to be grateful: the curls in Maggie's hair from the saltwater showers; the power of disinfectant to mask the stench of sickness in the corridors; the communal space on the top deck that allowed ample room for children's games and a good walk (contrary to stories they had heard of ships so crowded the passengers could only stand and sway like trees). And the real jewels: the lifting of the wondrous fog that had settled around the Lighthouse of Port

Said, and the whale and her calf breaching off the Sri Lankan coast before slipping in unison beneath the water's surface.

Unspoken, but at the very top of Frederick and Lili's list, was that in their home town of Budapest in 1939 they had not waited to see what was to come. 'If I was a younger man,' Levi had said to his son on reading news of the Second Jewish Laws, 'I would not wait.' The following night the young couple agreed it was a good time to visit a cousin studying in Bern, and packed their suitcases. They had not waited, not for news of more laws. They had not waited to see friends sent into the copper mines or forced to carry guns and battle the Russian winter. They had not waited to be given a number and put on a train, or for the country's leader to take a pistol to his head and declare Hungary a nation of trash. They had not waited for Eichmann. They closed the door to their apartment with just three small bags between them. At the station Frederick held tight to his father and said they would be together again at the end of the summer. Two days later they had arrived in Switzerland, and when the war was at an end they packed their bags again and caught a train to Lisbon. It was there, after another summer had passed, on the floor of their kitchen next to the refrigerator, that Maggie Varga was born.

Flying spoons into their daughter's barely open mouth and looking out to a horizon that beckoned to be reached, Frederick and Lili were grateful to be together for an hour every day, headed to a country at the other end of the world that had asked for people to come. They looked ahead, and tried not to glance behind them to their flat in Lisbon, to a family displaced over a continent, to the corpse of a father piled in a mass grave and all the days that led to his extinction. They looked ahead, and they were grateful—not to God, not anymore—but to the dead man who had told them not to wait.

It was cold when Maggie put the letter back into the envelope and threw it at the bin. When it lifted on a pocket of air and fell onto the floor she picked it up, scrunched it up and threw it again, this time with an accurate aim.

Because what remained was a simple truth. All those years ago she had let Martin take just a single suitcase, and after the month was out she had let him return, so they could begin again as they were. That was the best way, so she had thought . . . If he had buried it, she had been the one to pack the earth.

After that there had been late nights, some unexplained, and she had seen how the women flirted and how he let them. He was a handsome man; it happened. And there was the time at the party when Annie was upset and Maggie thought she must have seen something. When she confronted him, Martin laughed it off and made a joke about a drunk woman landing in his lap. Annie said she'd been drunk herself and couldn't remember it.

That was the bad stretch, his last few years at the bar. He didn't want to be there anymore; he was drinking too much and coming home in dark moods—rank, like something was rotting inside him. He wouldn't talk about it, and to stay afloat she cut herself off as best she could. She shuddered now at the memory of it. The blessing was that almost as quickly as it descended, the darkness lifted. He was appointed as a judge. They took a trip to India and Martin sat on a hillside at sunset in Rajasthan and told Maggie he wanted to travel with her like this every year. When they got home there wasn't the same need to work late; they went out again, to plays and exhibitions and restaurants, and started having Friday night dinner parties at home again. Maggie gave herself the whole day in the kitchen to prepare and they pushed their guests out the door in the small hours of the morning. Then into all this entered Finnegan, their beautiful grandson who came every week for an afternoon or a sleepover . . . And that was their life, full, overflowing, precious, and for every day of it she knew to be grateful.

Every day, until four months ago Martin drove into a street in La Perouse.

Now Maggie sat in her studio with a certainty he had something more to tell, another file for the cabinet. Asleep inside, the man who was left did not always know whether the day was beginning or ending. He was sorry but he didn't know for what. What need of proof was there now, she wondered, when in his mind the slate had been wiped clean?

It was two a.m. when she put down her pencil and her paintbrush. The eyes were filled, the portrait was finished, and Iris looked back at her from the page.

Part Four

A parked car edged into the traffic. Ethan slammed on the brakes.

'That's right, lady, just pull out . . . effing cow.'

From the back seat: 'Who's a cow?'

'Ethan, please . . .'

'Sorry. Sorry, hon. Sorry, buddy.'

'It's okay, Dad. She should learn how to drive.'

Ethan laughed.

'It's not funny,' Laini said.

'Oh, come on . . .'

'I don't want him learning it's funny to abuse people.'

'Effing is for fucking.'

'You see! You see what you've done!'

'I never told him that.'

More laughter from the back seat.

'Alright, I give up,' Laini said. 'How was your day?'

'A mediation. We'll settle. All good. Yours?'

'Not bad, actually. I spoke to the woman from school again about the blog. She said I wouldn't have to put much into a proposal before I took it to her boss. She thinks there's enough there, just to gauge their interest. She said she'd ask him if he'd have a look. Then I thought, God, he'll probably think it's a load of bloody rubbish. I mean, I can't write to save myself . . . I don't know why anyone's reading the thing in the first place.'

'That's why it's good. You don't think about it too much; you just do it. It's not try-hard.'

'Thanks, baby. You've never said it's good before.'

'Haven't I? I'm saying it now.'

'You only ever looked at it once.'

'That's because it's girls' business. I felt like I was snooping. You want me to read it, I'll read it.'

'I'm not forcing you. I'm just saying . . .'

'Come on, Laini, please. I had a tough day.'

'You said it was okay.'

'Yeah, the case went fine. But the same politics, you know, the same bullshit.'

'No, I don't know. Tell me.'

'Please, hon, I don't want to get into it. It's petty stuff, nothing to worry about. I've got enough to deal with tonight. Mum talked to the doctors today. She didn't go into it on the phone, but they're talking about the possibility of rapid onset . . .'

She reached over and put her hand on his thigh. 'Poor Maggie. This is rotten. It's not fair.'

And from the back seat again: 'What's not fair?'

'Nothing . . . Just Grandie not remembering things.'

'Is that why he fell off the rock when he was fishing?' Finn asked. 'Is it because something's wrong with his brain?'

'We don't know, Finn. We don't know why he fell.'

'And is that why he hit the dog? And why he tells the same story? Why can't he tell a different story?'

'It is because he doesn't remember.'

'But sometimes he remembers; he remembers lots of things. Why can't I go for sleepovers anymore?'

'Hang on a minute, buddy, Daddy has to concentrate.' And looking from the rear-view mirror back over his shoulder, he accelerated to move into the passing lane. 'This guy is playing funny buggers . . .' Behind them a horn blasted. 'You see that dickhead speed up when he knew I was trying to get in there?'

'Oh, for God's sake . . . Don't you dare eyeball him!'

'You saw that! He was miles back but as soon as he saw me indicate he sped up . . .' And just as the guy snaked up alongside them Ethan bent forwards and turned his way. 'Arsehole.'

'Ethan!'

'Come on, Laini, the guy's a dickhead. Can't you be on my side for once?'

The car went silent, the only sound the video game in the back seat. It wasn't until they pulled up to the kerb that Laini put in the final word: 'I just don't think all these people are idiots and dickheads.'

'Yeah, okay, I had a crap day. I'm exhausted, babe, I'm not sleeping . . .'

Outside the car she waited for him. 'Go inside, Finn,' she said. And once he'd gone: 'Come here, you . . .' She gave him one of her up-close-and-tight hugs, the 'we'll fuck later' kind. He melted into it, grateful. The goodies bag at the end of a bad party, sometimes it was all you needed to get you through.

Finn ran back out.

'Grandie's fishing on the beach. I'm going down.'

Ethan and Laini looked at each other; Laini passed him

her bags. 'Okay, let's go,' she said, and to Ethan: 'You go in. I'll wander across.'

Finn ran in front. Laini went as far as the bench on the headland.

He watched them, son and wife, pink clouds. There was nothing wrong. He loved her. She loved him. Tomorrow he would buy her a present; he would go to that shop and get her something expensive, and all would be well. That is what he told himself, but still he stared at her silhouette with the sense that if he took his eyes away, just as Finn disappeared down the hill, she might fade with the day.

'What are you doing out here?' It was Maggie. 'Come inside.'

He turned around, but didn't move. 'I just thought they might get cold.'

'They'll be fine. They won't be long, and Laini is there. Is everything alright?'

He didn't answer.

'Come on then, I've got something to show you.'

He took one last look, and followed his mother inside.

Maggie opened the door to the study.

'He's funny about me showing people, but I wanted you to see this.'

Laid out on the floor in rows the full length of the room were photographs, each row with a different subject. The first were in colour, Maggie swimming in the ocean pool, pieces of her: a single arm outstretched in freestyle, drops of water falling from her fingers, then one closer up, shoulder blade to elbow. Ethan had to look twice—the strength and definition in the body, his mother's body. The other photographs were softer, intimate—skin beneath the water—and the last identified her: the side of her goggled face as she took a breath, the water cradling her head like a transparent pillow.

In the row beneath, a dog on the beach sniffed the carcass of a seagull; and in the next black cockatoos lined up on the branch of a tree and then tilted their wings in tandem to take flight. Ethan got down on his knees to get closer to the photographs and picked them up, replaced them in sequence. He knew bugger-all about photography, but these were better than good.

'These are all Dad's?'

'He's barely picked up a camera since you were little. Then when we got back from the hospital he pulled it out, the old camera—not the SLR—the one he had in New York. I was amazed it still worked. He remembered everything, all the tricks. He started following me over to the pool in the morning, then he'd wander off down to the beach. It was the longest I could leave him alone; having the camera in his hands kept reminding him what he was doing. There are hundreds more, of the same things . . . He forgets what he's been taking, so I lay them out. They are beautiful, aren't they?'

'They are; they are amazing. And this is what he was doing when you met him in New York . . . God, why did he stop?'

For a minute she considered the question. 'He wanted it so much and then he wanted something else, or thought he did,' she said. 'He made a choice . . . I'll have to dig out his New York boxes. You've never seen them?'

'He told me he couldn't find them.'

Maggie shook her head dismissively, a sudden, surprising anger in her voice: 'Is that what he said? That isn't true.'

She knelt down on the floor alongside him and took a photo in her hand, the one of the side of her face in the water, shaking her head again and staring at the image like she'd forgotten he was there. The bookshelf behind her was stacked with the blue spines of law reports in year order; Martin had always preferred them to the electronic versions—'I like to turn a page'. He sat at his desk late into the night and Ethan lay in bed with a protective eye on the sliver of light that crossed the dark hallway. Still the smell of the room was the books—the faint, woody vanilla. It stirred a memory now—a night when the light was not there because Martin had left to stay in the Randwick flat. Unable to sleep, Ethan got out of bed and came into the study. There on the desk was an open volume, one of the law reports, and on the shelf, between 1975 and 1977 (he could still remember the years), a single, shadowy gap. For the longest time Ethan stared down at the book like it was a missing piece of a puzzle. That morning Maggie had sat him down and began: 'Your father and I . . .' He hadn't let her finish: 'Where is he?' he cried. 'Where is he?' Over and over as he threw every last apple from the bowl against the wall. The day before he'd heard her in the bedroom shouting about Marty's 'dirty secret'. 'It never stopped! You never stopped!', the same words muttered to herself long after she had slammed down the phone, and in the night, through his bedroom wall, the sobbing. He felt bad for her then, but only for a while, because in his mind she was to blame; she had given Ethan something and now she was taking it away. In the morning his father was still gone and her face looked blotchy, misshapen. That was why he didn't want to look at her. That was why he threw the apples at the wall. That was why he stared down at the blue volume on the desk, the question turning in his mind whether to leave it there or return it to the shelf, certain the right decision would help to bring his father home in a way his blast of boyhood anger had not.

When at the end of the month his father did return, Ethan had formed his own view of secrets: that they were better kept. He watched as his parents created a silence around what had happened, and with that silence—at first fragile, then firm like a resin—his life was again as it had been, as it was meant to be.

Casting his eyes now over the books on the shelf as his mother sat absorbed in the photos, Ethan caught himself checking each volume, hoping to find a year out of place so that he could return it to its rightful order.

'So did they book him in for another scan?'

'They tried, but he told the doctor he didn't need a fucking machine to tell him his fucking brain was dissolving. I don't know how I'm going to get him there. And this thing with New York is getting worse. He's there more than he is here.'

Ethan nodded. 'The other day I heard him telling Finn about that garden, how you wanted to go see it at nighttime.'

'Dear Lord.'

'Don't worry, Finn tells him when he's had enough. "That one's a boring one, Grandie," he says.'

She smiled, the anger gone. 'Oh, isn't he perfect . . .'

'And he started talking to me about the judgment again, like he still has to finish it . . . He thinks it's got something to do with the boat disaster.'

A boat of asylum seekers had collided with rocks and sunk off the coast of Christmas Island. Martin had been glued to the coverage: the delay in response time, how many rescued, how many bodies recovered.

Maggie nodded. 'He told me at breakfast it'll make a difference to the sentence, all these lives lost and whose fault it is.'

'What do you say to him?'

'You can't set him right. I nod my head, try to get his attention back to the camera.'

'So where are these photos, the ones from New York?'

They were in the basement, she said, in a green cardboard box—on the top shelf against the back wall. Outside now there were voices, Martin and Finn, Finn's laughter. 'Next time you come, Ethan, go down and find them.'

Martin had already disappeared into the bedroom. The bucket was empty but Finn shrugged it off. 'We found pipis,' he said. 'But we put 'em back.' And he ran off to wash his hands for dinner.

Ethan remained, alone in his father's study, the sound of his son running in the hall.

Further back, he remembered how it felt as a small child—the miraculous cocoon that formed around him when the friend from New York became his father. The picture was a shiny red fishing rod. The smell was stinky bait. The hook pricked his finger and Marty wrapped it up in a tissue because he forgot to bring band-aids. Sitting at the end of the wharf, the clouds turned murky and there was a grumbling of thunder, but Ethan felt safe. As they sat with their legs dangling off the jetty, he looked out to the water then up at the man sitting next to him, at his hands and his arms and his chest.

'I bet you could carry me on your shoulders if you wanted,' he said finally.

'I bet I could too,' Marty replied.

'In the morning, you could walk me like that through the school gates. You're allowed to do it.'

That was when Marty told him. He told him he wasn't going anywhere. 'I belong here with you,' he said. 'With you and with your mother. I know that in my bones. That's when you really know something. When you feel it in your bones.'

Ethan remembered that, the thing about bones. And as far as Ethan could tell they weren't just words. There was the day the bird got into his bedroom and crashed against his walls, dropping gooey brown shit all over his boyhood treasures; it was Martin who flapped it out and waited for the shit to dry white before scraping it off. And the time he was in trouble for letting Sam Gibson take the blame for the money missing from the tuckshop, then for keeping the lie going all the way to the school principal. When somehow the truth came out, Maggie cancelled his birthday party; everyone in the class was coming but she cancelled it and said he could spend the day in his room instead. So there he was, a lone outcast in his own house, the worst day of his nine years of life, and in came Marty. From the minute he opened his mouth—sitting down next to him on the carpet and asking how it happened, why it happened—Ethan sensed he was there to tell him not how bad he'd been but that somehow they were still on the same side and, sensing that, Ethan took his father through it, step by step, the stealing, the first lie and all the ones after that, how it became not just easier but more necessary with each lie, all the while Marty nodding his head as though it made sense. And then at the end of it, at the end of the story, came the biggest surprise of all.

'You know,' Marty said, 'when I was your exact same age, I did something along those same lines, the difference being—and it is a big difference—that to this day no one ever found me out.' Then he paused a while before going on: 'Now that I think of it, maybe you're lucky, you know . . .' And when Ethan asked why: 'Because it left a bad taste with me, what I did. And the truth is, I never really worked out how to get rid of it.'

Except for 'dinner is in ten minutes', that was it. Marty closed the door behind him and with him took the weight of the boy's crime, at least the best part of it, enough so he could go and sit at the table and look his mother in the eye and see the day as over and done.

When Martin brought his suitcase home from the flat, he sat down next to Ethan in that same spot on his bedroom floor and told him he'd done some bad things that Ethan was too young to understand, but that he was sorry and his mother had forgiven him. Ethan listened, unconcerned with his father's wrongdoing. It was nothing that had hurt *him*. His mum had told him it was a bump in the road, and that now they were on the other side of it, they'd move on like nothing had happened. The only difference he could see was that they didn't squish up and lie side by side on the couch anymore and for a while they didn't have dinner parties where the shouting and music kept him awake. Then Maggie won the big prize and Martin spent a whole day hanging one of her paintings in every room of the house.

It was only much later that Ethan worked out what sort of bump it was, and even then—whatever his faults, whatever his sins—to Ethan, Martin was and remained the father with big shoulders who fell from the sky.

And his love was in his bones.

On the floor, the dog with the seagull, the cockatoos . . . Ethan, alone again in the study: again there is the terrible weight in his chest, the fear of losing a father, and in a deeper recess, something heavier still . . .

'The chicken is overcooked,' Maggie said.

'No, Mum, it's fine.'

'And the potatoes aren't crispy.'

The potatoes were fine too. She was talking again about Martin's accident, about the dog that got killed; she had offered to buy another dog.

'Ah, good girl,' Martin said. 'That was on my list.'

'What list, Dad?'

'My list . . .' Martin shook his head. 'Lines with dots.'

Ethan smiled at his father then turned back to his mother—not to get an answer, but to make a point: 'And did they want the dog?'

Of course they didn't want the dog; they wanted cash, they just hadn't said it yet; they wanted to bleed her dry. He tried to hold his tongue, but now she had gone back again; now she was calling these people her friends.

'For Christ's sake, Mum, leave it alone. You don't owe them anything. Haven't we got enough going on here without you wandering around La Perouse? I mean, fuck knows who these people are . . .'

It was then that Martin spoke again. 'Don't look so worried,' he said. 'We'll find out who is behind this, you hear me? And we'll get the names of the people who have drowned, every last one . . .'

Ethan dropped his head into his hands, then raised it again, a teacher to a wayward pupil: 'Dad, I am trying to explain something to Mum about the people in La Perouse, not the people on the boat. She doesn't know them, Dad, so I am just wondering why the hell she is doing this.' His voice was louder than he meant it to be. 'I'm sorry. I'm tired. This is hard . . . I am sorry, Mum.'

At this, his father reached over and took his hand and squeezed it gently. 'Don't worry your head, you hear me . . .' He pushed himself up and walked out into the hall.

Around the table, the silence remained.

Ethan knocked on the door to the study.

'You alright?' he asked.

The door opened. 'Never better.' Marty turned back in. 'She showed you.' His voice was absent of concern. He sat down on the floor with his photographs, and when Ethan joined him: 'This dog is always by itself, never with an owner,' he said. 'When I go to pat him, he shivers like he is cold . . . I'm afraid he is used to being kicked.'

'I'm blown away by these, Dad, honestly . . . I don't get it: why did you stop?'

Marty shook his head, as though that wasn't the right question. His eyes flicked across the series of photographs of Maggie swimming. 'This is why I love it.' He tapped each image, ending with the outstretched arm touching the edge of the pool. 'Every second is different . . . Isn't that an extraordinary thing?' He looked up then with a sudden clarity, the thought jolting him into the purpose at hand: 'Where were we up to?' he asked. He was talking about New York, of course—how far he had gone in telling Ethan the story.

Ethan stopped to remember. 'You were at the party,' he said. 'You were just leaving.'

'Yes, that's right. I wanted to go back to the loft, but she said, no, she wanted to go to the garden. It was two a.m. but that was where she wanted to go, so I . . .' He stopped mid-sentence, picked up a photograph of Maggie and held it close to his face, then looked at Ethan. 'They always have a plan for us, isn't that the truth?'

In his father's gaze then there was something conspiratorial, something Ethan had seen in his eyes years ago and had chosen never to bring to mind. Late at night, in a grungy Newtown pub with his college friends, all blind drunk, but not too drunk for Ethan to see his father in a dimly lit booth at the back of the bar, and with him a woman. Ethan wasn't quick enough to look away. Their eyes locked for just a moment, before they let go and set each other free.

Martin didn't wait for a response from him now, but continued, and as he did, Ethan leant back against the wall and smothered the memory, gratified that this would be the end to the day: his father narrating the story of how he met his mother, a day spent together and a parting of ways, not fumbling for words or for meaning but telling it with humour and intimacy and a mastery of detail. Gratified, because his father spoke as a man with a mind at the height of its powers, and beyond that—what was so extraordinary to Ethan—as a man who could trace his path and, within it, find some truth.

Later, when Laini was asleep, Ethan sat down again in the dark at his computer.

At the bottom of the blog page he clicked on the archived file date and scrolled down to his comment. This was the third time he had checked for her reply, and now there it was:

'Maybe the two things are somehow simpatico, as you say, FaithlessJohn: maybe you are a better husband because you sleep with other women. It doesn't feel wrong to you, I get that. I am just wondering if it would be worth checking on *her* definition of a better husband. I suppose my question is: who gets to decide these things?'

He read it again, irked by the tone of the reply. Staring at the computer for a number of minutes, the domestic bloggess began then to take on in his mind an independent virtual persona, to the extent that he even caught himself thinking:

What would she *know about my wife's definitions?* Though he immediately recognised the gaffe (almost immediately, not quite), the words turned over in his head. *What would she know?* And like a torch knocked off a table, they shone a light on the question of knowledge from an entirely different angle.

'My wife holds the view that everything matters,' he began. 'I hold a different view, and over the years, in the context of our marriage, I believe I have been proven to be right. Truth be told, even though she's never said it, I think she is coming across.'

And with the words still flowing in this newfound light, he penned the next sentence: 'I think there is a possibility that at some level she knows what I am doing and that her silence constitutes a form of tacit consent.'

Ethan was, of course, having this thought for the very first time. To date it had never even crossed his mind. But there it was, pristine and full of potential: the possibility of an unspoken agreement . . . As he climbed into bed next to his sleeping wife, her naked body covered only to the waist by a sheet, it began to take root: *If she knows me so well, she knows this too* . . . He leant over to kiss the closest breast before putting his head down on the pillow.

It was enough to take him into his first half-decent sleep in weeks.

This is what I thought happened, as it was happening.

From a tenement window a dim corridor of light falls across the garden.

'Jesus,' she says. 'My head is swimming.'

'You okay?'

'I love it.' She stretches her arms to the sky. They walk the circle of paths to the centre of the garden where the air is mint and lime.

He sees the flag.

'Wait here,' he says, and he climbs onto the rubble and drags the mattress onto the outer path, then comes back into the centre, pulls the flag off its pole and throws it over the mattress.

There are lines he'd normally use now but words scramble, senseless (weed on speed). So he just faces her, she him. They step closer, not close enough for their bodies to touch but close enough to see in her flickering eyes that like him, mind and body, she is surging towards whatever is about to happen.

'Lie down,' he says. The words come out stilted, clunky, like a boy playing doctor, but the response is on song: she closes her eyes and lets herself fall flat against the mattress . . .

Only mid-air he remembers the broken springs.

'Oh fuck,' she shouts as she slaps one with the back of her hand. 'What was that?' Then she is laughing, a laugh that is raucous and reckless and it releases them, both of them, as the stripes on the flag wriggle into zigzag and the mud-stained stars disappear under her body.

He drops to his knees. The white shirt in moonlight, he begins to untie it. As he gets to the buttons she wonders without a trace of concern if they can be seen from the windows. And she laughs again. She looks young when she laughs, maybe too young.

'I'm straightening up,' he says.

'Is that a good thing?'

'I'm not sure. I just remembered who you are.'

'Oh, well, that's lovely!'

'You know what I mean. Not the girl I spent the day with. Maggie Varga, all the way from home . . . How old are you again?'

She sits up, an arch in her spine, behind her the broken rubble. 'Almost twenty-two.'

When he looks at her now he has the same feeling he had earlier, that she is in the lead and he is somehow part of her plan, but there she is, her shirt open on just one side and he is already imagining the dark nipple between his teeth. What does it matter? She is who he wants her to be. The girl at his door . . . He pushes the other side of the shirt across.

'Fuck, you are beautiful.' It isn't a line; it is just what he is seeing.

She rises up enough to kiss him and the day reads as fourteen hours of foreplay. His hand slides down between her legs and he thinks of other lips over the past months, other girls, other bodies, blurring . . . Then *bang*, there is a clamp around his wrist. She pulls away, brings him back. Like she's in his thoughts, she smiles. She knows.

'Start again,' she says, and when he does, her naked body feels fragile in his hands, like something he needs to take care with. As he moves around it piece by piece, it isn't strange to him; he recognises it like something he remembers—the freckle on her shoulder, the scar on her hip—something remembered, or something projected over years to come.

He holds her in his hands. She is not fragile.

Other girls, other bodies—he doesn't close his eyes like he does with them. He doesn't close his eyes to imagine someone else, to imagine Linda. He doesn't close his eyes at all because Maggie Varga doesn't let him. Like a demon . . . Maggie Varga, made of flesh, of air and fire, a freckle and a scar.

Maggie Varga will not disappear.

'Do you still feel like a visitor?' she asks, passing back his cigarette.

They are lying on the mattress, naked and spent, clothes scattered in the garden around them. The truth is he doesn't feel anything but post-coital oblivion. What just happened was far and away the best fuck he's had since he came to New York—one of those sessions when the planets align. In answer to her question, if he feels anything it is a sense of achievement. In that way he owns the moment: less visitor, more lord. But at the back of his mind is the knowledge that if he overthinks it, it will be gone. That is how all the good things slip away. Roll with it, Martin; don't start asking what it is. So he bounces it back: 'Do you?'

She shakes her head. 'No.'

'Yeah, I sense that. How did you get to be so fucking sure of yourself?'

'You say it like it's an insult.'

She's right; it sounded nasty. But the question was genuine. And though his standard move about this time is to roll over and slip out a stranger's door, he has the unexpected and overwhelming desire to understand her, at least some small part of her. He wonders if after all that he could still be a little stoned.

'I don't mean it like that,' he says, reaching over to stroke her thigh. 'I just don't get it.'

When his hand reaches her buttock he gets distracted, but she pushes it back up then slides in close again, her head against his shoulder, whispers, 'What don't you get?'

'Okay.' He will play. Why not? 'Like the painting thing for you—you don't have much to back it up, but you want something, and you're not afraid to say you want it. I'd like to know how that feels.'

She squints, trying to get a look at his eyes. 'Your photos . . .'

'I'm fooling around. I just got the idea in my head. But you . . . let me guess, you've known what you want to do since you were eight years old. Tell me I'm wrong.'

She falls back on the mattress. 'Nah, that's pretty much right.'

'So how the hell does that work?'

'You want to know?'

He does, and he knows this is entering a zone into which he rarely goes. Personal history on top of physical intimacy screams the beginning of something, and at least an in-principle commitment to explore the possibilities, but he proceeds with a safety net: tomorrow this girl is travelling back to the other side of the world.

'Okay,' she says, 'I'll give you the story I told to get into art school: I was seven. We were living in a camp for migrants—I was telling you about that. It was a bit of a tip—a bunch of tin shacks. The grass used to grow through the floorboards, and on the insides of the walls there were sheets of cardboard. Insulation, I guess. Anyhow, I drew pictures on them, on the cardboard. At first I got in trouble, but then my parents had to go to work and sometimes there was no one around to look after me. We never had any paper, so they told me that when I came home after school I could draw on the walls. My father bought me a box of coloured chalk, and when I was good he'd give me a new piece. It was like a treat, a reward. Then he started bringing newspaper home and I would use that, draw over the writing and find the bits of blank space.'

'And that got you into art school?'

She smiled. 'Nothing like a tough-luck story.'

'Okay, I get it. You're hardwired.'

'I suppose so.'

'Like a dog.'

She laughs. 'And let me guess: you were off leash. Roaming around your mansion.'

'Come off it, it wasn't a mansion. Don't start . . . I get enough of it from Linda.'

'Enough of what?'

'Silver spoon and all that.'

'Okay, your turn. What about the drugs?' she asks. 'Is that a typical night out?'

'Sort of, not really. For them it is. She is pretty crazy, in case you didn't notice.'

'I like her.'

'You do?'

'And you do too.'

He shrugs it off, lights another cigarette. 'She drives me nuts.'

'Yep. I bet,' she says, then laughs when she feels him harden against her thigh. 'Is that for me or for Linda?'

He takes hold of her hands against the mattress.

'You lie,' she whispers. 'You know what you want.' And she rolls her body over and up, back on top.

Later, as the first bird tolls the beginning of the day and the end of theirs, she says she has to go, but before she does, she has one more thing she has to say.

~

It was broken by the clatter of plates from the kitchen.

Maggie had overcooked the chicken but everyone said it tasted fine. Then there was more talk, but he didn't hear it. More often than not it was just a matter of watching mouths move.

But now it was only Martin and Ethan left at the table, and Ethan drew his chair closer.

'You know, Dad, I want to hear the rest of it.'

Martin looked towards the kitchen.

'They'll be a while,' Ethan said. 'Come on: you went to the garden, you had this wild night, then you just said goodbye?'

Martin leant forward and shook his head. 'I thought that was what we were doing, saying goodbye. I thought that was all there was left to do, but she had something to tell me . . . There was more to it all along, you see,' he said, almost a whisper. 'I lived the day, but I wasn't the one to say what it meant.'

'I don't understand. What did she say?'

But Martin didn't answer him, because already in his mind he had moved on to anticipate another, larger question, one that Ethan was entitled to ask his father and never had: 'Why didn't you come back?'

How best to frame the answer? In the end, hours after Ethan had taken Laini and Finn home, out in the garden in the middle of the starless night, Martin came up with just this: *There are people in life whose strength makes you weak and whose insight makes you blind. For me, that was your mother.*

The room was fluorescent-lit, a windowless box. Ethan tapped the table and looked at his watch, then at the empty seat. He shrugged.

'Her phone is off,' he said. Tina McCarthy was fifteen minutes late to the Family Court mediation that had been scheduled at her request.

Her husband smirked. 'She never turns her phone off.' A different tone, Ethan thought, to the handwritten note he pushed under Tina's door yesterday as he dropped off little Timmy. 'There's enough bad karma around this already,' the note read, ending with just: 'Please X'. Capital X: big, begging kiss.

At the end of the table the mediator smiled reassuringly, said the traffic was terrible, while opposite Ethan, Douglas Mott—Stewart McCarthy's lawyer—rose from his chair and turned around before breaking into a dry, hacking cough.

'I'm fine, I'm fine,' he said, blue veins pulsing in his temples. 'It's the change of seasons.'

Ethan suggested they keep the door open, then asked the mediator if they could get another room.

'This was it,' she said, casting an apologetic look over the walls. 'All booked up.'

Pulling at the loose folds of skin on his neck, Douglas suggested Ethan kick it off and explain why they were here, 'why this couldn't have been dealt with in a couple of emails'.

As Douglas tried to get the lay of the land and his client kept watch on the door, Ethan made mental notes of his own. In the eyes of Stewart McCarthy, either side of the scar still crimson in the middle of his brow, Ethan saw a different kind of wound, still raw and untreated, and beginning to fester. He couldn't remember a dispute where the opponent presented as quite so bent over the barrel, so damned and desperate he almost felt sorry for him . . . When Tina swept into the room in a feigned rush, spouting apologies and excuses, Stewart closed his eyes for longer than the blink required, and just managed to smile. In spite of what was about to happen—in spite of the grenade Tina was about to lob into this shitbox of a room—Ethan felt quietly confident that nothing would sway this man from his quest for immediate closure with his soon-to-be ex-wife. He had come to despise her, and worse still, because of that, he had come to despise himself.

Tina McCarthy tipped her head at Ethan and held his gaze, as one would to greet an intimate friend. Flushed in the cheeks, with less makeup than he'd seen her wear before—and maybe less a kilo or two—Tina McCarthy was a noticeably more attractive package. The hair was down and the dress was good—a charcoal grey wraparound that gently hugged her freckled, pendulous breasts . . . Standing up and directing Tina to the seat next to Sally—buttoned up to the neck again in her Victorian blouse—Ethan couldn't help but notice that in spite of the obvious contrast in styles, each called in its own particular way for a particular type of attention. When it came to Sally, he took note, but avoided eye contact. Over the last weeks the blouse had become her sign, her private message to him that should the opportunity arise, the door was (so to speak) open, with the result that the sight of Sally buttoned up all the way invariably implanted in his mind—cordoned off and open for viewing during strictly limited times—a particular image, minus the God-awful blouse and any other piece of clothing: Sally standing on the bathmat after her morning shower, wondering what to wear and thinking of him, dripping wet and bending over to dry her toes.

It wasn't just the sex. It was Sally, full stop. At home, Ethan was still twisting himself around in late-night sessions with Laini's blog, and the rest of the time she was consumed with turning her role as dispeller of darkness into a book deal, so when Ethan's head got all hooked up in the barbed wire of bad thoughts (take your pick: his dad's deteriorating brain, the bullshit with Max), Sally was his go-to girl, guaranteed to make him feel less alone, to raise him up and onward . . .

As per the agreement he had reached with Max, every second Wednesday Ethan was meeting in the boardroom with Marcella, the five-foot-nothing psychotherapist with arms like twigs. He wondered if Max picked her because she made him feel tall.

'So do you know Max?' he'd asked her. For their first session Ethan asked most of the questions. The answers were that she didn't know Max (or so she claimed), she wouldn't reveal who in the firm was her contact, and she only wanted to talk about his childhood if he wanted to talk about his childhood. 'Ask away,' she had said, her feet dangling off the ground in the chair that swamped her like a throne would a child queen. This could go on for a long time, he thought: *how much do you weigh?* But more questions would just mean more lunch dates with Marcella. As she explained her 'particular kind of process', he was trying to remember the name of the actress she reminded him of—the one who played the man and got thrown out the window in the Mel Gibson movie.

When her questions started he answered them as succinctly as he could. She did not seem suitably impressed when he told her he had made partner at thirty-one. Rather, she nodded, like it was a piece of the puzzle and she was mentally moving it into position. Same with his parents' dinner parties, the fact most Friday nights Ethan lay in bed trying to make out what was being said and what it all meant. That was another piece. Marcella nodded . . . The nodding was the worst part: horrible—fucking excruciating.

It was Sally who saved him.

'I think she thinks I am so hard on people because I fear my own incompetence. I think that's where she's going with this . . . I mean what sort of bullshit is that?'

Sally stretched out on the floor of the hotel room. 'Did she say that?'

'Not in so many words.'

'You are the best lawyer I know, Ethan. Don't analyse it, that'll just mess you up. Express gratitude for her insight, tick the box. Job done.'

'You are so right.'

'I know I am.'

'I am so the best the lawyer you know . . .' He dropped the smile. 'What would I do without you, Sal?'

She propped herself up on her elbow. 'Careful, Ethan. I'm not made of stone.' He went to say more but she put a finger on his lips, shook her head. 'I'm going to take a shower. We need to get back.'

And here she was today in the Victorian blouse, Ethan scrambling for a way to schedule it in but coming up empty—the meeting would take them to five, then he was racing home to get Laini and Finn and get them to dinner with the parents, cursed to wonder all the while what Sally was going to do with that pent-up energy.

As soon as Tina McCarthy took her seat, the mediator began proceedings—explaining the purpose and nature of the process and asking Douglas to recap on the offer that was presently on the table: the Mosman home—the latest valuation had come in at 5.6 million—and the 150K a year seasonally adjusted until the boy was twenty-one.

'And what has the response been to the offer?' Without looking at Ethan, she kept her pen poised over the page. She knew what the response had been—she had all the paperwork: a request for some further financials, some nitpicking on insurance and expenses.

'They seem like relatively minor matters, would that be right? Is there an issue with disclosure?'

Douglas: 'The last request was for the profit and loss of his brother's cleaning company.'

'Of which he was a director for nine years.'

'Ending in 1986. Ten years before they—' Mid-sentence, Douglas choked on his words and went into his second coughing fit.

'Sorry, I'm not contagious or anything. This has been hanging around for weeks.'

'Post-nasal drip,' Ethan said.

'Thanks for the diagnosis.'

Ethan shrugged.

'The directorship ended ten years before they even met, that is what I was saying.'

'In any event, they have it now,' the mediator said. 'But I understand, Mr Field, that your client has a few remaining concerns?'

'Thanks, that is correct. There are some ongoing expenses we'd like to see paid by your client. We've made a list.' Sally handed three copies to the mediator.

'Hang on a minute. That's one thing we have made perfectly clear from the word go,' Douglas said. 'My client wants a sum to be paid—monthly, quarterly, however Mrs McCarthy wants it. Then she can make decisions about day-to-day expenses, health insurance, maintenance of the property—whatever else you've got here—without having to consult Stewart. My client is eager to reduce dealings and avoid any situation that might create acrimony in the future. As you know full well, there is valid basis for his concerns, and as we discussed the sum was arrived at with that in mind. It seems to me that we are going around in circles here.'

Until this point, Tina had maintained a serene half-smile as she pretended to make notes on her copy of the list. With Douglas's last words, she shot him a look of pure derision, and when her gaze returned to the page she mouthed something, a word, maybe two; Ethan couldn't make it out.

'Is there something you would like to say, Mrs McCarthy?' Douglas asked.

Ethan raised his hand. 'My client feels as though she is being left with the burden of financial management, along with the burden of parenting.'

The mediator tapped her palm on the table. 'So if I could just understand this. Your client is prepared to take less in the form of a lump sum if it were compensated by way of Mr McCarthy taking over the payment of specified bills?'

'Well, no, given the change in circumstance, we are of the view those payments should be in addition to the lump sum.'

And there it was, a sprinkling of words—the safety pin pulled, the handle released.

Douglas pounced: 'The change in circumstance?'

'My client wanted to explain this herself—the change in circumstances, that is,' Ethan said.

Tina looked up from her list, cast her eyes around the table before settling on Stewart. And then, a single overarm throw: 'I am planning to have another baby.'

'Sorry?' And after Tina repeated what she had said: 'You can't do that. You can't use it without my consent.' The *it* he was referring to was the last remaining embryo of Stewart and Tina McCarthy, sitting frozen and lifeless in a sealed straw numbered 7634 in a cryostorage facility in North Ryde. It was the *it* Stewart had once prayed would be a sister to his son, an XX, a second miracle . . . Had he not seen the hopelessness in the eyes of the specialist, had he not witnessed what repeated failure and loss had done to his wife, had she not hurled the statue across the kitchen table . . .

'I don't need your consent. I'm using a sperm donor—anonymous. I start hormones next week.'

And for just a moment, a pin-drop silence . . . broken by Ethan: 'So obviously her ability to re-enter the workforce may well be compromised, and your client is aware of the costs of the treatment.'

Stewart raised his hands slowly and placed them over his eyes, and as Tina continued—a quaver now in her high-pitched homily—he slid them slowly around his face to cover his ears, in what appeared a last-ditch plea to see no madness, hear no madness.

'Timmy needs a brother or a sister and I am going to do whatever I damn well can to see that he gets one.' She was on her feet, her fists pressing into the table. 'Sorry, Stewart, if that doesn't sound convenient to you, if that doesn't fit in with your retirement plans—if that screws with your next surfing safari.'

The mediator's voice rose to the acceptable upper limit: 'Please, madam, sit down. We are still in mediation, and while we are here I am in charge of the proceedings.'

Douglas put up his hand. 'My client is not responsible for Mrs McCarthy's future plans. The prospect of further children . . .'

But Stewart wasn't listening; he was shaking his head, and he was getting to his feet. 'You think you can look after Timmy while you morph into a fucking basket case again? Who are you going to take it out on this time? You do this, Tina, and I want custody for the duration of the treatment. I will put it all in an affidavit, every fucking crazy thing you did, ending up with this . . .' Stewart pointed to the crimson scar on his forehead.

Tina's response was calmly delivered: 'At least I didn't drink myself into oblivion.'

And without another word, taking his coat, Mr Karma walked out of the room.

Ethan formed a smile, looked at Douglas. 'Take the list . . .'

But Douglas shook his head. 'Forget the list, Ethan. Our offer is good for seven days. Then it is off the table. All I'd add to that is the fact that following the assault my client didn't go to the police, as he was well entitled to do . . . as he's *still* entitled to do.'

'Mr Mott!' The mediator slapped the table with her hand. 'This is a court-ordered mediation. It is no place for threats.'

'Certainly, madam. Though I think we can safely say the mediation is over.'

When Tina left the room, Sally quickly followed.

While packing up his file, Ethan could feel Douglas watching him. It was only when the file was in his briefcase that he looked up.

'How are things, Doug?'

'Things are things,' Doug replied.

'That they are.' Ethan stood up, satisfied with the exchange. Still, Doug was looking up at him—squinting, like he was having a problem getting things into focus. With no interest in knowing why, Ethan got up and left the room before Doug had the chance to tell him.

Down on the street, Sally was waiting on the corner with Tina, thirty paces from Stewart, who was standing on the edge of the kerb and smoking a cigarette. The four lanes of traffic were at a standstill both ways, the air humid with idling engines and impending rain.

When Doug came out of the building, he took Stewart's elbow like he was more a patient than a client and began to lead him away; then he stopped and turned around and walked back to Ethan, and with the same squint of the eyes said quietly, out of his client's earshot: 'I'm just trying to work it out, Ethan. We were *that* close to settling this thing . . . until she went over to you. I've got to wonder, do you put these ideas in their heads? I mean, how do you do that? You just go around with a match and see which fire's going to light up?'

The man was attacking his professional ethics, accusing him of misconduct and a failure to fulfil his duty to the client and to the court, but what really had Ethan's attention was that behind him, watching the one-way exchange, smoke billowing out of his nostrils, Stewart had smoked the cigarette down to the butt, which he now had pincered in his fingers like a joint.

Ethan's back was against the wall of the building. Odd, he thought, in a David Attenborough kind of way, how the sweat bubbled on only a particular section of Doug's balding head.

One, two . . . he counted the seconds that the man stood there in front of him . . . three, four, five . . . until the bubbles weren't there anymore, not the bubbles, not the head, not Doug . . . Ethan had closed his eyes, and in place of his vision (and not for the first time) was a screeching black mass—like a flock of flapping magpies—and in that single moment, with the smell of smoke fading and the menace writhing in his brain, all he wanted to do, with every inch of his being, was to go to the hotel and fuck Sally senseless and smoke a cigarette and fuck her again and smoke another cigarette until he couldn't fuck or smoke anymore.

That, he thought or death . . .

It was just a moment, and just as quickly it had passed. But whatever the lead-up in the scenario playing out behind his eyes, when he opened them it had left a poignant blend of fear and sorrow. Having anticipated something quite different—anger, guilt perhaps—Douglas Mott was thrown. He took a step back and in the same lowered voice, he mumbled an apology.

He was out of order, he said; his head was pounding. 'This sort of thing is par for the course.' And looking back to Stewart

McCarthy. 'I shouldn't have played squash with the guy. You never want to know your client is such a bloody good bloke.'

'So what now?' Tina asked when Ethan joined them on the corner and waved a hand to hail a cab.

'We draft up the settlement. You two go back to the office so Sally can get those last financials.'

'With all the added expenses?'

'Every last one,' he said. 'Sally, can we get it to them tomorrow?'

'You're not coming back?'

'Nah,' he said. 'I'm done for the day. I need to get home—family stuff. I'll walk to the car park; I need a walk.'

'And what he said about custody?' Tina asked, worried.

'He won't do it.' And looking her straight in the eye as the cab door closed: 'He is too nice a guy.'

Watching the cab pull away, he was relieved to be alone, to breathe in the fumes of the city and stand invisible on its streets. As he walked into the park, the sun shone through the canopy of elms. Ethan stood beneath the glistening archway and inhaled long and deep—the smell of cut grass and decomposing leaves. He imagined Tina McCarthy in front of a mirror with a syringe full of hormones, injecting her pale, freckled flesh with her life-giving potion, and he imagined them side by side leaning over spreadsheets: Sally in her frill-necked blouse and his soon-to-be ex-client and her wraparound cleavage.

Sally—that fucking blouse again . . .

His thoughts faded to the sounds around him, the drilling of taller buildings, the rumble of a million steps and, closer in, buskers strumming bad guitar, the chatter of workmates, birds tweeting on the bird-shitty bench. With a couple of German tourists he stopped to watch the scavenging ibises feuding over garbage—their brutal black hooks, the precision of the swordplay.

As he reached the end of the central walkway, he stopped, looked up at the windows of the office buildings—his own office, his own window—and wondered if anyone was looking down, tracking his movements. *Is anybody watching?*

He was skating on the edge, granted. But in his mind the ground was firm. As long as he pushed himself back into the fray, as long as he wanted it, he was still in the game.

Whatever side, he told himself, the choice was his.

This is what happened.

He is lying down, and she is kneeling beside him.

As she buttons her shirt her hair falls over her face, and when she pulls it back he takes over with the buttons and tells her to come home with him; they can take a bath and sleep there until she has to go.

'No,' she says. 'Neither of us is going to be feeling any good. Best part ways here.' She smiles, holds his hand and, like she is reciting a poem he doesn't know: 'Here in the first pale light.'

'You are beautiful,' he tells her, without meaning to say it—maybe in gratitude for a clean break, he thinks, but from the sudden gnawing emptiness he knows it isn't that.

'There is something I want to say,' she says, and he is relieved to hear it, hopes she has a way to say it.

'Yeah, sure, me too. It was an amazing night. If you weren't leaving . . .'

'No, it's not that. It's not what you think.' She looks away and, seeing the garden around her as the sun peeks over the tenements, shakes her head. 'God, look at this place.' Then her eyes come back to him. 'And you. How did I get here?'

'You don't remember?'

She shakes her head. 'Yes, I remember.'

There is a flash of confusion in his eyes, and some trepidation in going forward: 'So?'

'So. I want to tell you something else, something I didn't tell you.'

'Okay, shoot.'

'It is something about when we were young,' she says. 'I didn't tell you but I want to tell you now.'

'So tell me,' he says, not knowing whether to make light of it. Her face is not light. But it is worth a go. 'Does it have a happy end?'

She leans down so that her hair falls forward again, this time touching the side of his face, and she whispers, 'It does: the end is now. Aren't you happy?'

Why the girl is spinning him around before she says goodbye, he doesn't know, but figures that in the end it doesn't matter. 'Sure I am. I mean, I'm happy.' She sits up again and he takes her hand. 'I'm sad too.' But again he senses he is missing the tone—the way she looks at him, like he is something edible and she is hungry . . . A curtain has come down on the night, but this is no parting game. 'What is it?'

'You said before that you remembered me, you remembered seeing me at your place when I was a little girl.'

'Sure, I remember.'

'Okay, so I used to sit there at the back door for hours when Lil did the dinners for your mum. I got bored. I helped a little, but I couldn't do much. I was only eleven. I wasn't allowed to get in the way.' She lowers her voice, holds his gaze. 'So I started looking out for you, waiting to see if you'd show up again.

'You did, one night. I saw you in the garden smoking a cigarette; there was a wooden bench under a magnolia tree—you lay down on it looking up at the sky. I saw the smoke rising up . . . You were there for so long I wondered if you'd fallen asleep. But then I heard the creak of the gate and you weren't there anymore.

'Another night I heard you fighting with your mother on the veranda and you threw a stone at the car. Do you remember that?'

A wave of adolescent memories is flooding over his creeping hangover. Though he has a question of his own—why is she telling me this now?—he doesn't ask it. 'I do, yeah, I remember that,' he says. 'It just seems a little strange that you do too.'

She isn't put off. She inches closer. 'You want to hear strange?'

He doesn't, but he will.

'I told you before about the photo on our fridge, the one of you and your mother.' He nods. It was an odd note even then, the mention of the photo. 'Well, your mother wasn't in the photo; it was just you. And it was never on our fridge. I took it from your kitchen. There were a bunch of copies, and I took one.'

She waits for him to ask the question 'Why?', then when he does she hesitates, and looks him straight in the eye.

'The truth? The truth is you were the best-looking seventeen-year-old boy I'd ever seen.'

There is no response from him beyond an awkward smile, but as she knew they would—as she had intended—the words sing to his vanity and settle him in for the rest of the story.

She took it home, and she stuck it on butcher's paper on the inside of the cupboard door in her bedroom. And she started doing drawings from it, lots of drawings, each with a different view of him, a different angle—as though she were writing a secret journal, inventing a coded language. When the paper was full she tore it down and threw it in the garbage before Lili could see it.

When he turns away she waits for him to look back at her. 'Then imagine today when you handed me the charcoal and sat down on your stool . . . You wondered why I laughed. I mean, I couldn't say—not then. I couldn't tell you I'd drawn you all those times before. But now I think, what the hell, I'm not going to see you for, like, forever, so why not spill it? The truth, I guess, is that you were pretty much my first love.'

Her eyes are glazed, shining. But the pupils are minuscule now . . . *hardwired*.

For a minute there is silence but for the sounds of the waking street. Finally he finds the words. 'That is one hell of a story.'

He tries to remember back to the little girl at the house. He can remember the mother, the dinner parties, but the girl is just a shadow at the door . . . He can't remember her at all.

'And you think I'm crazy.'

'No, well, a little bit, sure I do.' The words come back: stalker girl. 'I mean, not mentioning it earlier—letting the whole day go by, the night . . .'

She puts two fingers to his lips, presses down then slides them away as she kisses him, soft and long, and final. 'I gotta go now, Martin,' she says. 'I don't regret a bit of it. If I could have dreamt it, this is how it would have happened. And already it feels like it never did . . . That's always the way with the best things.'

She ties her shirt and smiles, and it dawns on him if this is a hit-and-run then he is the guy left lying on the side of the road. It is happening again; he is a character in someone else's story. Behind what happened here, there was an intention, and with that intention, an inevitability . . . She leans down, more a brush of the lips than a kiss, and then she is on her feet, standing over him. All that is left now is the slow fade of her smile as she turns away.

When she is gone, in her place there is a chiding sadness—an old man sitting among scattered photographs, shaking his head and telling him it is a mistake to let her go and it is a mistake to follow her home; it is a mistake to think that he can match her, because he never could, he never can.

Out a window, it is daylight, and like the line between the cliffs and the sky, the time to speak was clear.

In the study again, there she was, smiling at the door, bag on shoulder, keys in hand.

'Where are you going?' he asked.

'To see Iris,' she said.

But he shook his head. He knew her; she was never one for blinkers. 'You are foraging.'

Her smile faded. She looked surprised, but not unpleasantly so.

'Perhaps you could just ask,' he said.

'Ask what?'

'Why I went there.'

'I did. You didn't remember.'

His next words came without forethought in a voice that knew more than he did: 'Then for heaven's sake, Maggie, ask someone else.'

Coming through Iris's gate with the finished painting, Maggie remembered walking up the same steps to the same open door four months ago. She remembered how afraid she had been, how she had looked inside, down the hallway to the scribbled walls.

Come, Maggie, she had said to herself. *What is the worst it could be?*

Just four months, the same door, and now all she felt as she knocked was a reluctance to wait—an impatience to see Iris, to see the look on her face when she saw the finished portrait.

Without waiting for an answer, she entered.

Walking down the hall, she stopped at the stairs to call for Iris then continued to the kitchen to find it empty. Dispirited, she stood at the bench and wondered whether to wait. She put it down, the large plastic sleeve tied with blue string, and after a couple of minutes untied it herself and removed the top sheet to look at it again. Though each stroke on the page was her own, already she was outside it. That was the way she could always judge a painting: if it was poor or incomplete, the faults and omissions were hers, but once worked to a point where there was nothing more she could do, the painting stood alone. It didn't always follow, not by any means, that it was a great piece, just that she was no longer its caretaker.

She checked her watch; Iris could be hours. Ready as she was to hand it over, Maggie returned the top sheet and turned back down the hall.

Strange, she later thought, how one day life can be so gentle in allaying our fears, and the next so brutal in obliterating expectations. Months ago she had stood at the door, consoling herself by asking what the worst could be, and what had she found? A little girl in purple underpants with a texta lid stuck in her nostril, and Iris, the old woman who refused to take payment for her shell-covered box. Then today, with the painting under her arm, she found only an empty house, and now, as she was leaving, something more: an occupant returning—and finally an answer to her question as to what the worst could be.

There in the doorway was a woman, the same woman who had rushed past her and out the door on her first visit. It was, she now knew, Kayla: mother to Tyson, daughter-in-law to Iris. Maggie stopped halfway down the hall.

Unable to see her face, Maggie recognised her only from the same green tracksuit and streaked, matted hair. To hold herself up, the woman was gripping either side of the doorframe with her large brown hands. Like a dead weight, her head lolled forwards, though at the sound of Maggie's steps it raised up, a slow reveal of her face: first the mouth, the tongue lying flaccid on her lower lip, then the half-open eyes rolling from side to side before settling on Maggie, and when they did, when they found their focus, the tongue retracted to form the question: 'Who the fuck are you?'

Fear rising in her throat, she could feel the woman's eyes burrowing into her own. 'I am Maggie,' she said. 'A friend of Iris's.'

In response, the woman's head lunged forwards again, as though in an effort to nod she had miscalculated its weight.

'You must be Kayla,' Maggie went on. 'Iris told me you were moving back.'

Looking up again, the woman separated her words as though she was being forced to repeat them to a simpleton, ending in a crescendo. 'I—am—not—moving—back—to—this—SHIT—HOLE!'

Maggie took a small step forwards, edging towards the door, the door that was blocked—'If Iris isn't in, I'll . . .'—but Kayla paid no attention, her words now slurred together: '. . . This fuckin' zoo up here, everyone watching like you're a monkey in a cage.' Her eyes flickered. 'Like you . . . like you, watching me . . .' And again: 'Who the fuck are you?'

With that, her eyes closed, and as they closed, she leant against the doorframe and slid slowly down to the floor.

Maggie stared down at the woman, her thoughts blocked by a creeping paralysis. Here it was, the ghoul she had feared when five months ago she had stood in that same doorway and remembered the warning: it wasn't a street where you went around knocking on doors. Here it was, previously imagined so that now it felt to Maggie like something remembered, something known to her, and as for her judgment—her condemnation—for that she could look even further back, to a day long ago when just down the hill and a stone's throw from the snake man she had been dragged from the jetty and had gone home to scrub herself clean. This woman, damaged and drug-addled, laying blame everywhere but at her own feet . . . The rising stench of stale sweat and tobacco was as abhorrent to Maggie as everything she had done: her abuse of herself, her neglect as a mother . . . So it flowed, all the reasons why the line between them was a wall—*I am not her, this is not me*—all the reasons why her instinct told her to get out of here, and to get away.

How then to step around the woman without stirring her back to life?

As she considered the question, Maggie noticed a new drawing on the scribbled wall: a road that went all the way to the doorframe, and on the edge of the road a house and above the house a yellow sky and in the corner of the sky a black moon. The road was green and the house was red—a world of its own, Maggie thought, no matter what played out around it. Like the picture on the wall of the migrant centre: The Land of Tomorrow . . .

She stepped closer to the door, and the moment she did, the eyes opened. When she went to take a second step, Kayla made a yelping sound as though she'd been kicked. 'Don't touch me,' she shouted, and as she shouted her head began to shake violently, like she was in the middle of a convulsion. It lasted only a few seconds. By the time Maggie grabbed her phone to call an ambulance, the woman had clamped her head in her hands to make it still, looking at Maggie now with pleading eyes and simple, quiet words: 'I can't be here.'

'Is there someone I can call?'

Kayla seemed to consider the prospect before dismissing it. 'Ty-son!' The first syllable of the name was lost under her breath; what was heard was only the shrill and desperate cry for her 'son'. Maggie turned back to the door, hoping that the boy would appear, but no one did. When she looked again at the woman on the floor, she was staring back at her now, teeth bared in a smile.

'You the judge's wife,' Kayla said.

Maggie nodded.

'How is he, the judge?' she snarled, and began to laugh, a horrid, high-pitched laugh. Then she covered her face with her hands and shook her head, lost in a memory, all the while laughing. Only when Maggie stepped closer to the door did Kayla speak again. When she did it was more a hiss: 'So what you people trading now?'

Maggie stood silent and stunned in the face of the woman's contempt. Just as she was forming the words to ask what she meant, the boy appeared at the door, and behind him a brown dog.

He flashed a look at Maggie then knelt down and took his mother's face in his hands to look into her eyes. 'You alright, Ma?'

'Tyson, my baby,' she said, and to the dog: 'Fuckin' mutt.' She kicked out at it but missed and hit the wall.

'Come on, let's get you up.'

And as he went to pull her arm over his shoulder, he looked at Maggie nervously. 'She's fine,' he said. 'She's been doing okay, I promise.'

Realising she had been mistaken for someone who needed to be convinced, someone with power over their lives, Maggie told him he needn't worry about her. 'You don't need to explain. I'm just . . .'

But her sentence trailed away. The boy was the same height as his mother, and they were both stick thin, but there was more colour in his face, and next to her sunken eyes his shone large and luminous against the chestnut brown of his skin. His front teeth were slightly crooked but no bar to the fact he was a strikingly beautiful-looking boy.

'I'm just here to help,' Maggie finished. 'I'm a friend of Iris's, that's all.'

He hauled his mother up from the floor, and Maggie followed them back into the kitchen, where he propped Kayla into a chair.

'We'll be right,' he said.

Kayla formed a last smile on her lips before falling asleep in the chair, a sliver of dribble sparkling at the corner of her open mouth. The boy took her wrist and felt her pulse, nodded. 'She'll just sleep a while,' he said with the despairing confidence of a physician treating a terminally ill patient. 'That's all she needs.'

As though the animal had waited for the all-clear, the dog now made its entry, and immediately lifted its leg against the leg of the chair in which Kayla slept.

'Aw, hell!' Too late, Tyson scooped up the dog and ran it out to the back courtyard. When he came back in, Maggie was kneeling on the floor, wiping the chair leg with a paper towel.

'I'm Maggie,' she said.

The boy nodded.

'I did a painting of your nan.'

'Yeah, she told me.'

'And I wanted to talk to you. That's why I came here in the first place.'

'Yeah, she told me that too. But she already got me the dog.'

'He is a lovely dog.'

'Except she's pissing all over the place. I can't let her inside. I gotta train her somehow.'

'I am sorry about the other one, the other dog.'

He nodded. 'Yeah, I heard.'

'I am very sorry about that, about what happened that day.' After all this time the words sounded abstract and hollow, but on hearing them Tyson looked at her more closely, curious.

'What did you hear about it?' he asked.

'I spoke to the ambulance officer.'

He nodded, looked away. 'So you know. He told you what happened.'

Not sure what he meant, Maggie cast her mind back to the conversation, and remembered how it ended. 'You mean about kicking the car?'

Still looking down at his feet: 'I knew that was why you came.'

Maggie shook her head, told him it wasn't the reason, but the boy wasn't listening. She reached out and took his arm. 'That isn't why, Tyson. I don't care about the car . . . Do you hear me? I don't care about the car one bit.'

He looked down at the hand on his arm, then back at Maggie. 'I just wanted someone to help, that was all. I didn't mean to kick it. I didn't mean nothing.' He looked at her then, as though trying to gauge whether she believed him, as though it mattered. 'No one would help,' he said. 'No one helped.'

Maggie searched her mind for an answer to that, for some kind of assurance that it wouldn't be that way again. 'Your nan . . .'

Shaking his head, his eyes filled with worry as he turned to gesture to his mother. 'Nan reckons Mum's blood's full of maggots. I heard her say it. She said she'd be better off locked up.'

And there it was, the fear of the boy laid bare. 'She doesn't want that,' Maggie said. 'It's the drugs; she just sees what they're doing, like you do.'

He shrugged. They were words he had heard before. Kayla started coughing and he took her a glass of water and made her take a sip, then helped her up and took her down the hall to the couch in the living room. When he came back, he appeared stronger in his mother's absence. 'You finished the painting?'

Maggie nodded. 'I brought it today. Do you want to see it?' She didn't wait for an answer, but pulled the painting out again and laid it on the bench. Tyson stared at it a while but his eyes gave no hint as to his judgment.

'She should put it up on the wall here in the kitchen,' he said finally. 'So everyone can see it. It might stop 'em nicking stuff, with her eyes on 'em like that.'

For a while he didn't say anything, just stared and nodded. In the painting there were two images, both of Iris, one in the foreground against a wall made of shells and stones, and the other walking in the distance along a road. 'It's weird, how you got her,' he said, looking up now at Maggie.

'Well, I tried. There is a lot to get when it comes to your nan.'

His eyes softened. 'Yep . . .' He stopped there, though he clearly had something more to say.

'What is it?' Maggie asked.

'You worked it out,' he said. 'Her secret.' He waited for Maggie to ask what he meant, then pointed to the painting, to the image of the woman on the road. 'She can be there—' and then to the foreground, against the wall '—and she can be here.'

'I'm sorry, Tyson, I still don't understand.'

'I thought you did.' He didn't look disappointed that he had to explain, but excited, like a small child with a story to tell, and for a moment she could see it, the child that he had been, and the child that he still was. 'Someone's sitting and talking with Nan in Dubbo, then next minute you see her walking across the street in Mount Druitt. You just got to ask where she's been and soon enough you work out there's no other way she could've done it.'

'Done what?'

The boy hesitated. 'It isn't just me that's worked it out. I heard other people around here say it.' Maggie didn't prod; she waited until he spoke again, more a whisper. 'She can be in two places.'

In the corner of the next room his mother was slumped on the couch, the drool having made its way down the side of her face and caked now into a white trail, but in his mind the boy was a world away, a world in which anything was possible, a world in which selfless souls travelled across space with magical powers . . . Maggie turned away but the boy saw the tears in her eyes.

'I'm not crazy or anything,' he said.

'No, it isn't crazy, not at all.'

'So you believe me.'

'Yes, I do.' She looked him in the eye. 'I believe you.'

'That's good,' he said. 'I don't tell many people that.'

'Thank you, then,' she said. 'I am glad to know it.'

When Maggie went to leave, she again asked about Kayla, if there was anything she could do. The boy shook his head. 'She's hooked up with a new guy. He's coming to get her.'

'Are you going with them?'

'Nah. He doesn't want me around. Suits me alright.'

And as she turned to leave: 'Hey, Maggie . . .'

'Yes?'

'Nothing, don't worry.'

'What is it?'

'Just something Aunty Peg said.'

'What was that?'

The eyes shone bright when he smiled. 'She said you might get me some shoes.'

It wasn't until she was almost home that she had moved backwards in time from the boy to his mother; it wasn't until then, sitting in the car outside her house with a pounding heart that the words returned to her.

You the judge's wife . . .

So what you people trading now?

On the morning news there was a story about the link between a ten-year-old girl's abduction and her photos being tagged on Facebook. Laini wanted him to turn it off.

'No photos of Finn on your blog, okay, babe?' Ethan said.

'Of course not,' she snapped. 'I'm not stupid.'

He didn't need to say anything else and fuck knows why he did: 'I mean the dog's fine, just not Finn.'

She finished her mouthful. 'How do you know there's photos of the dog on there?'

He shrugged. 'I saw them when I looked that time.'

But she was straight onto it. 'No, you didn't. I only put them up a month ago.'

He put his hands up. Caught. 'So shoot me, I took another look. Can't I be interested? I mean since the publisher's come on board . . .'

She smiled. 'Sure, but why not tell me?'

'I'm telling you now. It looks great. The book will smash it.'

The conversation was over, but still she looked at him across the table, a bemused expression in her eyes, and then the thought: *Would she recognise me?* In his head he could see it, her mind ticking, and the dots beginning to join . . . *He reads it. He reads the comments.* How far a jump was it to the possibility he had made a comment? Of course, he always deleted his browsing history (he made double sure of it again after she went upstairs), but still he hadn't been able to get those damn dots out of his head all day.

Now it was late lunch in the hotel room, and he was still doing his best as he thrashed it out with Sally in the shower and on the bathroom floor, and that was all good (better than good), until it happened—the afterglow cut short by an event to which he would react—an action and a reaction with the potential to bring the whole hoopla crumbling down into an ashy heap.

Lately he had heard the idiom repeated too many times. It must have been on an office calendar, or one of those Google quotes of the day—Max was the last one to give it voice, yesterday afternoon as he sipped his sencha tea: It isn't what happens to you—so it went—it is how you react. 'You heard it from me,' Max said, and Ethan smiled back, while mentally in a single, swift motion he reached across the tearoom table and snapped Max's birdlike neck.

With her ecstatic scream echoing against the cold tiles, Sally sank her nails into Ethan's arse, the shot of pain sending his climax skywards, and for a moment that was all it was, a blissful blend of pain and pleasure . . . just a moment, before it was blasted away as she ran her hand over the broken skin and said it—after a single action, a single word: 'Oops.'

All afternoon, Ethan had been forming an explanation in his mind as to what lay behind his reaction. His reaction: a chemical combustion, or, more aptly, a brother to the neuronal activation that had preceded it by only minutes; he could see in his mind one of those diagrams with the feeder bubbles joined by transmitters and in the centre, the big box, the big bang—the exothermic, the ejaculatory response.

'Oops,' she said, and he reached back to feel for himself, five little crescent welts.

The feeder bubbles, with the benefit of hindsight, all on the back of his blunder with the blog.

The marks, the position of the marks, there was no way to explain it to Laini—fingernails at the centre of his right buttock—and there was little chance of concealment. (Behind this, the discarded possibilities: a tryst with the neighbour's cat, a pyjamas comeback . . . discarded because he had never been near the fucking cat, and they were naked people; they slept naked, they went to the fridge naked . . .)

In the seconds that followed her short and painfully inadequate expression of regret, Ethan felt the odds stack against him. Odds-on chance, the game was up . . . It was the end.

And then: the end of what? Out of that bubble, two feeders.

First, the end of Sally . . . There she was, Sally, stone-faced in her frilled blouse, packing up her desk.

And last, the end of marriage. Laini and her hot, phlegmy tears.

'Oops.'

The reaction.

He closed his eyes and began to count again, and again the feathered darkness was forming, the screeching menace in his brain, because something was being taken from him . . . What Ethan did then, worst of all: he clenched his fist. There he was, teeth gritted, clenching his fist to contain the instinct, the instinct to inflict pain. In all his life, in all the fury, it had never entered his mind, not a woman . . .

And at that very moment, the very woman reached up and put her hand on the side of his face.

He didn't move, but permitted the instinct to flow into his words: 'Don't touch me.' And a second later, making sure she was looking back at him, dead straight in the eye. 'Don't fucking touch me. Not ever . . . again.'

He pulled himself up off the floor and got dressed. As he opened the door to leave, Sally stepped in front of it. 'Ethan, stop . . . Stop this. It's me here. I know you, and I know what's happening here.'

She waited, but he didn't move or respond. As she spoke the next words, her mouth hardened. 'You are having some kind of breakdown.'

Finally, a minute's silence. She stepped back, and Ethan walked out the door.

Strike four: a partner fucking a junior solicitor.

The end of it all.

Martin was sipping tea at the kitchen table when Maggie entered.

As was now his way, he took continuous sips until the cup was finished. Once something was put down, it was too often forgotten. Better to keep it in his hands, like his camera. Same principle.

He smiled up at her and didn't notice that she didn't smile back. 'Ah, that was good,' he said when he was finished. 'I could almost have another. How about I make us both one?'

She watched him as he pulled the milk from the fridge and the sugar and tea bags from the cupboard and returned everything to its rightful place. The wires, it seemed, were connected. There was no reason to wait.

'Thanks,' she said, taking the tea—just how she liked it, the lemon sliced thin. 'I went to Iris's today.'

He nodded. 'Up on the hill.'

'Yes. Up on the hill.'

'The old woman there up on the hill.'

He had taken to repeating words or phrases when he liked the sound of them. With Finny, it was the bear hunt: 'Swishy, swashy, swishy, swashy . . .' She waited to see that he was finished.

'Yes,' she continued, 'but she wasn't there today. Someone else was though. A woman named Kayla.'

What Maggie expected in response was a glimmer of recognition and then a failure of memory (or at least a claim to it), but she got more than that, much more. With Martin's reply there began one of the most difficult conversations of her life.

'Tell me what you know,' he said, matter-of-fact. 'I'll work out what is relevant.' And when he saw that Maggie hesitated, he continued as though he were turning now to a professional matter: 'There is no need for you to filter it. Please, take a seat.'

Maggie looked back at him. Though his mind had jumbled the context, there was not a skerrick of confusion on his face, and though her instinct was to correct him, to remind him what the pieces were and how they fitted in, she had the sense that in front of her now was a window, and behind that window there was the truth. All she had to do was reach inside and take it.

She sat down.

'Very well,' she said, now sorting through the facts in her mind to find the shortest route. 'Rodney is Iris's son. Rodney is in prison. His partner is Kayla, and their son is Tyson.'

At this Martin shook his head. 'No, no, I don't know about the son, not yet. Don't jump around. Get to the charges. What are the charges?'

Cautious of treading in a minefield, Maggie slowed. 'They were . . . they *are* robbery charges.' Martin nodded, waved his hand in a circle to direct her to continue, which she did.

'There are a number of them, but one is very serious. A boy was stabbed.'

'But Rodney is granted bail.'

'Yes, he is the only one to get bail.'

'And that's why they want to keep the lawyer. They have faith in him.'

With his use of the present tense and now the third person, again her instinct was to correct him, but it seemed already they had a pact, that this was the way it would be told: this way, or not at all. 'Yes, that's right,' she said. 'So he stays in it. He remains in the matter.'

'A messy business,' Martin said.

'Yes, the stabbing—though it wasn't Rodney with the knife.'

Martin shook his head dismissively. 'Please! Not the stabbing. If you want my help with this, you must stop jumping around it . . . Not the stabbing. The payment of fees, get to that.'

Not knowing what it was she was meant to get to or how she was meant to get there, Maggie felt certain of only one thing: that Martin, finally, had something to tell. She searched her mind, her memory of everything Iris had said, about the plea bargain and the sentence, but nothing about fees. And then the words returned to her again, not the words of Iris, but of Kayla. *What are you people trading now?*

'You were a Queen's Counsel.' She forgot the rules, the tense, the pretence. 'You didn't do Legal Aid matters—you were barely doing any more crime. Legal Aid wouldn't pay your fees.'

He allowed it. He nodded. Maggie was now asking the questions.

'You did the bail application pro bono.'

He nodded again.

'But the rest of it . . .'

'There was to be a trial . . . It was a messy business.' There he stopped and looked at the empty cup on the table. 'Did we have our tea?'

'Go on, Martin.'

'I told you, Maggie: ask someone else.'

Maggie paused, as one with a last chance to turn back. 'No, Martin,' she said. 'There is no one else. You remember this, and you can tell me.'

He shook his head. His eyes widened, the flash of a cornered animal. If she pushed, it would scuttle away . . . 'Let me keep going,' she said. 'I will tell you what I know, what I know about Kayla. I know that she is an addict. And I know that she lives in Redfern, but that she used to live up on the hill in La Perouse. When you acted for Rodney, that is where she lived.'

'Is that all?'

'There is one more thing, something she said.'

He waited.

'She asked me if I was the judge's wife, and when I said yes she began to laugh. And then she asked me what we were trading; she said: "What are you people trading now?"'

Martin listened carefully, nodding his head long after she had finished speaking. 'I see. Is that all?'

'Yes. Do you know what she meant?'

'No, no,' he said. 'That is not the place to start.' He tapped his forehead and looked down at the floor. 'Where to start . . .'

It was a moment before she realised he wasn't thinking out loud, but asking her a question—that he was playing witness, and would not proceed unless prompted.

'Start when you met Kayla.'

'Yes, that is best.' He seemed almost grateful. 'I saw her at court with the rest of them, just briefly. I didn't recognise her when I saw her again.' He stopped, waited for the next question to come.

'Where was that?' she asked.

'In a bar, in Surry Hills.'

'And you didn't recognise her.'

'No, not at first. The face was familiar, but no.'

'But you talked to her?'

'She approached me, and I remembered then seeing her at court.'

'What did she want?'

He looked up. 'I don't know what was in her mind. You can't ask me that.'

'Sorry,' she said. 'What did she say?'

'At the bar?'

'Yes, at the bar.'

'She said she was Rodney's girlfriend. I didn't want to talk to her, but she sat down with her friend. They wore tiny skirts. I soon left.' And he repeated. 'I didn't want to talk to her.'

Again he had reached a point where unless prodded he would go no further—as though there were still a chance that could be the end of the story.

'One wanted to help, you know . . .' he said, the digression made in earnest. 'The fellow wasn't a bad sort.'

'You mean Rodney?'

'Yes, Rodney.'

'You told me that before. You said he was just mixing with the wrong people.'

'Yes, I said that. And that is true, that is—and of course the drugs had a hold of him . . . But there was another thing: he was scared of something, like he was being chased. It was as though he'd had a glimpse of what was to come, if you believe that sort of thing. One wanted to help. One hoped one could.'

'And you did, you got him bail.'

'Yes, and after he got bail he was alright for a little while, but he stopped reporting to the police and they picked him up pinching batteries or something like that. The matter had been passed on to someone else by then, one of the public defenders. But the family thought I was some sort of magician . . . The irony was that as a lawyer I'd never felt more powerless.'

'But you took it up again, and you got him a good deal.'

'Well, yes. Good in that he ended up with two years instead of four, but either way the die was cast, wasn't it? I knew he'd be in and out then, just as he knew . . . And we were right, weren't we? You tell me he's in prison now.'

She pulled him back. 'What about Kayla?'

He went to speak, but stopped, looked her in the eye. 'It is ordinary, Maggie, very ordinary. The truth is more ordinary than you ever thought it could be.' A last look: in it there was something pleading, but in the way she returned it there was nothing permissive. All that was left was for him to go on.

Martin was in chambers after a few too many at Friday night drinks. 'And she turned up—Kayla. It was just after he'd breached his bail. Someone let her in, brought her into my room. She said she had something to tell me about the case. I told her another barrister was looking after it, but she said he didn't want another barrister, and they could pay me; they'd find a way. I agreed to take it, I told her I'd do it without a fee—I'm sure I told her that—and she left.

'It was just chance—I thought it was—when I saw her again, later that night, in that same bar in Surry Hills. Rodney was back inside, she said . . .'

'You said that. I know that. What happened then?'

'His mother gave evidence at the sentence. She said he had seen terrible things . . .'

'Not in court, Martin—the bar in Surry Hills. What happened there, with Kayla?'

'She started crying.'

'Why was she crying?'

'She hadn't any money, her purse had been stolen, I think that is what she said. She had no money to get home. We went outside to the street so I could put her in a taxi and pay for it, but it was raining and there weren't any taxis, so we went to my car, and we drove . . .'

'Up the hill.'

'Yes, up the hill.'

'Into that street . . .'

'Yes, that street. There was a house with a yellow door.'

'And you went inside.'

Told simply, it sounded like a story from a children's book.

'The mattress was leaning up against the wall because the roof leaked,' he said, and shaking his head: 'She was such a skinny thing . . .' He stopped there, jolted back into the present. 'I don't seek to explain. I don't pretend I can. Not my part in it, anyway. As to the girl's, you have surely guessed it already. In any event, the postscript will explain.'

And he completed the story.

The end was this: the week after Martin drove up the hill and had sex with his client's girlfriend, the matter was listed for mention. Kayla was sitting in the back row of the courtroom. From the dock Rodney pointed her out to Martin and asked if he had talked to her about his fees. 'That's Kayla, my missus,' he said. 'She's the one who's gonna make sure you get paid.'

Outside the courtroom Martin was talking to the prosecutor and Kayla walked up to him and shook his hand and introduced him to a cousin as Rodney's lawyer: 'the best that money can buy'. They never spoke again.

'And there we have it. It seemed without knowing it I had received payment for services rendered.'

Martin went to rise from his chair but sat back down again. 'You know, I thought about giving it all up then. After what had happened, and day after day putting on the wig and the gown like a galah. I felt like such a terrible fraud . . . I didn't think I could keep it up. But then, of course, the matter was taken out of my hands.'

Maggie stared blankly.

'I was appointed a couple of months later,' he said. 'That was the year I became a judge.'

'So why did you go back up there?' Maggie asked.

He said he didn't know; he didn't remember. He said there was nothing more to tell. And then he said: 'She was the last.'

It took a moment for the words to settle. Again, what Maggie had expected of this conversation and what she got were two very different things.

Martin did not look at her, but at the empty cup in front of him, which he began now to move in circles, slowly at first, then in a sudden motion he picked it up and turned it upside down on the table, like he was trying to catch a bug. She didn't stop him. She watched the dribble of milky tea run over the edge of the table onto the floor.

Martin watched too, then he turned away from it towards the empty seat at the table, and nodding his head in agreement with a silent shadow: 'The worst till last,' he said. 'I never did go for skin and bone.'

And he walked out of the kitchen, down the hall and into their room, where he closed the door behind him.

Maggie didn't move from the table.

She sat with the missing piece—or the *pieces*—until the information began to trickle down, drip by drip, not as something toxic or fatal, but as something stale and, yes, ordinary. What it left her with was the feeling she had eaten something that she shouldn't have. To relieve it she poured a thumbnail of scotch, looked into the glass and downed it in one before pouring another.

The pieces. The house up on the hill with the yellow door . . . He had been revisiting the scene. She remembered back now to the first time Martin had driven and got lost and called her from the service station. Then the day he hit the dog, the day of his stroke.

And she remembered the year he had spoken of today, the year he was made a judge. Maggie had been commissioned for a public work and was painting night and day all through the winter. She remembered his moods and his drinking, how some nights she'd look up and see him standing at the door to her studio and staring down at her. Sometimes he turned away without saying a word; when he did speak, she wished he hadn't:

'How long have you been there?' she asked one night.

He was holding on to the door. 'All these symbols of yours—this secret code . . . I'm never meant to get it, am I?' And then: 'Why don't you ever paint something erotic?' More belligerent than curious, more accusation than question.

'Would it help?' she asked.

He shook his head as he turned, his answer trailing behind him: 'I don't know.'

She let herself believe him when he said it was about work. If New York had been about stepping outside his comfort zone, it seemed to Maggie that the rest of his working life had been lived with a view to staying inside it. She went on with her painting, that night and the weeks that followed, refusing to be dragged down with him. (It was in October that she started to swim her daily laps.) Then the appointment to the bench, a raft thrown to a drowning man. A purgation . . . a fresh start.

What haunted him now, Maggie thought, staring into the glass in her hand, was not the infidelity but the insult, the assault on his manhood. *Payment for services rendered . . .* This morning she had heard how the woman slumped in the doorway laughed at the memory, and wondered if Martin had heard that same terrible sound.

The woman in the doorway: there was one more question in Maggie's mind. Her grey skin and sunken eyes must have made her look older than her years, but Maggie could see that even now she was still young. Ten years ago when Martin drove her up the hill and went into her house, how old was she then?

With the drink in hand, she opened the bedroom door, but found him fast asleep and strewn across the bed, mouth agape and palms out to the side. Even then, he did not look weak; he was not weak. Weakness was no explanation. To remain faithful to her there had been no internal fight that had been lost. It was his want and his way.

And the others? She remembered now the night Annie had been upset at the cocktail party; Maggie had suspected she had seen something, something Martin had done with one of the drunken wives, and Maggie had let herself believe his explanation.

Then Sonia Kirby and the arse that was bruised like a peach . . .

She stepped closer and studied his sleeping face as she sipped her drink, measuring the distance between his eyes and between his mouth and nose, assessing its proportions, looking down as though she were seeing it for the first time—without attachment. His mouth closed, and from time to time, his eyelids quivered and she wondered what projections his mind was making beneath them, what story was being told to make sense of the one that had just now ended.

When she had finished her second drink, Maggie walked outside into a blustery afternoon and got into Martin's car. When she arrived at La Perouse she was relieved to find that her friend was at home.

Maggie untied the blue string and pulled the portrait from its sleeve.

'Should I look then?' Iris asked.

'Please.' Maggie slid it closer and Iris looked down at the painting for the first time. Maggie watched as her eyes moved over the page.

'My mum always said I had a big head,' she said finally.

Maggie laughed.

The old woman stared down a while, expressionless, then squinted as though to look closer. Shaking her head, she smiled and looked up at the artist. Her eyes welled with tears. 'I ain't ever seen anyone do that in a painting,' she said. 'I don't know how you done that . . .' And when she saw that Maggie was blinking back tears of her own, she pulled her chair closer to the table and placed both hands on her forearm. 'You seen me, Maggie, these last months sitting up there in my room; it's right here on the page, that big head right there,' she said. 'And I seen you too. I don't pretend to know what it is that's been chasing you all this time, and I don't ask. But I reckon now you been ducking it for too long. I reckon it's time you let it catch up . . . That's all I'll say.'

She looked down at the painting again. 'What's the rocks for then?' In the bottom corner of the painting, against the wall made of stones and shells, was an outcrop of rocks.

'There's something hidden,' Maggie answered. 'You have to find it.' She smiled. 'I call it *The Lost Cat.*'

The old woman smiled with her. 'It's a shame your pigeon lady ain't here to see it.'

'It's enough that you are, Iris. It is more than enough.'

~

Across the park the next morning, Maggie stepped over the platform of rock, grateful the sea was calm and the pool empty. The temperature had dropped the last few days, unseasonably for December; yesterday it was down to seventeen. Raising her arms above her head, her body remembered it and rebelled, the lungs compressing to strangle the oxygen mid-breath even before she hit the ice-cold water. For the full length of the first lap she repeated an underwater curse against the cold with every outstretched arm, then, as she turned into the second, came the relief of numbness, and halfway back there it was: the rhythm in her stroke. As she turned about a second time and a third, her mind functioned only to recognise her senses, the taste of salt, the flow of blood, the glimpse of sky. The events of yesterday, her mind permitted them only fleeting space. Today the sea was calm; other days the waves crashed over the wall and she swallowed the water to battle them. It took more from her, more of her will. But not today; today, once she had adjusted to the cold, it let her be. Today there were moments as Maggie completed her thirty laps that she felt almost graceful.

As she walked back to the house the cockatoos took flight. Heading north, but not far, she thought, and not for long, certain it was the same flock that returned daily through the winter.

In her studio, Maggie picked out some fresh paper, and started sketching, just as she had done as a child after taking the photograph from Martin's mother's kitchen, and again when she had come home from New York. At first the sleeping man: seven sketches with his eyes closed. She opened them gradually, moved through pages of half-open eyes, to the moment when the world was at last perceived again, anew, the moment of revelation: Martin staring into the vast and inglorious unknown.

Over the days that followed Maggie worked in her studio, morning till night; it was the shortest period in which she had ever finished a picture. Three days. And there it was, completed but not delivered, the portrait that Martin had always wanted, with a secret code all of its own.

'What are you working on?' he asked her, for over those days she had barely emerged from her studio.

It was not out of spite that she did not tell him or let him see it. The act of withholding was an act of healing. Eventually she would have showed him, she later thought. Had he lived longer, on a chosen day she would have sat him down in the studio and let him see his final portrait.

Martin heard Maggie open the door to their bedroom and then close it again.

The place he went to then was not the place he wanted to be. As it turned out, he had no say in it; it was the same unseen force that had led him there months ago, up the hill and to the house with the yellow door. *The undercurrent* . . .

Now he understood. This was the place it had been taking him all along.

They are alone inside her house. Outside it rains.

Ask yourself, Martin: What are you doing here?

It isn't a place he would usually take them. He can't dim the light because there is no light—there is no globe—but still he flicks the switch back and forth as his eyes adjust to the murky dark.

'Why is the mattress against the wall?' he asks the girl.

''Cause the roof leaks.'

'You live here alone?'

'With Rodney—like I told you: I'm his missus.'

'You look too young to be anybody's missus.'

She said she was old enough to be anything she wanted to be. 'You want some speed?'

He laughed. 'I haven't had speed in a long, long time.'

There is a moment then, after he has pushed the mattress down onto the floor, when he takes her tiny wrists in his hands and he wonders what is in it for her.

'That's a fancy watch,' she says, and he knows then she's never had a man like him in her house, never had a man like him at all.

He wishes he'd worn a fake one so he could give it to her.

'You're real strong,' she says.

Afterwards, streetlight through the window casts a line across the bubbling plaster on the ceiling and the darker patch of mould. He is staring up at it and cursing the drugs: it was the speed that had messed with him . . . In the end he'd given up on trying to come. But it is only when the first drop of rain hits the edge of the mattress that he realises his real mistake, the reason why this is different from the rest of them—all the way back to the woman at the bar the night of Maggie's big award. (Something about that whole hoopla had made him want to jump off a cliff, and jump off the cliff he did.) After that there were others like her, women he had never met and would never meet again (crimes without trace), but others too, those who had their own reasons to keep a secret—because they were married (Sonia always said it was safest to stick it to the other judges' wives), or in the case of dear Annie because she knew Maggie, because she loved Maggie, and she couldn't bear for her to know.

Martin and Annie: neither had planned it, both had regretted it. She was having a horrid time with Jack and Martin had given her comfort, and then for four months they had been the most careful of all: a hotel room, and only once in a while. Then, like the idiot he was, he drank too much at the cocktail party and grabbed her outside the bathroom, grabbed and wouldn't let go . . . She cried and said that Maggie was her best friend in the world. Of course, she was right, her eyes steady and clear: 'We are terrible people.'

And then: 'Why do you do this, Martin?'

As for the girl lying next to him, Martin thought as he waited for the sound of the next drop on the mattress, this was different; this would be a big story (a Queen's Counsel in my bed, the Rolex . . .), a story she could tell to anyone who cared to listen. He turned to her, watched her as she slept. Too young, he thought, and worse, worst of all, she might want him to come back; Christ knew with these young ones . . . He started framing the conversation, the directions he would give her when he shook her gently out of sleep. He would keep it vague but authoritative in a paternal kind of way, how it would be best if this was all forgotten . . . He reached across to touch her shoulder, and just as his hand made contact, there was a sound in the next room. Her eyes opened. The sound was a cry.

In a room down the hall behind a door that had been closed . . . 'Hush, Tyson,' she whispered. Martin got a glimpse of the baby sitting up in a cot (the grounds of the bail application coming back to him: Rodney had a son)—just a glimpse before Kayla closed the door again, and before he had the chance to say a word, she had said it all.

'You should go home now, Martin.' The voice was different from the one that an hour earlier had told him he was strong; the voice was different, and the message. 'We are done here.'

Elsewhere, under a faraway sky, it was a different time of day.

The earthmover lunged forwards and the birds screeched as they fled from the walnut trees. There were still posters on the surrounding walls protesting what was about to be done, the demolition of a community garden to make way for more buildings. The driver looked at what was in front of him, the staked vines and cornstalks, and thought in his mind, *It is a shame.* He knew downtown kids who used to play here and take cucumbers home from the garden. He was just glad the people had stopped with their pickets so he could get his job done, which he did, levelling the entire block within an hour and fifteen minutes. The last to go was the big one in the centre, the Chinese Empress tree.

'Greetings,' he says, 'my name is Dave . . .'

And he laughs. It is not the first visit, but the last. He is sitting at the window by his friend's hospice bed and with the weight inside even then Martin knows he will never feel for another friend the love that he feels in this moment. Where once the lesions had raged there are now flakes of skin like silver scales, and beneath the surface, a maze of capillaries. With the pale light falling across his face, Dave's skin is luminescent, like the venation in the wing of an insect.

'The circles will bump into the building,' he says, 'and the buildings will come down. Waves of energy will seep through the city, through the whole fucking world. It is everything . . . You feel that, Marty?'

He nods then, as he nodded when they were back in the garden between the tenements, and then, as now, he wishes that he understood.

Ethan felt around for the light switch to the basement before he remembered that it wasn't inside the door (as logic might dictate) but at the bottom of the stairs.

Just a couple of steps down and he could smell it, the treasured dirt, the musty gold of a childhood tomb. For an instant he remembered the rush when he and his schoolfriends closed the door behind them, the possibilities . . . Perhaps it was then that he overstepped, in a surge to recapture his youth: overstepped and failed to regain his balance, stumbling forwards and swiping the stand of garden tools before landing on the stone floor on outstretched hands and one knee, the other foot grounded with a straight leg, like a sprinter at the start of a race—in which position he remained to assess his injury (inconsequential) and, as the objects around him emerged out of darkness, to ruminate briefly on how the fall slotted into the week's trajectory.

Somehow, even in those few moments before the light came on, Ethan sensed there was more to it than a slump from bad to worse. Even in the dark of the basement, Ethan maintained a flickering faith in his ability to come back from the brink.

When he'd returned to the office after the hotel yesterday, Sally had left for the day, and this morning she had called in sick. Ethan had kept his lunchtime appointment with the counsellor and had talked about his frustration with his accountant's file management system. He had left early to get home so he could surprise Finn by picking him up from skipping training. The only thought he had allowed himself in relation to Sally was to plot her exit, assess the minimum amount of time after which she could hand in her resignation without raising suspicion. There would have to be another job offer, but that shouldn't be a problem, not with a résumé like Sally's and a rock-solid reference from the firm.

Now it was a Wednesday dinner at Mum and Dad's, and the wheel kept spinning . . . The honey cake was the best he could remember, but the dinner hadn't ended well, no argument there, and through no one's fault but his own.

After his second piece of cake Finn left the table, giving Laini the opportunity to tell Maggie about his trouble at school.

'Finnegan threw a rock at a boy and it hit him in the head, just missed his eye. A dozen kids saw it and said it came out of nowhere; the boy was just playing handball with his friends.'

'Oh, I don't believe that,' Maggie said. 'I just don't believe that.'

'The school is making a big deal of it,' Ethan said. 'It's like he planted a fucking bomb in the toilet.'

'What did Finny say?'

Ethan smiled. 'You know what he said? He said the boy's a little criminal.'

Throughout the conversation Martin had been staring down

at the glass in his hand, a world away, but on hearing Ethan's last words, he suddenly looked up. 'Who is a little criminal?'

Laini repeated the story. When she had finished, Martin shook his head and said firmly, knowingly, 'There is a back story to this.'

When Laini asked him how he could be so sure, his response was short and final: 'Because in my experience, there always is.' And without taking further questions, he excused himself so that he could find Finnegan to start their game of UNO.

'Christ, Mum, this must be a nightmare for you,' Ethan said once his father had left the room. It was only then he saw how tired she looked, almost frail. 'Are you okay?'

'Yes, I'm fine.' She rubbed the papery skin around her eyes. 'It's been a hard day, that's all.'

Laini asked if she was working on a portrait. 'I just finished something. It is being framed.'

'A commission?'

'Of sorts,' she said, then changed the subject. 'How is work, darling?'

'It's okay. I'm jumping through their hoops.'

'What sort of hoops?'

'Oh, you know—any kind, any shape . . .' Tonight Laini was driving, so he'd had more to drink than usual. That was the only way he could explain how he let the next sentence dribble from his lips. 'Then I go see my midget counsellor and tell her when I stopped wetting the bed . . .'

Mother and wife, one over the other with a demand for particulars: What was he talking about? What counsellor?

In the name of diplomacy, he answered the wife first. 'I told you, babe, I've been having a crap time. That was what was crap about it.' And to his mother: 'Like I said, it's just a hoop. The managing partner set it up. I don't really want to go into it.'

Laini said that was his problem: he never did; that was why they wanted him to see a counsellor . . . 'Blood out of a fucking stone, I swear.'

The best he could muster: 'There isn't much to tell, alright? I've forgotten how to say hello to people in elevators. Apparently there is an art to that.' He was hoping to leave it there but when Laini's face started to blotch up he sensed a better idea would be to try to explain. 'Max says I am not nice to people. And he wants me to see a counsellor to work out why. It's alright. It's just stress. I'll sort it out.'

'Sweetheart,' Maggie said quietly, 'you need to listen. You really need to listen.' She looked worried now. He didn't mean to do that, make things harder.

'Please don't worry, Mum. We'll take a holiday. I promise! Okay, leave it.' And to Laini: 'Please, babe, I'll talk to you later, I will. Let's just leave it now.' He put his arm around her and gave her a kiss on the forehead. 'Let's book Fiji.'

Laini served herself another helping of cabbage salad as he talked about the best month to go. When he was done, Maggie looked from her plate to her glass, then to each of their faces: 'I have something to tell you,' she said.

It was the night, it seemed, to lay it all out on the table.

'I went to see Iris again today, this afternoon.'

'Oh, you are good, Maggie,' Laini said. 'With all you've got on.'

Maggie's smile was patient. 'I don't go to see Iris because I am good. I go because she is my friend.' She loaded a fork then left it resting on the plate. 'When you asked before about the portrait, the answer is that I was painting Iris.'

There was silence. Ethan poured himself another glass of wine.

'Sorry,' Laini stepped in. 'I didn't mean to . . .'

'No, I know you didn't. I just want you to understand she is not my charity case.'

Maggie had been keeping up the visits. Every so often she would tell them something about Iris, something she'd said or something that'd happened over at her place. Ethan had tried to see it Maggie's way: she was a bleeding heart and felt bad about the dog, fair enough. Once she took over paints and canvases for some kids. In the context of what was going on with Marty, the visits got Maggie out of the house, and they made her feel good. No harm done, he'd told himself, and it wasn't as though they were going to continue ad infinitum . . . But somehow these people kept conning her into going back. And now the portrait: odds on it would end up winning a bloody prize and be worth fifty grand and then some. Did she really think the old lady would hang on to it then? Someone had to start asking the questions.

'So I'm guessing there's no commission on the painting,' Ethan said, 'and I don't remember you saying she put up an argument about taking any of those art supplies.'

'Iris has had eleven children in her care, Ethan. She was in no position to argue.'

'I think it was lovely—a lovely thing to do,' Laini said. 'They need all the help they can get.'

Maggie nodded. 'I quite agree.' And again, a pause as she looked from plate to glass, then to Ethan. 'So I drove over today in Martin's car . . . And I left it there, as a gift.'

'What, the painting?'

'No, not the painting.'

Ethan leant forwards so that his face was just inches away from hers but in spite of it—or *to* spite it—Maggie held his gaze. 'The car. Tomorrow I'll get the papers to transfer it legally.'

The car.

'It isn't worth that much,' she went on. 'You've always said it was a heap. We have no need of it. Dad can't drive it anymore . . .'

The table went silent, and in the silence, he could feel it shift: this was no longer a story about what was happening to his mother, but part of the week's plan, part of a week gone wrong.

'That is a fucking cracker, that is,' he said softly, but still felt better for saying it, like he was warming up, and with that giddy warm feeling spreading into his face, he slapped the table and cupped his head with the same hand and, with eyes half closed, he began to paint the ugly picture as he saw it—not a portrait but a landscape of syringes and welfare checks and, in the middle of it, his mother, duped by her white guilt into giving away her possessions. 'From the day you turned up at her door, this is what they've been working at . . . It would've been quicker if they'd just smashed the window and hotwired the fucking thing.'

Throughout, Maggie remained calm, and only when he started to slow down did she interject to ask if he was finished.

'No, I don't think so.'

'Can I speak?'

'Go ahead.'

'*These people*, as you call them . . . Please, Ethan, look at me.'

He looked.

'*These people* have asked me for nothing beyond a pair of shoes. Iris travels for miles around the state—there isn't a week she isn't getting herself to a funeral or a bedside or a new baby. She is seventy-four years old and she has chronic diabetes; she catches trains and buses and her legs swell up like water balloons . . .'

'Okay, Mum, that's all well and tragic, but I'll tell you what will happen now.' Ethan stood up from the table with his fork in his hand and heat rising into his face, not the warm giddy kind. 'They'll sell the painting and the car, and you know what they'll do with the money? They'll drink it, or they'll shoot it into their arms, any way to piss it up against a fucking tree.'

As he finished, Finn appeared at the door with Marty behind him.

'What is all the shouting about?' Marty asked, on his face a misplaced smile.

'I'll let Ethan explain,' Maggie said, then turned back to her son. 'Maybe you are right in what you say, Ethan. Maybe. Or maybe Iris gets a car. In the meantime, let's see if your counsellor can work out where all this bile comes from. God knows, your mother never could.' She rose from her seat, and when Ethan tried to say more she stared him down like she did when he was twelve. And she started to clear the plates.

So, no, dinner hadn't ended well.

And rewind further back, to yesterday in the hotel room.

It isn't what happens; it is how you react. For a moment he tried to imagine the events as they happened, minus his input: action without *reaction*. There was no argument—tonight with his mother, and yesterday with Sal. It looked a whole lot better.

And here he was, in the dark basement, at the bottom of the stairs, with enough time having passed for his eyes to adjust. He let the straight knee bend to the ground and, kneeling, checked his wrists, then stood to put weight on his knees, and to brush himself off.

It was only now that he thought back to what he had said to Sal, to the way he had said it and what lay behind it . . . With distance, he hoped, with time . . .

Finally he found it, there on the wall next to the stand for the tools: the light switch.

When the room came into view, savoured memories stirred again.

This was a place he used to come as a boy, by himself and with his friends. The door was on the side path to the clothesline so they could meet without having to come into the house. They'd never locked it because there wasn't anything worth stealing, but one time he remembered someone got in there and made a mess rifling through the boxes. For Ethan and his mates it was even better after the thief had been, a better atmosphere. One day they heard a scratching sound behind boxes and they thought they were going to bust the bloke for sure, but turned out it was just a baby possum thumping its tail on dried leaves. Ethan's friend Johnny tried to pick it up (bloody moron) and got the crap scratched out of his arms. Other stuff they did in the basement was suck helium and do séances or swap shit they'd nicked. They hung a red scarf over the light and sat knee to knee on their beach towels because the floor was a dust heap, and in the trusted sandstone of the basement it was cool even on the hottest days of summer.

The room was smaller now, not just because of the passage of time but because it was filled with more boxes, many with his name on them and a year or a description. He would have to pull some of this stuff out some time, show Finn. On the ground leaning up against the wall was a framed *Star Wars* poster—Darth Vader. The glass was cracked clean down the middle of his mask, cutting his cape and his light sabre in two.

On the back wall, on the top shelf, just like Maggie had said, there was a green box. When he reached for it, the cardboard was soft and damp in his hands. He carried it down to the trestle table, imagining all he would find would be photographs ruined by time and neglect, but when he opened it he found a plastic container, and in the container, within a foolscap envelope, the photographs, layered in between sheets of paper, in perfect condition.

And just as he began to lay them out, he heard the footsteps coming down the stairs.

Ethan turned around to see his father standing over the tools strewn at the bottom of the stairs. He explained the fall, and his father stepped closer, looking at the pile on the table.

'What have you got there?' Martin asked, and without waiting for a response: 'Let's have a look, shall we?'

Ethan laid out the first four images and with his arm ushered his father in closer to the table. 'We've got to get them out of here, Dad, get them framed. I could hang them at home.'

As Martin passed over each of the images, he nodded his head. Boys screaming in the subway, a man at the end of a tunnel of light, a boy on a mattress on a fire escape. The SoHo skyline. Then he returned to the first, and picked it up in his hands.

'I need to keep this one. I sold it, you know. This lot—' he pointed to the boys on the subway '—they said, "Yeah, man, go ahead, take the photo," then they screamed like monkeys.' Martin put the photo down and looked around the basement, to the pile of boxes and the slabs of stone. 'I need a darkroom now,' he said, and with an uncertain smile and the politeness of a stranger: 'Are you someone who could help me with that?'

When Ethan did not answer him, the ageing man held his gaze. 'I'm sorry, is that why you are here? Did Maggie make the appointment?'

This room stored memories, but it could not store all of them. The cold of the basement suddenly leeched inside his bones and with it the rage of the forgotten son in a house minus a father. His mind flooded with signposts, all the reasons Martin should remember, a sea of blurred history. *Please, not this.*

Please, he wanted to scream, *don't do this.*

His father's smile faded, and Ethan could see now that his lips were trembling, like a child on the brink of tears who had found himself alone in a place that was not known.

When the words came, there was no rage. Ethan's voice was weak. 'I can't see why not . . . I'll ask Mum.'

And just as quickly as Martin had lost his place he seemed to find it again in a flash of recognition, as though he were just now opening a door to greet him. 'You look so worried, Finny,' he said. 'Don't let them bully you.'

'Marty, it's Ethan.'

Martin cupped his cheek in his hand and smiled. 'Of course it is.' But behind the smile was the wreckage of what was lost—if not yet, then when? And that was where Ethan was left, sinking . . . He leant his weight on the table but it did not hold him; his knees came down to the floor, and there he was again and somehow it was better to be there, down with Vader, safe and low in a place where he had cried the tears of a boy.

When he looked up, the silver-haired man towered over him, smartly dressed in his collared shirt, blue eyes staring down in consternation from a broad, tanned face. He pointed a finger at Ethan, though all the while kept his eyes on the photographs on the table. 'The boy on a beanbag in a striped shirt . . .' The voice was deep and mellifluous, and between each pronouncement he paused as though to make certain of the next. 'In his lap there is a bowl of popcorn. Maggie reaches down to switch off the TV and introduces me as Marty . . . And you, four years old, you put your bowl down on the carpet and climb off the beanbag to stand up as tall as you can, and you smile and you hold your salty hand out so that I can shake it.' He smiled, long and warm. 'Do you remember it?'

He did, in part, not the shirt or the popcorn, but he remembered sitting on a beanbag and looking up at the man his mother had brought into the room.

'There was an agreement of sorts between us, you and I,' Martin went on. 'Like father, like son . . .' *An agreement of sorts*: a conversation in a bedroom about getting away with lies, and a sighting in a grungy pub where his father sat in a darkened booth with a woman with wavy hair. Neither of them had ever spoken of it, not until now. 'All that ducking and weaving,' Marty said. 'I'm not so sure, Ethan; I don't think you can live like that anymore.'

As he began then to pack the photos away, Marty turned to his son to make sure he was still listening, an old man at his workbench, working with all that he had left. 'The second hand is the one to watch,' he said. 'The rest of it doesn't much matter . . . And even then, it plays its tricks.

'This one,' he said suddenly, pointing to the photo on top as though stopping a spinning wheel. It was a man in a subway tunnel with a tiny light at its end. 'This one I took the day before I met your mother.'

'Are there any of the day she came?' Ethan asked.

'You know, I didn't take a one. Isn't that a funny thing?'

As he followed Marty back to the basement steps, Ethan stopped to pick up the garden tools on the ground. There were two rakes—one fan-shaped and made of green plastic, the kind he used to rake the lawn with for his pocket money, the other a flat bar with metal tines. It was lucky, he thought to himself, he hadn't landed right on top of the thing . . . a passing thought, and it almost got away, but right at the last, he snapped down: if he had landed on top of it—the metal tines piercing into his arse, like fingernails . . .

For a moment full recovery flashed before his eyes. *I can come back from here.* What the situation required was a measured response: with time, with distance . . . Five fingernail marks did not mean his downfall. He felt the rusted points and played it through. He would agree he'd need a tetanus shot; he would stop his game on Laini's blog. And once it was all done, he'd talk to her again, lay his cleaner soul bare the way he used to . . . Ethan took a deep breath (poor Sal, she had seen the worst of it), then let the rake fall back down to the ground. Following his father up the stairs, he heard that he was still muttering.

'I'm not sure you call that living at all.' And at the top step: 'The light is still on. Would you?'

Ethan went back down and flicked the switch, and there, in accordance with his father's wishes, he sat in the dark of the basement waiting to see what would bring him to his feet again.

He is lying on a blanket on the lawn next to the garden bed. This is where he comes now when he wakes in the night. The smell is grass and mulch and salt—salt because he lives by the sea.

God's country.

The witness holds up his hand and swears by Almighty God.

This is where he comes when he wakes and he waits for her to come.

Finally, tonight, he hears her steps.

'What are you doing out here?' The voice isn't angry like it was before.

Before was the study when she told him to go to bed. At first he couldn't remember what he had done wrong. He waited, but when she spoke it was into the air.

'There isn't any point,' she said, then she talked about putting something into a drawer and shutting it, nice and tight. She shouted too. 'Can't you even look at me?'

He couldn't, because he was looking through the box of photographs of New York he and Ethan had brought up from the basement. The time capsule. She shouted about that too. 'If I hear you dredge up that day one more time . . .' No, 'fucking day', that was what she said, or 'fucking time'.

Then she was crying and telling him she didn't mean to shout and that she loved him but sometimes she couldn't bear the sight of him. He didn't respond because the room was suddenly small and airless.

Only when the house was quiet again did he remember that she was angry because of what happened in La Perouse between him and the girl. She was angry because he was a liar, because he came home from New York a liar and because once a liar he stayed a liar because that was what he was.

She repeats: 'What are you doing out here?'

'It was your idea to come to the garden,' he said. 'That's why we came.'

'It's cold.'

'No, it's not, we're fine. This is the best part. You remember?'

She shakes her head. 'Please, Martin, enough . . .'

He holds his hand up in the air, extending it towards her. 'The only reason I am telling it is that you will listen,' he says. 'I had to start from the beginning, don't you see?'

For a time she is silent, but somewhere her eyes soften with sadness. She takes a step closer and looks down at him. 'Alright, you tell me: what is the best part?'

'You have to lie down. You remember?'

Lie down.

And she does, she lies down next to him, and staring up at different stars, she asks—finally, she asks. 'Where are we up to now?'

He tells her that they've woken up and she has told him the story about drawing on the cupboard door. 'Like you did on my wall.'

'Yes, the wall of the loft.'

'A graffiti artist.'

They smile together. There is a reason to dredge up the day.

'So tell me then, what happens next?'

'You had another story. You remember?'

She nods. She remembers. 'Does it have a happy end?'

The sun peeks over the tenements. 'Of course it does,' he says. 'The end is now. Aren't you happy?'

'Oh, Martin . . .' Each time as she repeats his name the sound is a different one, each a different kind of pain. The first is fresh, the second is old, the third is quiet. Then she smiles and closes her eyes. 'You were pretty much my first love.'

There it is, the best part.

Now he knows, but he didn't then. From that day he had made a mistake, a mistake he carried forward. From that day he had thought he could never match her, and all those years he had never tried.

'I was wrong, Maggie.' That is all he says, and what he means. In the end—since that night with the girl in La Perouse—he had matched her. In the end, since then, with as much certainty as she had loved, so he loved too.

He doesn't stop her leaving. Her smile fades and the girl is gone and he is alone in the garden that lives and breathes with the sense he has lost something before he ever really had it.

On the walk home he stops at the shopfront of Mrs Bess, sits on the sidewalk facing the building. The closed door is covered in graffiti—words and pictures, the tag of the running man, straight up and sideways and upside down. The eyes are the windows, burnt-out holes. The words are overlaid in colour and the letters end in arrows.

Against the door a pair of stone-eyed pigeons huddle, waiting for it to open. They remain immobile, as though he were not there at all. His head is aching, but it is someone else's head.

The memory is there again. The old man is younger, in a place he doesn't belong, a dark street. The mistake is fresh, still bleeding . . .

The man is not a memory, nor the mistake.

It is raining. He is on the street, in the passenger seat of a car driving up a hill to a house with a yellow door. That is where the day must end.

And if the day ends?

~

She sleeps.

As he watches he thinks not of the girl in the loft but the woman who crosses into the reserve every morning and walks down the rock ledge, cap and goggles in hand. A swimmer's shoulders.

When he stands up, it feels for a moment as though he has woken from a nightmare to find the abyss is not real. *This* is real: a box against the steps full of his grandson's toys and, hanging on the clothesline, the frayed rug they hauled back from Istanbul and were forced to leave in customs. For four weeks Ethan stayed with his Nanna while they toured Greece and Turkey, and when they finally put the rug on the floor just a few weeks after they'd got back, Nanna had a heart attack and died. Ethan was ten and he ransacked his toy cupboard, furious at her betrayal, throwing all the bears she had given him into the hallway.

Nanna was Lili. They'd had a lovely trip, but Maggie never could speak of it without tears.

~

Next there is a seeping light and the birds begin their call.

Martin follows the sound down the side path and out the gate, across the road and onto the reserve. The grass beneath his feet is long and wet and wavy. *Swishy swashy, swishy swashy . . .* But it is just a detail, along with the splitting trunk of a banksia tree, the white paint peeling from the timber railing, the spotted rock and the tanned cliff, like paints on a palette beneath a grand canvas. Martin looked out at it—the edge of pale yellow light unveiling the day. As he reached the cliff there was a memory, fingers fumbling with lure and bait, numb from the cold. He cast, and just as the flight of the cast passed vertical and the motion stopped, he released the line and marvelled at its distance, at the pink ripples in the surface of the water.

Across the water, the call of the cockatoo: dots forming in the distance, then nearing, they seem to cease flight mid-air, to descend like rain into the single tree near the cliff's edge, suddenly silent, unseen.

And if the day ends?

This is the answer. I play it backwards.

Like so, the sky his screen:

The freckle on her shoulder, the scar on her hip.

A big blue hat and a little skirt.

The drink spills.

She smiles, he follows.

So what are you going to do, Maggie Varga?

And finally, to begin again, she stands across his doorway.

A last wave of blood rushes into his chest.

Without fear of falling he is suspended in the liquid air, and in the branch of the single tree, sidestepping towards him with the watery eyes of a lonely boy, is a black cockatoo. It is for his grandson Martin reaches now. If he could scribble a message on the bark of the tree, if he could finish the conversation they had started . . . And then it ebbs, this need to make right. As he extends his hand, his fingers touch the branch to form a bridge, permitting the bird to continue its way until it is near enough, and when it is, it dips its head down to Martin's ear and whispers, chortles.

All he can make out from the limerick is the sound of its taunting rhyme, and all that is left on this last of gentle days is for Martin to laugh along.